"Layers of a mysterious past must be unraveled to solve a murder in the present in this intimate journey through time. Ann Lambert's novel is an honest rendering of Quebec life and a faithful tale of one woman's experiences when confronted by danger, by life's daily complications, and psychic mutations."

—JOHN FARROW, author of *The Storm Murders Trilogy*

"Riveting and elegantly written, with secret histories and crimes past and present, this marvelous novel surprises at every turn."

—AYELET WALDMAN, author of *Love and Treasure*, *Red Hook Road*, and the Mommy Track mystery series

"*The Birds That Stay* feels on the one hand like one of those intimate, emotionally meandering phone conversations with a close friend that the protagonist Marie is nostalgic for and on the other hand like a suspenseful piece of deliciously escapist fiction. It strikes a familiar chord in its depiction of uniquely Québécois subcultures but also in its frank portrayal of universal themes: family dynamics, aging parents, midlife erasure, trauma, and regret. I devoured the book in 72 hours and am impatiently awaiting the next installment."

—MICHAELA DI CESARE, award-winning playwright of *Successions* and *8 Ways My Mother Was Conceived*

"*The Birds That Stay* is not only a masterful mystery novel debut, but also a thoroughly pleasurable adult read. Ann Lambert creates an utterly convincing crime setting in a seemingly calm Laurentian town outside Montreal, where suppressed secrets from the past violently ricochet into the present. I can't wait to read Lambert's next one."

—MEGAN WILLIAMS, author and CBC Correspondent

THE BIRDS THAT STAY

A Russell and Leduc Mystery

THE BIRDS THAT STAY

Ann Lambert

Second Story Press

Library and Archives Canada Cataloguing in Publication

Lambert, Ann, author
The birds that stay / Ann Lambert.

ISBN 978-1-77260-091-9 (softcover)

I. Title.

PS8573.A3849B57 2019 C813'.6 C2018-905145-0

Editor: Wendy Thomas
Book design: Ellie Sipila

Cover photos: karnaval2018 / shutterstock.com
and Tatjana Zlatkovic / stocksy.com

Printed and bound in Canada

The author gratefully acknowledges A Nature Lover's Almanac: Kinky Bugs, Stealthy Critters, Prosperous Plants & Celestial Wonders *by Diane Olson, illustrated by Adele Flail, Published by Gibbs Smith, Utah, 2012 as the resource for nature-facts on pages 7, 138, and 139.*

Second Story Press gratefully acknowledges the support of the Ontario Arts Council and the Canada Council for the Arts for our publishing program. We acknowledge the financial support of the Government of Canada through the Canada Book Fund.

ONTARIO ARTS COUNCIL
CONSEIL DES ARTS DE L'ONTARIO

Canada Council for the Arts
Conseil des Arts du Canada

Funded by the Government of Canada
Financé par le gouvernement du Canada
Canada

Published by
Second Story Press
20 Maud Street, Suite 401
Toronto, ON M5V 2M5
www.secondstorypress.ca

For my mother, Thérèse Bourque Lambert, 1922–2011
And my father, Russell Edward Lambert, 1919–1980

À la Claire Fontaine
M'en allant promener
J'ai trouvé l'eau si belle
Que je m'y suis baigné

Il y a lontemps que je t'aime
Jamais je ne t'oublierai…

And, of course, for David,
my partner in everything worth doing.

When will redemption come?
When we grant everyone
What we claim for ourselves.

SHE WAS JUST SETTLING into her evening tea, a minty concoction she made herself from that wildly invasive plant that threatened everything trying to survive around it. She sank into her ancient armchair and realized she'd forgotten her crossword puzzle from that morning in the kitchen. She heard a noise outside. Then she heard it again. Must be that pesky porcupine that liked to chew on the side of her house. She wasn't unsympathetic to it. All rodents had to constantly keep chewing as their incisors never stopped growing. Porcupines, too. She just wondered what it was about her cabin that appealed to this one so much. The wood stain? Salt in the wood stain? Because it was there? The upside to this was she was offered a close-up view of a distracted animal—one she could photograph and then recreate in charcoal at her leisure afterwards. She peered out into the blue light of dusk—it came earlier and earlier now, and she had to brace herself for the low-grade depression that stalked her from November to March, when the light returned. Nothing there. But still she called for Kutya to join her—just the presence of a dog, even a toothless, timorous one, could often persuade a wild animal to abandon its mission. She lifted her plaid jacket from its hook and slipped into her old leather boots by the back door. It was probably five below zero out there tonight and the chill no longer seeped into her bones—it invaded them with sticks and knives. She stepped outside and took in the cold air. It was as though the season was changing at that very moment. The stars were just coming out, a crescent moon dangled low in the southeastern horizon. How many more nights would there be like this? She shone her flashlight along the edge of the house where it met a few tufts of rogue weeds, now brittle underfoot. There was nothing there. She turned to another sound behind her. And then she understood.

One

LOUIS LACHANCE EASED into the driver's seat of his ancient Toyota pickup and turned the key, grateful that he'd had the muffler replaced a week earlier. He had a little job to see to that morning, but he had to escape his house, undetected, first. The engine sputtered to life, and the tires crunched along the gravel driveway as slowly as a hearse. He felt quite safe that Michelle was still asleep, her mouth slightly open, snoring like a man. If he was lucky, he could be done and back home before she woke up.

Louis Lachance was a retired *homme à tout faire.* Except retirement had been Michelle's idea, not his. He still loved driving the dirt roads he knew like old friends and working for the few customers who really counted on him, year in, year out. He closed down houses for the winter and opened them up again in the spring for *les anglais* from the city. He fixed pipes burst by early freezes, replaced locks with lost keys, fixed jammed windows. He was not a crook like those guys from town—charging people hundreds of dollars for a few hours' work. He was an honest man. A trustworthy man. And at eighty-six years old, an old man.

He was especially fond of Madame Newman. Even after all these years, she never insisted he call her by her first name like so many did now. She always had a good cup of coffee ready for him when he was done, and a homemade muffin—banana-chocolate, his favorite, another thing forbidden to him by Michelle. Madame Newman was old—almost as old as he was—but she had the most startling blue, round eyes, and golden-gray hair that she knotted into a perfect *chignon* as though she'd woken up that way. She was always in her garden, which was one of the most efficient and intelligent ones he had seen. She grew enough food in that little plot of land to see her easily through her year, and then some. She always paid him in cash and didn't follow him around pretending to understand what he was doing. They never talked much—it was clear Madame preferred the company of her dog and garden to that of humans—but Louis Lachance understood that well. Very well, indeed. Everyone today talked too much. Talked too much about too little. *Ça parle trop pour rien.* He sometimes imagined himself arriving at Madame's house in the late afternoon, with a bottle of wine, and the two of them watching the sun disappear behind the hill from her back porch, while listening to the afternoon birds singing their diminishing song to the trees.

He turned down the unmarked road to her house, passing an overturned garbage can. The bears had obviously gotten to it, the last big feast before hibernation. He would clean that up for her on his way out, if he had time. His window of opportunity with Michelle would open only so far. He turned into Madame's driveway and was surprised not to be greeted by her dog, Kutya, barking from nose to tail so ferociously his whole body spasmed with the effort.

The sun was almost hot now, unusual for a late October morning. The leaves were well past their prime, but still glorious and radiant against the deep blue of the sky. He hoisted his tool belt from the back of the truck and stepped carefully down her uneven flagstone walkway to the side door to the kitchen. He could not afford a broken hip at his age. She was usually waiting for him, working on a crossword puzzle, sipping coffee. The paper was on the table, a pencil resting on it, next to her coffee cup. The radio was on, a honey-voiced host explaining the piece of music he was about to play. Louis was uncomfortable entering her house without permission, although he knew she wouldn't really mind. He stepped into the kitchen and called her name. Her little gray Subaru hatchback was parked in its usual place. But where was Kutya? They must have gone for a walk. Louis turned to head out of the kitchen, grabbing a muffin on his way. Then he put it back. He did not want her to think he had no manners. And Michelle would be furious. Well, she was going to be furious anyway when she found out he'd been out on a job, another strictly forbidden activity. (For a few months, Michelle insisted she tag along if he refused to stop working. He made her help him carry a hundred-pound water tank, which she dropped in mid-move, almost killing him, and breaking her toe. But she was a stubborn woman, and now he only took jobs in the early morning when she could be counted on to sleep in.)

He glanced out the kitchen window to the garden, but there was no one there. He was tempted to just walk through it—even in late October it was beautiful. The hydrangeas had dried to a delicate pink, the winterberries a brilliant orange. A larch tree glittered gold in the sun. Louis headed back to his truck, feeling more disappointed than he should have. He had to admit that in another life, he and Madame Newman might have been very good friends. Just then, a splash of something bright red interrupted the thought. It was a pile of rags over by the compost bin. And there was the dog, Kutya, lying down next to it, panting in the hot sun. Louis limped closer to investigate. Kutya stretched to his feet, approached Louis, his tail wagging cautiously. It was then that Louis realized the pile of rags was a person, and as he hobbled closer, he saw it was Madame Newman, lying face down in an empty flower bed. He turned her half onto her back and knew immediately that she was dead. Her skin was leathery and cold. Her lips were blue, but not as blue as those open eyes that he was too terrified to close, like they do in the movies. The dog began to whimper very quietly, as though the mourning process could begin now. Louis Lachance, married for sixty-four years to Michelle Dupuis, sat on the dew-damp earth beside Madame Newman and began to cry.

Two

AFTER THE MALE HONEYBEE ejaculates, he leaves his genitals—which remain in the female—behind. This kills the rest of him. Be glad you're not a male honeybee, kids. Could she use the word *ejaculate* in a nature book for kids? Why *was* she writing a nature book for kids? Because that was one of the "new and exciting" projects her publisher had decided she should tackle during her sabbatical from the college. Could she include all the more *eccentric* sexual behavior of the natural world? Like the dragonfly, the serial rapist of the insects. First, he has sex with himself, then attacks a female and removes all the other enemy sperm from her. Then he impregnates her by dragging her around in violent flight. He might do this *a hundred times a day*. Or maybe she should write about earthworms, who are hermaphroditic and thus able to mate twice—at the same time.

She began to draw an exploding honeybee and was again reminded how important it was that she never illustrate her own work. Marie had been determined to finish this chapter today, but when she glanced at the clock she realized it was time to pack it up and get on the road. She closed her sketchpad (she always wrote her books on unlined sketch paper) and whistled for the dogs. *Dog.* Even after all this time, she felt her throat catch with emotion. Loki, her beautiful black Labrador, had died five weeks earlier, on his eighth birthday.

That day began with him refusing to go for a swim in the lake. Marie knew something was wrong, but didn't pick up on the next cue, when Loki went off into the woods by himself and did not return when she whistled for him. Instead she scrambled up the hill behind her house, found him lying in a thatch of leaves, and took him immediately to the local veterinarian's, where he was kept overnight for tests. He died early the next morning, by himself, in a cage. He had inoperable cancer and had obviously been trying to go off into the woods to die, thoughtful and selfless to the very end. She shook that haunting image from her mind and went to fetch her other dog, a puggle named Barney, who was too incorrigible to even consider taking along with her. Marie was going to drop him off at her neighbors' house; they for some reason did not seem to mind his lack of house training, his garbage-can dumping, and general bad dogginess, which had gotten much worse since Loki had died.

Marie stepped onto her porch and took in the commanding view of—trees. And through the now mostly leafless trees, her little lake. Well, not hers, exactly, but the only other houses on it were at the far end, and they were just for weekenders, so she often had it all to herself. She loved to kayak around its nooks and coves hoping to spot the lone kingfisher who cackled and hovered over the water, or the two resident loons. They were her favorites. She and Daniel often used to say they were like the loons—mated for life and crazy. They got one-half of that right, anyway. Marie's friends were often critical of her choice to move to the weekend cabin after her marriage ended and live here in such isolation. One recently told her she'd be way too creeped out at night to stay here alone. She was appalled that Marie had no curtains on any of the windows. "Who's going to see anything?" Marie had asked her. "What's there to see?"

She left Barney on the porch while she went back inside to switch on the Weather Channel for a last-minute look at the forecast. She was packing light and wanted to get it right. When did people start watching the weather on TV? She used to think this was the pinnacle of vapidness, but now she rarely left the house without a check-in. Probably around the same time we all started drinking *bottled* water, which at the time seemed like an insane thing to do. She triple-checked that the stove was off, cranked all the windows shut, dropped Barney in the back seat of the car along with his doggy bed, squeaky toys, and special cuddly, a rag of a teddy bear that he'd had since he was a puppy. Maybe it was time she got some grandchildren. Her daughter had just broken the heart of the man who was perfect for her, after four years together. Her son had dated a succession of girls as physically beautiful as he was. Then he seemed to lose interest entirely. Her ex-husband had started speculating that their son was gay. But then he moved in with Maya, a woman he met online (!), who informed Marie at their first meet-the-parent supper that having children was immoral, that she would adopt a kid if she decided she really needed to have one. Marie didn't care how she got a grandchild. But this woman who called her son "babe" and still smoked cigarettes did not seem like good parental raw material. Marie knew she was not trying hard enough to like her.

Marie returned to lock her house, and the key stuck as usual in the old lock. She had tried WD-40, but to no avail. She would have to call Louis Lachance again and suffer his grumbling about how they should have torn down this old wreck and built something brand new. Why would anyone want a moldy old farmhouse when they could have everything new, with windows that closed tight and doors that kept the cold out? During the Quiet Revolution of the 1960s in Quebec, everything old was seen as backward. So everything old got torn down and replaced with brand-new, prefab box houses with vinyl siding. The Catholic Church went, too. Women used to have ten, twelve, fifteen children. Now Quebec had the lowest birthrate in the world. A socially progressive era came to Quebec, and never really left. But the architectural landscape took a beating and never recovered. Even now, driving along a highway, many of the houses were soulless, ugly, and *ketaine*, until you crossed the border into Vermont or Ontario, where you were catapulted a hundred years into the architectural past.

As Marie turned down the road to her neighbors' house, Barney began to tremble violently with delight. He loved visiting Joel and Shelley, cheerful old hippies who still smoked a joint every day and remained resolutely hopeful about the world, despite all the evidence to the contrary. He was the great-grandson of chicken farmers who had fled Russia during the pogroms of the late nineteenth century. She was the daughter of considerably more aristocratic Iraqi Jews who had run from Baghdad during the expulsions of the early 1950s.

Shelley came out to greet them and spoke directly to Barney about the lovely chicken soup she'd made them for lunch. As if on cue, a chicken scuttled by, chased by their rooster. Marie startled. When she was in grade 3, her school had visited a local farm, and the barn rooster had tried to attack her, his talons just missing her face. "Our boy is a lover, not a fighter," Shelley reassured her for the umpteenth time, steering Marie toward the house. Marie was still frightened of him. Joel waved down to her with a hammer from the top of a silo stuck to the side of their hybrid barn-house. It seemed to Marie that he was much too old for that kind of thing, and she felt a shiver at the sight of him up so high with no apparent safety device. Barney licked Shelley's entire face, including her lips, which, amazingly, she seemed to enjoy. She carried him into the house, as Marie schlepped his stuff behind her. As much as she wanted to stay and get caught up on the local gossip (Shelley and Joel were the official local *yentas*—they knew all the gossip from Ste. Lucie to Montreal and often well beyond), Marie was on a schedule. She hovered in the doorway and tried not to smell the freshly baked something that Shelley had clearly just removed from the oven. She had promised her mother she would arrive before suppertime. As Barney was already gobbling up something forbidden off the floor, Shelley looked Marie in the eye and launched into a story about another weekend neighbor, Pierre Batmanian, a billionaire restaurateur and real estate tycoon.

"His entire empire just went tits up. Just like that! Who knew?" Marie detected a kind of glee in Shelley's voice—nostalgic, anti-capitalist feelings, no doubt. "And that twelve-year-old wife of his? Apparently, she's already hightailed it for greener pastures. That'll teach him for trading in his first wife for a newer model," she said, with the delight you feel when vindicated for predicting something correctly. Shelley had long said Pierre's wife was much too young for him.

"He's already put the house—I mean *estate*—on the market. Guess how much?"

"Oh. I don't know. Um…a million?"

Shelley's jaw dropped.

"A *million*? Have you seen his place? He's asking 2.7 million. And he'll probably get it. Disgusting!"

Before Shelley could start in on her contempt for the uber-rich and socially irresponsible, Marie checked her nonexistent watch, exclaimed loudly, and declared she had to go. Shelley took her hand and squeezed it gently.

"Good luck this week. Just remember we love you. And don't worry about this little guy."

Marie headed out to her car. Shelley waved from the kitchen window with Barney's paw. Joel had disappeared from his ladder—by choice, Marie hoped. She waved back at the window, smiling at the thought of this couple. Kind. Eccentric. And entirely devoted to each other—each was the center of the other's emotional life. She felt another pang of regret. No, not regret. Anger. Disappointment. Before her marriage had come to an abrupt end eight years earlier, Marie thought she and Daniel were going to grow old together. Retire and have projects. Have grandchildren. Travel to Africa and teach. Instead, she was informed that he had not been in love with her for a long time, and he needed to be *in love* again. He needed to know what a first kiss felt like *again*. Wasn't that redundant? He insisted there was No

One Else, but within three months he had moved in with another woman with whom she supposed he did a lot more than kissing. For the sake of their kids she had tried to be "friends" with him, but it was a struggle. Now, she couldn't understand what she'd ever really seen in him, but she figured that was a pretty common reaction. In fact, she often felt repulsed by him, especially when he casually touched her hand or called her to complain about his new wife. She had fantasies about killing him, actually. Vivid, ultra-realistic movies that she sometimes made up for herself for hours on end.

As she ducked into the driver's seat, she paused to breathe. Marie hated leaving the country for Montreal. As she got older, she had less use for the so-called attractions of city life. Ste. Lucie, the village of eight hundred or so souls about six minutes from her house and an hour northeast of Montreal, was named for a fourteenth-century saint who blinded herself because she could not bear to witness all the sin in the world. Or she had popped her eyeballs out herself to discourage a persistent suitor, having sworn to preserve her virginity, of course. Every July, a few hundred Italian Montrealers emptied out of yellow school buses and paraded her statue (a woman carrying her two eyeballs on a platter) through the four streets in town. This all culminated in a mass at the quaint little church that almost no one attended now, followed by a hugely festive picnic. It was the only action Ste. Lucie saw all year. Like everywhere else on this planet, young people didn't want to live in small towns anymore. Ste. Lucie now consisted mostly of retirees, gardeners who called themselves "organic" farmers, minor criminals, and hippies who never grew out of it.

It was late October, so most of the leaves had given up and fallen. There were still a few aspen leaves trembling nervously on nearly bare branches. Her mother always said that you could see a tree's real character when its leaves were gone. The bird feeders were swaying with the weight of squabbling birds that stay—chickadees, nuthatches, juncos—stuffing themselves before the long, long winter. The sun, which had been almost hot that morning, was now smudged by clouds roiling in from the northeast. The wind was gusty, snapping off desiccated larch needles, which fell in showers around her. It was like the weather had decided to make itself a symbol of what lay ahead.

She made the first hair-raising turn onto the 329, accelerating like a torpedo not to get rear-ended. Driving in Quebec was unlike anywhere else, really. Crosswalks? Don't even think about it. Drivers *tried* to hit people in them. She passed Au Kazou, the tiny and wildly popular local *casse-croute*. There was the usual crowd packed at the window, clamoring for hot dogs *stimés or toastés*. Or Quebec's particular gastronomical claim to fame: poutine, the traditional version of which consisted of french fries, covered in melting cheese curd, drowned in brown gravy or *"la sauce brune."* Marie was surprised the snack bar was still open—they usually closed Thanksgiving weekend and reopened on Victoria Day. The unseasonably warm weather must have kept them open a few weeks longer. She hesitated, but only briefly. Her days of wolfing back a couple of steamies slathered in mustard and onions, washed down with a Coke, were over.

A pickup truck zoomed past her, two yahoos in backwards baseball caps and orange camouflage jackets in the front seat. Probably moose hunters. Marie had never even seen an intact moose, only their severed heads strapped onto car roofs, or the butt end of one disappearing into the roadside bushes. In the woods out back of her house, she sometimes heard the wail of coyotes and sometimes, she liked to hope, wolves. She spotted bear scat frequently, often blue and oily from their decimation of her blueberry plants. She imagined a huge black bear, delicately nibbling at the tiny fruit—there was often not a single berry left once the bears had their way with them. Marie found lots of scat on her hikes up in the hills, but never once a bear. She was just fine with that, having read too many accounts of gruesome attacks. Louis Lachance claimed there were even cougars in these woods, returned from extinction. Or maybe the rural legend that they had never really died out was true.

Marie decided to take the shortcut to the highway. She wanted to avoid the road construction work ahead that had been going on for months longer than it was supposed to. "Road work" in Quebec consisted of half a dozen men, leaning on their shovels, chain-smoking, while one guy did what seemed like most of the "work." The contractors the government hired were notoriously corrupt, so nothing ever got done competently, or even inadequately. This was the subject of many a raging radio show host across the province. She turned off the paved road onto a hidden dirt road that cut though some very pretty, hilly terrain. This is where you lived if you really did not want to be found, Marie thought. Her Bruce Springsteen CD was blasting away, and she realized she was driving way too fast when her car fishtailed on the soft shoulder. Marie had always loved to drive—she got her license the day she turned sixteen and never looked back. She downshifted as she approached the next, blind curve and practically slammed into a police car.

There were at least six of them, Sûreté du Québec police cars parked haphazardly on the road and by a house a few hundred feet back, their red and blue lights flashing. It was a pretty bungalow that Marie had driven by countless times, but she had never seen the people who lived there. She watched one officer wrapping yellow tape around the recycling bins at the end of the driveway. Another signaled Marie to drive on by, so of course she slowed down to get a better look.

"*Qu'est-ce qui se passe?*" she asked the policeman, who looked about fourteen years old. He shook his head.

"*Continuez, Madame.*"

Reluctantly, she pulled away, glancing in her rearview mirror as long as she could before they disappeared. Marie wondered if it was some big grow-op bust. An unusual number of pot growers lived up in the Laurentians. Nobody bothered with them much, especially the cops, who for years were in on the business until *they* got busted a few years earlier. Or maybe they finally decided to arrest the infamous Jumeaux Thibodeau, local twin brothers who had broken into practically every weekend house of (mostly) anglophone Montrealers. The scuttlebutt was that the twins had crossed the Rubicon in the annals of small-time local crime. It was one thing to steal from a bunch of rich weekenders who could afford to lose a television or a nice sound system. It was entirely another to steal snowmobiles from the Mohawk First Nations reserve just outside Ste. Lucie. According to Joel and Shelley, if the Thibodeau twins were ever caught by the Mohawks, they'd take them out to the woods, tie them to a tree, and leave them there. Forever. Maybe the cops were doing them a favor by arresting them. The Mohawk reserve Tioweró:ton was in fact the traditional hunting grounds of the Kahnawake and Kanesatake Mohawks of Montreal. All non-Mohawks had to ask permission to enter, but very few wanted to. The Mohawks and French Québécois had a long history of hostility that went all the way back to the "discovery" of "Canada" by the Europeans. The Mohawks were the traditional allies of the English, and that antipathy still played out in more subtle ways in the twenty-first century.

Marie remembered with a smile an encounter she had had with her son and one of the local Mohawks. The only Ste. Lucie convenience store, or *dépanneur,* was owned by a Chinese family—recent immigrants from Guangzhou—who came to Canada probably hoping to be settled in huge, English, and very Chinese-flavored Toronto. Somehow, they'd ended up in Ste. Lucie much to their horror, she imagined. But they seemed to make the best of it, greeting customers cheerfully in incomprehensible French while Chinese soap operas played on a tiny black-and-white TV behind the cash. When her son, Ben, was about eight years old, he was looking for material to make a bow and arrow. He was obsessed with anything Indigenous at the time and imagined himself hunting in the woods out back. He had carved his bow and arrow, but had only string to complete his bow, and it had no elasticity. Marie drove to the dépanneur, and as they entered, there he was, at the cash paying for some milk and bread—a massive man, with an actual Mohawk haircut, clearly from the reserve. Ben's eyes opened as wide as his mouth, thrilled to see a real live Indian. The guy looked pretty scary, covered in menacing tattoos and pierced with lots of metal, but Ben was unstoppable. He asked the man what made the best line for a hunting bow. Marie started to stammer an apology, but the giant leaned down to Ben's level, mumbled something, and disappeared to the back of the store. He returned with fishing line, which he showed Ben how to attach properly. He even paid for it. Ben talked about that day for months. Marie remembered watching the Mohawk and the Chinese man at the cash, and how much they resembled each other. They had the same high cheekbones, lanky black hair, brown eyes, olive skin. They could be brothers. Both were immigrants. One recent, one from 10,000 years earlier. It was a funny old world.

As she turned onto the entrance near the highway, Santa Claus Village/*Village du Père Noël* loomed up ahead. It was closed now until a brief few weeks around Christmas, the animals shipped off to various winter petting zoos, the cheesy gift shops shut down, two giant candy canes and a derelict igloo looking forlorn, Santa's throne covered in plastic tarp. Marie used to take her kids there when they still believed in Santa, but then they started asking too many questions. Her daughter, Ruby, had her heart broken when she asked Marie point-blank if Santa Claus was actually *her*. Marie just could not lie right to her face. When she said yes, Ruby's lip started to quiver. "What about the Easter Bunny?" Marie answered yes again. Ruby finally howled, "And the *Tooth Fairy*?" What else could Marie do but tell the truth? Nonetheless, for Ben's sake, Ruby agreed to pretend, and they made one last visit to Santa Claus Village, but the last straw was when Ruby climbed onto Santa's lap to make her gift request, and he fell off his throne with her still clinging to him. He was stinking drunk. Not that Marie could blame him, really.

She hit the highway and to her relief, traffic was light. She passed the several ski hills readying themselves for the winter season. They were sprawling, wintery versions of Las Vegas on what were referred to as mountains but were really hills. What they lacked in size they made up for with unabashed development. She passed what was once a lovely old town now almost entirely overrun by clothing factory outlets. Then a water park, closed for several years now after a terrible accident. Its landmark was a giant faucet at the top of a 60-degree waterslide—the faucet now turned off forever. Despite all the crass exploitation of this gorgeous countryside, the trees, more in leaf the farther south she drove, were still resplendently, breathtakingly beautiful.

She flicked on the radio—a CBC talk show was crowing about a new Canada after eleven years of right-wing paranoia, viciousness, and ideological blinders of the outgoing Conservative government. She sincerely hoped so. The last government had basically been climate-change deniers, muzzling its own scientists and anyone else who sounded the alarm. The new prime minister at least talked the talk of doing something about it. Marie spent a lot of energy trying to convince herself that it wasn't already over for her species. Because it clearly was for so many others—she hadn't seen a bat in three years, when there used to be hundreds around her house on summer nights, each bat eating one thousand mosquitoes *an hour*. Tree swallows that she used to watch feed their babies on the wing had disappeared. Wild turkeys, never before seen in the Laurentians, were now routinely spotted. On second thought, maybe global warming wasn't so bad after all.

The traffic slowed to a crawl for exiting shoppers from

the brand-new mall—another gargantuan stack of big box stores, packed with people on Sundays, especially. Just how much can people shop? How much can you possibly buy? An atheist since the Vatican changed all the rules when Marie was twelve, she would still rather go to church than a mall on a Sunday morning.

Marie hit Highway 13, and before she knew it—sometimes she drove so completely on automatic pilot that it was a miracle she'd never had an accident—she was in the leafy West Island suburbs of Montreal, where all the streets had nostalgic, Norman Rockwell names like Maple Crescent, Fieldfare Avenue, and Basswood Road. And then she was turning down her old street, the street on which she'd grown up. About three blocks from the shores of Lac St. Louis. It sounded idyllic, except for the fact that swimming in the lake had been prohibited since 1967 due to toxic amounts of PCBs and raw sewage embedded in the lake bottom. It was the street that held in its leafy branches the dreams and nightmares of her childhood. Woodgrove Avenue.

Three

ROMÉO LEDUC, chief homicide investigator for the district of St. Jerome, pulled up alongside an SQ patrol car and zipped up his jacket before he stepped out into what had become a much colder October day. He reached instinctively for his breast pocket and then felt his heart sink as he remembered. He had quit smoking six days ago. He fumbled in his pocket for his Nicorette gum—and violently chewed up two pieces. This was not going to be a good day. A baby policeman hastened over to him, speaking self-importantly into his shoulder walkie-talkie. Good, now they all knew he was here and maybe, just maybe, would not contaminate half the scene before evidence could be gathered. A possible homicide in this neck of the woods was quite rare, and the police here were pretty excited, which sometimes led to careless crime scene preservation.

Roméo was trying not to be resentful of being asked to take on this case. A more junior detective had already been assigned, but Roméo had learned that the guy had contracted flesh-eating disease, and that he had been airlifted to a Montreal hospital. Given what had befallen his colleague, it was hard to stay resentful, but Roméo was three days away from his first real vacation in three years—he was going where most Québécois went to get some sun and sea, Punta Cana in the Dominican Republic—and he was counting the minutes until his departure. He'd got an indecently cheap deal at a five-star all-inclusive hotel, a sprawling compound of swimming pools, tennis courts, beachfront, and restaurants with enough toys to satisfy even the most spoiled brat for a week. Roméo planned to do nothing but eat, swim, drink, and sleep. Then wake up the next day and do it all over again for exactly seven nights and eight days. He had mentioned to his superior that taking on a possible homicide was unwise at this juncture, but his objections were set aside. Roméo Leduc had been the junior investigator on a series of sexual assaults and murders of middle-aged women in the Laurentians and the West Island of Montreal fifteen years earlier. It was Roméo who had gone back to the crime scene and had discovered the incriminating boot print that tied the murders together. It was also Roméo who had made the connection to a series of rapes in the trendy Plateau neighborhood of Montreal by a "handyman." William Fyfe was eventually arrested and was now serving many life sentences in Millhaven.

Roméo had got the call about this case while he was just pulling his suitcase from the crawl space in the basement, fishing around for his swim trunks from the last time he'd actually gone swimming—was it two years ago? He hoped they still fit. Even six days without cigarettes can cause weight gain—he already felt the beginnings of a paunch, *une bedaine,* start to tighten his pants at the waist. Not to mention the nicotine-withdrawal nightmares. He hadn't had an actual full night's sleep since he quit.

As he stepped toward the waiting patrolmen, he noted how beautifully maintained the grounds were; they reminded him of the farms he had hiked past in the Swiss Alps many years before on his honeymoon—so perfectly groomed, as though an army of garden gnomes worked at them night and day. This was not the home of a Hells Angel, or a grow-op guy, or one of the low-life break-and-enter assholes who inconvenienced everyone. The possible victim was Madame Anna Newman, eighty-two years old, found dead in her garden on the Fourth Range Road. Was it a robbery gone awry? Senior citizens did not routinely get murdered in the Laurentians. Roméo had a feeling this one was not going to be simple. He felt that Dominican beach was not going to be his this year. Again.

The ambulance guys were leaning on the hood of their truck, smoking and waiting for Roméo to take a look at the body. He headed to the garden straightaway. He would save the interior of the house for later. Roméo guessed it had been about twelve to fifteen hours since the woman had died. Rigor mortis had dissipated in the fingers and toes, through the arms and legs, and then up through the chest to the neck and face. He would wait, of course, for the coroner to confirm this, but he was pretty sure. Near the body was an old ladder propped up against a small toolshed. Had she fallen off it? She had received a trauma to the head, perhaps hitting the boulder protruding out of the frozen ground where she'd fallen. Roméo squatted beside the body and examined her. She may have been climbing a ladder at night, and she may have fallen, but something else had probably killed her, and there it was. Fresh bruise marks circled her neck. She was wearing a flowery nightie and a plaid lumberjack shirt—nothing else. One leather boot was still on, the other several feet from the body. Roméo hoped there had been no sexual assault. She was about the same age as his *grand-mère*. Not that rape at any age was acceptable—he had seen too many women destroyed by it, young and old, but he hated the thought of telling her family if that was what the examiner discovered. There were several sets of footprints in the garden—they would have to sort them out later. No obvious murder weapon—except perhaps a spade that had been found by the toolshed that they would test for blood.

Roméo signaled to cordon off the area and requested that a forensic team be dispatched immediately. They needed to get to work examining, dusting, spraying, and photographing the crime scene, and looking for clues in the blood, hair, and skin on the body. Roméo noticed an old man sitting with one of the baby police officers by a patrol car. This must be the one who found her. With violently trembling hands, he was trying to put a coffee cup to his lips, while the officer took his statement. Probably for the third or fourth time. Roméo would get to him soon.

The house was a compact, two-bedroom log bungalow with a screened-in porch. The front door was unlocked. Roméo put on his latex gloves and pushed the door open. The small living room looked like some giant hand had lifted and shaken it. The sofa was overturned and cushions were strewn about the room. One leaned comfortably against the woodstove. An old but solid armchair had toppled onto its back. Drawers in a small buffet were pulled out and tossed. The rest of the room, however, seemed intact. There were about half a dozen needlepoints framed and hanging on the wall, another in a large wooden frame that had been overturned. Roméo had to admit that he, too, had little appreciation for the domestic arts. His ex-wife, Elyse, used to drag him to various craft fairs, and for him they were a special kind of torture. He would stand there bored stupid, while she would ask his opinion of a teapot, a fruit bowl, a quilt. He supposed he should have taken an interest. But he couldn't. There are just some things that he could not force himself to do. He guessed there were a few too many of these moments for his marriage to have survived—including accepting the fact that Elyse had been sleeping with her high school sweetheart for a year before he found them in his and Elyse's bed one morning when he came home early with a flu. A cliché right out of a bad movie if there ever was one, but that is exactly what had happened. Roméo often felt like his life was a bad movie.

As Roméo surveyed the walls of the living room, he had to admire the work here, though. These needlepoint landscapes were stunning. Exquisitely detailed, pointillist explosions of color matched by solid composition. He noticed a photograph pinned by the frame—so that's how she did it. She took the picture first, and then needlepointed the picture. He looked around for a camera. It was in an opened drawer in a cabinet side table. An ancient Minolta. Roméo remembered a Minolta he once had. It took great pictures. When the whole world went digital, he lost interest in taking pictures completely. Those happy accidents that produce a compelling photo were now largely eliminated. What did a great photo matter when you could take a thousand, leave them on your computer forever, and never look at them again? Or when you could Photoshop them into anything you wanted? He felt grateful for having been born early enough to remember actual photo albums—the painstaking record of the past, not the disposable world we lived in now. He would of course have the camera checked.

Despite the fact that someone had opened the cupboards and done a quick search of their contents, Roméo noted that the kitchen was impeccably clean—like the homes of observant Jews during Passover. When he was a boy growing up in Outremont, Roméo had been a Passover *goy*, helping Orthodox Jews on certain holidays by turning their lights and stoves on and off, work they were forbidden to undertake on those holy days. There wasn't a crumb on the counter, not a dish out of place, the tea towels neatly folded. He looked into the fridge—even that was spotless and almost empty—there was butter, milk, two wrinkled apples, a few carrots, homemade jam, ketchup, and a case of Boost energy drink. It seemed like Madame Newman preferred her food in liquid form, although a plate of half a dozen muffins sat on the kitchen counter under plastic wrap as if waiting for guests. On the table beyond that, a half-finished crossword puzzle, a pencil, and a coffee mug.

Although her assailant had rifled through her drawers and a few storage boxes from her closet, her small, single bed was still made, or had been remade, and with military precision. The whole bedroom was as immaculate and spartan as the kitchen. Even her little vanity table contained just a few old lipsticks, one vintage perfume bottle, and a monogrammed hairbrush, with a few golden-gray hairs still in it. Roméo picked it up in gloved hands and looked closer. On its silver back, elaborate, curlicue initials were engraved: E.N. Roméo's grand-mère had a similar set of brushes and mirrors. It was so extraordinary that people once owned such things—that such things were actually made and treasured and passed down through the generations. He wondered what he would pass on to his daughter. An old cell phone? Cheap golf clubs? He had no jewelry, no real money. He rented his house. This was getting depressing.

Roméo noted that the closets were sparse as well. A couple of old shirts, two pairs of neatly folded pants, one sensible cotton dress, and two pairs of shoes took up about a tenth of the space. It seemed she had exactly what she needed, and nothing more. It occurred to him the world would be a much improved place if more people lived like Madame Newman. On the floor by her bedside, a single enormous book lay opened and face down. Roméo picked it up gently and laid it on the bed. It was bound in very old leather, its title illegible with age. Roméo opened it. The pages were almost brittle, the print tiny. It was *The Complete Works of William Shakespeare.* As he delicately turned its pages, looking for a note or a letter that her assailant had not discovered, Roméo noted that Madame Newman (or someone) had underlined and annotated almost every page. Otherwise, the room was empty—there wasn't a photograph, a painting, a *tchotchke.* That's what was so odd. Despite the artwork in the living room, the house so far had no evidence of a long life lived. It seemed empty of a past. Bereft. Roméo opened her bedside drawer a bit farther; there was an embroidered handkerchief with the same monogram and some Jergen's hand cream. That was it. Had she been heading to bed when her killer appeared? Had she gone outside to climb a ladder at night when her killer showed up? Why had her bed been left undisturbed? Or had her killer made the bed after he searched through it? If so, her killer was either once in the military or had been in prison. One thing was sure—out here in the middle of nowhere, a murderer could take all the time he wanted, Roméo concluded. Tidy up the house, have a nice meal, watch a little television. Roméo's overall feeling was that someone was trying to make it *look like* they were looking for something.

Roméo was just heading for the bathroom when he heard his named called. They were summoning him to the garden. A baby cop approached him, flushed with discovery. He can't even grow a beard yet, Roméo observed. "We found something."

Roméo followed him to the garden. Another cop, a young woman, held something up for him.

It was a necklace.

"I was the one who found it—I mean, it was here." Baby Cop pointed to a spot just steps away from the body. "Embedded in the dirt. Probably torn from her neck?"

Roméo took it from the gloved hands and examined it more carefully. It was a gold necklace, the chain broken into two pieces. The charm was a simple, golden *chai*.

"This is a letter in Hebrew," Roméo explained. "It's a symbol of life in Jewish numerology."

The baby cop peered at it. "Really? I've never seen that before. So, the victim was Jewish?" There were no other signs suggesting this anywhere in the house—no mezuzah at her door, no Chanukah menora, nothing. Had her killer snapped it off her neck? Had she torn it off the neck of her assailant? Or had Madame Newman lost it years ago, while working in the garden? They would of course check it for fingerprints, but after a quick glance around the yard, Roméo had a sinking, gut feeling that this killer had left few traces.

Roméo decided to have a talk with the old man who found her. After a few minutes clarifying some details of his account, it was clear Louis Lachance was completely shocked by his discovery. It was also clear, however, that he was very fond of Madame Newman. Roméo assessed the old man. Was he in love with her? Who could ever understand the secrets of the human heart?

"We'll be calling you in to answer a few more questions, Monsieur Lachance," Roméo explained. "Are you planning on leaving town any time soon?"

"Not much chance of that," Louis responded, still trying to sip his hot coffee with trembling hands. "Last time I went to Montreal was seven years ago. To see a Canadiens hockey game." A grateful weekender had given him the coveted tickets for preventing his pipes from bursting one frigid weekend. Louis had taken Michelle, and even though the Canadiens lost to some team from the southern United States, where hockey is not a religious experience as it is in Canada, he still thrilled to the crowd, the lightning pace of the game, the shock of how much a beer and a hot dog cost.

"Once was enough. I don't need to do that again," Louis declared. Roméo had a lot of respect for that. "But what about the dog?" Louis asked. "Madame loved that dog so much. Who will take care of it now?"

"The next of kin will be searched for and notified, and then the dog could be put in their care. Until then, he'll be taken to the local animal shelter," Roméo explained. "Monsieur Lachance, would you like to keep the dog for a few days?" Louis did not answer at first, then slowly shook his head. There was no way Michelle would not hear about this, which was bad enough. But to bring a dog home *en plus*? It was out of the question.

"*Non, j' peux pas. Pas de question.*"

Roméo and Louis looked over at the dog. One of the policewomen was trying to lure him into a police car with a handful of kibble but ended up having to grab him by the collar and force him inside. If only a dog could testify. Or pick a suspect out of a lineup, Roméo thought. The paramedics leaned against their ambulance, still smoking cigarettes like their lives depended on them, waiting for the medical examiner to arrive. Roméo felt a craving so powerful he had to walk away. He watched as the two uniformed cops squatted by the body, peering at her as though she would suddenly sit up and explain everything. *What happened to you, Madame Newman?*

Four

MARIE KNEW ALMOST no one on her old street anymore. At least half of them had taken off down the 401 to Toronto following the election of a secessionist government in 1976. Most of the rest followed after the first failed referendum on independence from Canada in 1980. Many of the few who stayed were very old and had already moved into seniors' homes or hospitals or were dead. Marie had no idea who lived in these houses now, and some had changed almost past recognition, but she mostly remembered each house and the stories lurking inside. Memory fragments floated by as she passed each one, like snapshots from an old photo album—the kind that made her wonder if she actually remembered a moment, or just a photograph of it.

Right off the highway was her friend Linda Couchman's old house. She had lots of street cred for being an orphan and having a demusked skunk as a pet. Linda was raised by her grandparents, who Marie remembered were incredibly kind and solicitous of her friends. Marie remembered lots of grilled cheese sandwiches and Campbell's soup from the can—a thrilling meal for Marie, and something her own mother would not dream of serving.

There was Bobby Gauthier's ramshackle house, now probably worth at least half a million. Bobby was one of ten kids. His father used to beat the crap out of all the kids, but mostly him. He could be annoying and failed grade 6 twice, but Marie remembered him as hilariously, outrageously funny—in the way kids who had nothing to lose were, who would do *anything* for a laugh. Marie had learned years ago that Bobby had done some hard time in prison, then died of AIDS.

There was Mrs. Daley's old house, once a simple cottage now tarted up with a turret and a gazebo. Mrs. Daley was their long-suffering, elderly babysitter. Marie remembered her waddling down the street still in her housecoat when her mother called, frantic, needing someone to watch Marie and her sisters—more often than not when Marie's father, Edward, was stuck somewhere drunk again, and her mother would have to go get him, or pick him up at the police station. Mrs. Daley had had her legs amputated from diabetes, and they didn't see much of her after that.

The McConaghys' beautiful ranch-style bungalow. He was a soccer star in Ireland and apart from a career-ending knee injury, his tragedy was siring five daughters and not one son. Every day after school and most weekends you could see those five girls out in their front yard, getting soccer balls kicked at them, bounced off their heads, or occasionally bloodying their noses.

There was Timmy Ebert's huge house, once surrounded by giant oak trees, now entirely shorn of anything but a golf course of a lawn. Timmy, a few years younger than Marie, would eat anything they dared him to, even road kill. He also submitted to many "medical" examinations performed by their gang of girls when they played doctor. Did kids still do that? Or did they play IT expert? Were they still afraid of quicksand? Play Cowboys and Indians? Nazis and Americans? Marie and her friends played that even though they were Canadians. Marie remembered someone telling her that Timmy Ebert had become a surgeon and had moved to California.

There was the Kovaks' house. They were refugees from the failed uprising against the Communists in Hungary. Mr. Kovak was a bull of a man with a thick head of wavy hair and a booming voice. Mrs. Kovak was a bit of a mouse. She was much younger than her husband, had watery blue eyes, and was very thin, very nervous. She didn't like to talk much because of her accent, but he never minded even though his was much worse. Marie mostly remembered Mrs. Kovak at church, her perfect blond hair covered in a lacy black veil, like she was in mourning, her rosary laced through her fingers. Her family always sat in the fourth row of pews. Their daughter, Magda, was a year older than Marie. Their son, Tomas, Marie's middle sister's age. Their claim to fame was the nuclear bomb shelter Mr. Kovak had built in their basement. And the accident. Marie looks at the pool that is still there. It is empty now and covered in sodden leaves.

The Donergans at 67 Woodgrove. Mrs. Donergan was the perfect mother. She looked like Mary Tyler Moore, made fresh Toll House cookies after school, and despite having five children, including two sets of Irish twins, never lost her temper. Ever. And their house was impossibly clean all the time. Their house was a sitcom set. They *were* a sitcom, without the laugh track. Later on Marie learned that Mrs. Donergan had a powerful Valium addiction ("Mother's

Little Helper," as it was called at the time) and later went through a horrific divorce during which it was revealed her husband had been going to prostitutes for years.

The Mitchells were an octogenarian couple across the street, and the nicest people on the street. Mrs. Mitchell had snow-white hair and smelled like baby powder. Mr. Mitchell was tall, angular, with kind, bony hands and matching white hair that he meticulously upcombed with Brylcreem. All Marie could remember was that all the Woodgrove kids fell over themselves to do chores for the Mitchells, the same chores they'd resist doing at home—raking infinite numbers of leaves, mowing their lawn, carrying their groceries into the house. The Mitchells lived well into their nineties, and then Mrs. Mitchell died of a stroke. Mr. Mitchell died in his sleep two weeks later.

The Posners' house. The only Jewish family on the street. Their only child, Betty, the only Jew in Marie's Catholic school, which was odd, Marie thought, as she learned later that Montreal Jews almost always went to Protestant schools. Betty's family owned the local butcher shop—exotic in and of itself, but to be *Jewish*? Most of the kids felt sorry for Betty because she didn't get Christmas, didn't get gifts, didn't get to compete for the dream role of the Virgin Mary in the annual Nativity play. She did get to skip Friday morning mass, where if you were a girl and forgot your hat, a teacher would stand at the doorway and drop a *Kleenex* on your head. But to *not* believe that Jesus Christ was the son of God and our Savior who died on the cross, so we could be cured of Original Sin? And saved from going to hell? Hell to six-year-old Marie Russell was a real place, where if you committed a mortal sin you were heading to directly—flames roasting your toes, then your legs, pausing somewhere around your waist—for all eternity. Marie distinctly remembers being afraid for Betty's soul.

The Marcottes, the Boxers, the Schlondorfs. The people in those houses were referred to by one name, as a singular unit. Marie turned into 74 Woodgrove. The Russells. Claire and Edward. The driveway badly needed repaving, the trees pruning; the garden was terribly overrun with...everything. The little cabin they "camped" in during the summer was listing pretty seriously. The lilac trees her father had planted were all but gone now, as were the apple trees in the backyard. The house needed at least one coat of paint. Marie immediately felt a stab of guilt like she always did visiting her house. She was the only one of her siblings who had stayed in Quebec, and she could not keep up with a job, her kids, and her own and her mother's house. Their old neighbor, Mrs. Davis, always asked why they didn't see her more often and often reminded her that her mother could sure use more help. Marie tried to visit every two weeks. And called her mother every day. Definitely every other day. She parked in the carport and sat for a minute before committing to getting out of the car. She thought of the nasty e-mail she'd gotten from Louise, her older sister in Calgary, who refused to fly out and help, even though she was retired, and as far as Marie could tell, spent most of her time obsessing over her toy poodles, Humphrey and Bogart. Every Christmas Marie received a calendar from her sister—with each month represented by a picture of her dogs playing famous actors in different old movie settings. This is what kept her sister too busy to come home and help out. Marie knew she had been her mother's favorite even though she was an unexpected addition to the family. Born six years after her older sister, and three years after the middle one, Marie was the child who missed much of the fallout from her father's alcoholism. Her mother had had two miscarriages between Louise and her, and so Marie was seen as a gift from God. Louise never got over it. Madeleine, the oldest of the three sisters, had died of liver cancer two years earlier. They say one in three children of alcoholics will get the disease themselves. Madeleine was the one who had lost the genetic lottery.

Marie had a clear memory of her mother, ironing her father's shirts while *Days of Our Lives* was on TV, crying over her ironing board. Marie always thought it was something that had happened to one of the characters that made her so sad. When her father was committed to the Douglas, the local mental hospital where at that time alcoholics were sent to "dry out," the TV soap operas ended—and the real-life soap began. Her poor mother—married an upwardly mobile aerospace engineer with all kinds of future, only to find herself stuck in the suburbs with an alcoholic, two babies, and neighbors who saw her being French as an act of hostility. When her mother had moved out here to the English suburbs of Montreal from her cramped cold-water flat in the French east end of the city, married to this handsome English engineer with a great future awaiting him, she must have thought she'd hit the jackpot. Little did she know what awaited her.

Five

AS ROMÉO PULLED OUT of Madame Newman's driveway, the setting sun was just beginning to impale itself on the pointed balsam firs that circled her yard. The forensic team was still working under the lights and would notify him immediately if anything urgent was flagged. Despite the baby cop's initial assessment that *la vieille folle* fell from her ladder and hit her head hard enough to kill her instantly, Roméo had a bad feeling about this one. What he saw at the house did not add up. Madame Newman was clearly an unusual person, eccentric perhaps. But why would an old woman go out at night and climb a ladder? What on earth was she doing on a ladder at any time of the day, for that matter? There was no tool, no paintbrush, no broom near the body to suggest she had some task in mind—cleaning an eaves trough, for example. Or repairing a broken shingle. Maybe she had a stroke and fell. Maybe a heart attack. But Roméo didn't really believe any of it. He would have to wait for the coroner's report on cause of death, but she most likely had been strangled to death. If he was correct, he knew his trip to the Dominican Republic and a never-ending flow of margaritas was about to be seriously compromised.

He was just pulling onto the 329 south, the main road to his house, when he realized he wasn't ready to go home. Home meant facing his daughter, Sophie, who used to live with Roméo on the weekends, but fifteen months earlier had reversed that arrangement. She now lived in St. Jerome with Roméo during the week to attend college there, and weekended with her mother and stepfather in Montreal. Her stepdad, a professional *bon vivant*, had a huge house in Outremont with an indoor pool, outdoor hot tub, billiard table, astoundingly well-stocked bar, and a lifestyle devoted to the pursuit of hedonism. He was handsome in a Cary-Grant-gone-to-seed kind of way, had retired at fifty-five from the public relations firm he had built himself from scratch. The more Roméo thought about it, the more he realized why Guy was a more attractive option for his ex, who was never shy to admit that the unfair distribution of wealth did not trouble her. Roméo had to endure countless pictures of the two of them on Facebook—posing poolside in some expensive, exotic place, drinks in hand, with gangs of good-looking friends. Everyone looking insanely happy. Or posing before a fireplace in some expensive, exotic place, drinks in hand, with gangs of good-looking friends looking insanely happy. Roméo spent his weekends alone, trying to catch up on paperwork and chores. On Saturday nights he watched the hockey game and drank Scotch until his own snoring woke him up several lost hours later. He knew he ought to ask someone out, go online for dates, at least go to the local bar and try to be social, but he could never locate the will to do so. With Sophie gone on weekends, he often didn't even cook anymore, just warmed up leftovers or pulled some food fossil from his freezer. No wonder the two women in his life had abandoned him.

Sophie had announced to Roméo just two days earlier that she had quit college with only one semester to go, to move to Costa Rica and "help" villagers. Roméo couldn't imagine what help she and her anglo boyfriend (who called Roméo "dude") could offer in the way of "help." Maybe teaching them how to roll a flawless joint, Roméo guessed. Roméo couldn't face his daughter's backpack on her bed, her summer beach clothes all laid out so carefully and hopefully. He couldn't face his daughter's refusal to see why quitting school now was just stupid. She was so much brighter than what's his name, had so much more going for her—but she was in love for the first time, and nothing could stop her. Certainly not her middle-aged, tired, and aptly named father—in respect to romance. This trip was yet another way Sophie had thought up to punish her father for the divorce. She was waiting for him to approve of her decision, but what choice did he have? She had her own money (that her stepfather gave her, buying her affection, or at least tolerance). She was nineteen, almost twenty. By her age, Roméo had already quit school twice, hitchhiked out to California and then all the way to Nicaragua, met and proposed to her mother, something Sophie reminded him of frequently. Maybe Roméo was mostly upset because everyone else seemed to be living their lives fully. Except him. And Anna Newman.

Roméo pulled off onto the shoulder and U-turned on the 329. He needed to pay a visit to an old acquaintance before committing to home. He drove mindlessly past the little houses along the dirt road to Ste. Lucie, which was sadly like so many little towns in Quebec. The government had invested in and rebuilt much of the crumbling public services and infrastructure in the hopes of enticing people back. But Roméo noted the empty tennis courts, unused hockey rink, vacant kiddy park—it was like the town had thrown a party for itself and no one came. He passed the old church on his left, the life-sized figures of the Nativity *crèche* still out on the front lawn. No one had put it away from last Christmas, and now they might as well leave it out. At least someone had removed the baby Jesus from the manger because it was simply not done to have him appear until Christmas Day. Mary needed some serious touching up, as one of her eyes had disappeared. Joseph was still looking fine for such an old guy. Roméo wondered who in town was responsible for restoring the crèche. Surely not the elderly priest who already tended to two other flocks in the Laurentians? Roméo passed the derelict Jeannette's Bed & Breakfast and the Casse Croute Skidoo that hadn't survived the last exodus of people from town. Even the winter snowmobilers who roared through town every Saturday and Sunday couldn't revive the business. Roméo headed toward Mohawk territory and bulleted down the road that ran through the reserve like someone had taken a knife and cut a straight line through the fir trees. A misspelled sign that read "Shoting Range" hung crookedly from a balsam tree. Roméo smiled to himself as he considered whether that range included the road he was driving on.

Roméo turned down the back road to the town of Val David. Within a few minutes his car bumped into a gravel driveway and he pulled up to the house, a small pre-fab bungalow with no character or charm whatsoever. Two old cars sat on cinder blocks in the yard, obviously cannibalized to outfit the third car, a souped-up Ford LTD that had recently been given a fresh coat of red paint. Several old stoves and fridges sat like sculptures in the yard. Something that had once been a small greenhouse had lost two supports and was kneeling on its side, overgrown with weeds, its plastic sheeting snapping in the wind. As soon as Roméo emerged from his car, two dogs came tearing up to him. He jumped back toward his car door until they reached the end of their chains and got snapped back to safety. They looked like a cross between a pitbull and a wolf, and both strained at the very ends of their tethers, barking hysterically. Roméo looked past them at the house and saw the sheet tacked up in the window flutter slightly. His arrival had been noted. The front door opened to another dog—this time a snarling, trembling Chihuahua the size of a small housecat. Roméo reached down and offered the top of his hand, which it promptly bit. It drew no blood, just a laugh from its owner, who beckoned for Roméo to come on in.

Roméo had known Ti-Coune Cousineau in high school in Montreal. He and his sister were famous for running away from their alcoholic, abusive mother. And her equally alcoholic and abusive boyfriends. They were finally taken in by so-called Child Protection Services and for a year or so got shuffled from one foster family to another. One day, when they had run away for the umpteenth time, they were hanging out at Alexis Nihon shopping mall, known for its busy day trade in teen prostitution. They were spotted by a biker who had once "dated" their mother. He felt sorry for them and took them in. They lived in the bikers' clubhouse above a bar in the Plateau, now a very trendy, gentrified neighborhood, for almost two years.

Hélène was only fourteen at the time, a bit too young for a biker chick, so she was under their dubious protection.

Ti-Coune was only twelve years old and told Roméo he remembered the bikers as being mostly kind—probably because Ti-Coune and Hélène did what they were told, like dropping a package off when they were asked to, or making themselves scarce when the clubhouse was being used for activities no kid should witness. They had to share a bed in a little back room—it was filthy, but relatively safe. At least it wasn't the streets, where a girl like Hélène wouldn't last a week without falling into the teenage sex-trafficking circuit. She was unusually beautiful. The bikers called her *Hélène de Troie*. Helen of Troy. None of them knew the kind of abuse she had endured until she'd decided to run away. Not one of them was as tough as Hélène.

Roméo remembered her pulling up to Outremont High School on the back of a Harley-Davidson. They would all stare as her "father," a tattooed, bearded, and ponytailed beast of a man roared off into the leafy streets. No one messed with Hélène Cousineau. Ti-Coune ended up getting flagged by one of his teachers and put back in foster care. Hélène told a sobbing Ti-Coune that she could never go back into the system. At fifteen years old, she hitchhiked all the way across the country by herself and, as far as Roméo knew, was living in Edmonton.

Ti-Coune had moved up to the Laurentians to get out of the city, where he had mostly hung out with low-lifes, trying not to drink himself to oblivion, and failing most of the time. He was a small-time break-and-enter guy, mostly to support his dope and booze habit, sometimes to pay off a few favors. It was widely believed by those who give a shit about these things that Ti-Coune was tight with what remained of the local Hells Angels chapter—but Roméo knew better. To become a "full-patch" Hells Angel, you had to first spend time as a "friend," then a "hang around," then a "prospect," and finally after many byzantine initation tests, you could wear the infamous death-head logo on your back. Ti-Coune was tolerated because of his past experience with the Hells in Montreal, but he was no more, and never would be more, than an *aspiring* "friend." He was a peripheral guy—always around, always hustling for a few bucks, a fast talker, but a slow thinker. Roméo often wondered about fetal alcohol syndrome where Ti-Coune was concerned. It was a small miracle the guy was still alive.

Ti-Coune Cousineau was the same age as Roméo, forty-nine, but looked much younger and older at the same time. He was very fit—Roméo noticed bulging triceps and abs through his stained white T-shirt, and absurdly developed forearms with fading sleeve tattoos. There was a poorly executed Wonder-Womanish version of Hélène, a few names and quotes Roméo couldn't make out, and then a clearly drawn swastika by his elbow. He exuded a kind of explosive, nervous energy, not unlike his dogs. Ti-Coune's face, however, clearly bore the ravages of booze and way too many drugs. Deeply lined, pockmarked, and a shade of yellowish gray, it was as though his head had been removed from a much older man and attached to an athlete's body. The effect was disconcerting.

The house smelled like skunk and body odor. A torn, vinyl La-Z-Boy chair faced a woodstove that burned lazily. A coffee-table was covered in newspapers, filthy coffee mugs, beer bottles, and several empty frozen food containers. On one wall was a torn poster of a bunch of dogs sitting at a table playing poker. On another, a Confederate flag was tacked up, and just below it the blue and white Quebec *fleur-de-lys*. Strange bedfellows, Roméo thought. He tried not to look at the kitchen, which clearly had not been cleaned in weeks, possibly months. The two doors off the living room were hastily closed by Ti-Coune, who swept some "girly" magazines off an old armchair and invited Roméo to have a seat. The Chihuahua leaped onto Ti-Coune's lap and directed a low, persistent growl at Roméo.

"*Tais-toi, Pitoune*," said Ti-Coune tenderly, although he was now holding her jaw shut. The growling continued, muted. He turned to Roméo, raising his chin. "*Pis? Qu'est-ce que tu veux*?" Roméo asked him what he knew about Madame Newman.

"Not much. She's a mystery, her. I know that she been living there about. Oh. *Criss*. About twenty years. She don't talk to no one. She makes paintings. She makes good money with that, I think."

"You know any of her friends? Any family?"

Ti-Coune shook his head. Pitoune had finally stopped growling. Now she just trembled violently. "I never seen her with no one. I mean, she don't even say hello at the dépanneur, *t'sais*?" Ti-Coune looked at Roméo carefully. "Why you wanna know about Madame Newman?"

"There's been an…accident. She's dead." Roméo watched Ti-Coune's reaction.

"Me, I'm not surprised. Old lady, living out there all alone. She got no one. Shit happens."

Roméo leaned in. "Think any of your buddies might know something about this?"

"*Ahn*? No. We got nothing to do with that. An accident, you said?"

"Maybe. Maybe not." Roméo removed two twenty-dollar bills from his pocket and slid them under the ashtray teeming with cigarette butts and spliffs. He would have to take a shower as soon as he got home. "*T'es tu certain*?"

Ti-Coune hesitated, then offered one nugget. "I heard she had money. A lot of money. *Les juifs, hein?* People think she keeps money in the house. That's what les juifs they do."

Roméo raised an eyebrow. "Oh? I thought they just ran all the world's banks. And Hollywood."

Ti-Coune nodded. "They run the banks for other people. To take their money. But they keep their own money in the home." Ti-Coune leaned in. "*Ils ont tu fouillés dans sa maison?* Did they take something?"

Roméo stood up and brushed the dog hair from his pants. "If you hear anything—anything—call me. Right away. *Compris*?"

As Roméo backed out of Ti-Coune's driveway, he was uncertain whether Ti-Coune knew something about the Newman case. Ti-Coune had a way of twisting the forelock of greasy gray hair over his right eye when he was lying that was entirely absent today. But Roméo was intrigued by the idea that the locals thought Madame Newman was rich, and given to hiding her money in her house. Nothing like a little garden-variety anti-Semitism to fuel rumors. Roméo saw it all the time in Quebec, where its roots ran deep and tenaciously. It was definitely worth looking into a little further.

Six

MARIE KNOCKED at the front door and waited. She noticed the mailbox was clinging to the wall by only one screw. The Welcome mat was worn down to read V LC ME. She resolved to fix both those things immediately. But the house was already sold, so it didn't really matter anymore, did it? Marie waited a few more seconds, then pushed the door open. "Mum? *Maman?* It's me!" There was no answer. Marie went into the kitchen and noticed the stove burner was red hot, but nothing was cooking. As she turned it off, she called to her mother again, much louder this time. Where could she be? Marie felt her panic rise when she checked the bedroom and her mother wasn't there, either. Had she wandered off again? She raced into the bathroom—maybe she had slipped and was lying unconscious—but the bathroom was empty. Now she was screaming for her mother, a terrible sense of dread overtaking her entire body. She ran two stairs at a time to the upstairs TV room—her mother still sometimes watched the afternoon soaps—and came to a sudden stop in the doorway. There was her mother, lying on the couch completely motionless. On the television Luke and

Laura from *General Hospital* were looking meaningfully at each other, but when they spoke no sound came out. Claire often watched TV with the sound muted now—maybe she found it easier to make up her own dialogue. Marie tiptoed over to her mother, who was snoring delicately. One hand was tucked under her head, cupping her cheek, like a sleeping child. If only she could stay like that, Marie thought. Undisturbed and unburdened by the sense that the world has shifted out from under her, and is never coming back. Marie looked closely at her mother's hands—the fingers bent with arthritis, the veins raised and blue. She leaned in to take one of them in hers, but thought better of it. She would let her mother sleep a little while longer.

She turned off Luke and Laura, went downstairs, and left through the side door to retrieve her bag from the car. The day was definitely getting more blustery. Marie could smell that snow was on its way. She glanced at the fence, now coiled and bent with rust and age, that separated their yard from the nearest neighbors. How many times had she and her friends climbed over that fence and taken off together to roam the neighborhood in search of adventure? That was in the 1960s, when Marie and her friends had freedom unimaginable to most kids today. There were no such things as "play *dates.*" Marie just dropped in at friends' houses like they were her own. No one locked their doors, except for the Kovaks, but they were Hungarian. "Playing" wasn't supervised or regulated or mediated. In the summer, Marie and her friends were kicked out of the house by nine in the morning and were ordered not to return home until lunch at noon. They would go to their park where, by today's standards, death awaited them everywhere. There were *see-saws. Concrete* merry-go-rounds. *Metal* monkey bars. They would ride to the park on their bikes with banana seats and monkey handlebars flying sparkly rainbow streamers. They did not wear helmets. No parent accompanied them. After lunch, which for Marie always consisted of homemade soup and a sandwich, inhaled while watching *Johnny Jellybean* on their black-and-white TV, afternoons were spent at the pool when the sun had warmed up the day to make that frigid water almost bearable. They were not allowed to come home until four, when sunburned and waterlogged they would stagger into the house, starving and foraging for whatever snacks they could find before the torturous wait for supper at six sharp. Repeat for two months. That was summer circa 1968. Marie thought of her own children's highly regulated lives. How *did* that happen? She wouldn't dream of letting them do *half* the things she'd done. What the hell had happened to her generation that they were such a bunch of anxious control freaks?

Marie climbed the short flight of stairs to her old room, which was now the guest room, although there were never any "guests" anymore. She could still remember what it looked like when it was her room. Royal blue and white bedspread. White French-style rococo dresser and matching mirror, pink Princess telephone (her mother's idea), a white desk, with matching chair, the *de rigueur* shag carpet—royal blue, of course. A few trophies for track and field, swimming, and public speaking. Over her bed, a poster of David Cassidy, later Che Guevara. A picture of her dog framed by her bedside, which was later replaced by a picture of her boyfriend, changed every few months or so.

Now the room was beige. The bedspread was lighter beige on dark beige. The curtains were off-beige. The carpet was beige and pale blue. There was a painting over the bed of abstract beige shapes with a few white ones thrown in. Marie seemed to remember her mother had called in a decorator to redo the room when Marie had gone. She'd like to hunt her down and get her mother's money back.

Marie sat down on the edge of the bed and looked out her window. The yard was huge by today's standards, probably close to an acre. A cedar hedge lined the far end, and a few old maple trees still stood. The blue spruce tree her parents had planted when her oldest sister, Madeleine, was born was now over fifty feet high. The yard had once been filled with apple trees that her father had planted, but Marie's mother had them all cut down. She had always disliked the mess they made—stinking rotten apples everywhere, covered in drunken wasps. When Tommy Ebern's sister, Laura, had gotten stung multiple times and went into anaphylactic shock, Marie's mother took action. They were all gone within the week. Marie remembers weeping for those trees. Their pink blossoms were like a special gift her father had given her, just her. Every spring she would wake up to the vision of them out her window, and she felt loved by the world and, especially, her father.

Marie opened her worn suitcase on the beige bed and slid a few of her clothes into the small beige dresser. The bed was new, not the saggy mattress she had slept on for years that made a squinking noise when any movement occurred. She remembered sneaking her boyfriends into her bedroom through the backyard door, and the terror and thrill of possibly being caught by her parents. Once in the wee hours of the morning when Marie was enthusiastically enjoying herself with a new boyfriend, her father opened her door and just stood there, watching them. They didn't notice him for. *Oh my God. How long…?* They scrambled off each other, pulled the sheets up to their chins, and stared at Marie's father. Marie thought she was going to die of humiliation. There was an endless moment. And then her father closed her door and disappeared without a word. He did not look her in the eye for a long time after that, which in almost every way was worse.

Marie suddenly felt very sleepy. She noticed that more and more, she seemed to need an afternoon nap. She lay down on the beige bed, crossed her ankles, and looked over at their next-door neighbors' house. It seemed so much smaller than she remembered. The Atwoods used to live there but like almost all the others, were long gone. The Atwoods had disliked Marie's family. They disapproved of them. Marie's father's drunken debauchery was legendary, and Marie's mother was just too…French. Lucy Atwood was Marie's best friend and spent every single day after school at the Russell house, every weekend, and every Wednesday night because they always ate out at Vesuvio's, the local Italian restaurant. On report card day, Lucy would head to the Russells' house first, to confess to Marie's mother why she'd got too many Bs and Cs, before she had to face her own mother's wrath. Marie's mother had this gift: she could make anyone feel better almost immediately. She could make Charles Manson feel better about himself.

To Marie, the Atwoods were pretty much the most normal family on the block. They had three kids, a big goofy dog, they went camping in the summer and skating in the winter. Marie knew that Mrs. Atwood didn't make *boudin* for breakfast, or *escargots* for dinner like her mother did, but

Marie had never been invited to their house for any meal ever. Mrs. Atwood seemed to spend most of her time sitting in her backyard, reading her stack of books with her hair in pin curls, something Marie's mother would literally not be caught dead in.

But one day. One extraordinary day. Mrs. Atwood told Lucy to invite Marie to have supper with them. Marie's first-ever supper at their house. She had been there only three or four times before, when Lucy and Marie would try very hard to play quietly with their Barbies until Dr. Atwood would emerge from his study and say, "Keep it down, girls." (Marie's father didn't have a study; his room was called a den, and all he did in there was fall asleep watching the news while Marie and her sisters waited to make sure he was good and out before Marie's sisters would change the channel to *Hogan's Heroes*. Or *The Beverly Hillbillies*.)

Marie's mother, of course, gave her usual instructions: "Don't forget your please and thank you's, don't sap, elbows off the table, help clear the dishes, eat everything Mrs. Atwood puts in front of you." She looked Marie right in the eye and said, "She always has people in her house from all over the world. Because of Dr. Atwood, I think. They might be very different from us, from you. So be careful what you say." It was true. Dr. Atwood was actually a doctor—a professor of comparative politics at McGill. The Atwoods often had people staying with them—students from India, Thailand, Rhodesia, Ceylon, as well as young men, and sometimes young couples from the United States. Marie thought now that's why Mrs. Atwood's own children were sometimes overlooked and neglected. She'd wanted fully formed people living with her, not people she had to raise.

When Marie remembered sitting down to Lucy's dining room table, she recalled almost weeping with joy at what she'd seen: iceberg lettuce in a bowl, with a container of Kraft's Creamy Italian dressing beside it. White Wonder Bread in a basket, with a tub of margarine waiting to be slathered on it. Glasses of Coca-Cola. Already poured. It was…heaven. At the table was Mrs. Atwood, making polite conversation. Lucy's big brother, who just kept calling them retards. Her big sister Tracey, who sat there in a coma of sullenness. Mrs. Atwood was being very nice, trying hard to please because Marie was there and was Lucy's best friend, and this was an occasion. There were also two other people at the table. A young couple from the United States. From New York. Lucy whispered to Marie that they were living at her house for a while, and that they were *draft dodgers*. Marie had no idea what that was. Lucy whispered again that the husband didn't want to fight in Vietnam, so they ran away and came to live in Canada, and they couldn't go back home. Ever.

The draft dodger's wife, as it turned out, had made the meal. Not Mrs. Atwood, which Marie's mother would've found insulting. But after the promise of the iceberg lettuce and the bread, everything went downhill from there. The main course was spaghetti with tomato sauce, all mixed together in a giant green plastic bowl sitting at the center of the table. Mrs. Atwood did serve the spaghetti though, which was difficult, as it was very watery. They all started to eat, although, truthfully, having been raised on her mother's spaghetti Bolognese (she mixed veal and pork), this was not what Marie would call spaghetti. Suddenly, the draft dodger stood up, slid his plate over to his wife across the table, and declared: "This is not edible. This is disgusting. What were you doing all day? Couldn't you have done more than dump a can of Heinz sauce on this...excuse for spaghetti!" They all froze in their chairs. No one said a word. No one breathed. Except Lucy's older brother, who said, "This is bullshit" and left the table. After what was probably a few seconds, but seemed much longer, the draft dodger's wife, in a tiny voice, said to her husband, "If—if you don't like it? Don't eat it!" To which he replied, "Okay. I won't!" At that point he stood up, grabbed that giant bowl of spaghetti, and overturned it on her head. The entire bowl of spaghetti. It dripped down the sides of her face, slipped inside her shirt, got caught on her ears, and then mixed, horrifyingly, with her tears. The worst part, Marie remembered, was she just sat there. She did not remove the bowl from her head. She just sat there and wept like a little girl. Marie realized that she could not remember what happened next. Her memory stopped right there, with that sobbing young woman from New York, and her total inability to move. Or speak.

What Marie remembered of the aftermath was this: she ran home before dessert and told her mother everything that had happened. Surprisingly, Claire Russell was not as entertained or pleased as Marie thought she'd be at this turn of events. All she said was "Poor soul." Marie's mother always said that, and now, almost forty-five years later, Marie finds herself saying it too. She was never invited to the Atwoods' for supper again.

The next thing Marie knew was that her pillow was damp with her own drool. She wiped the side of her mouth with the pillowcase and opened her eyes. Claire Russell stood at the foot of the bed, staring at her.

"You finally made it, Louise!"

"Mum. Louise is in Calgary, remember? It's me. Marie."

A slight hesitation. "Of course I know it's you!" Claire smiled like it was a joke they were both in on, but Marie knew the truth. She noticed that her mother had a large yellow stain on the lapel of her cardigan. Probably old mustard. And it was buttoned the wrong way. Marie's heart broke for her mother again. Until her illness, Claire had always been so fastidious about her appearance, never left the house without at least applying her lipstick. She would be mortified if she knew.

Claire squeezed Marie's foot. "I think my program is starting now. Would you like to watch with me? Could we have a TV dinner?"

Marie's mother always watched her "programs"—mostly British sitcoms, so odd for a French Canadian. Her current favorite involved some man dressed up as an old, foul-mouthed granny. Claire would laugh uproariously, leaning into the television like she wanted to join the party. Marie had read in a magazine that people with Alzheimer's who once enjoyed witty, ironic humor often preferred slapstick and pratfalls as the disease progressed. Marie's mother was a case in point.

Marie heated up a couple of Lean Cuisines—inedible low-fat frozen food that she knew would leave her hungry within the hour. Claire had stacks of them in the freezer. She poured her mother a glass of tomato juice and struggled not to pour herself a stiff Scotch. She wanted to keep her wits about her, as Claire could be quite difficult when it came to bedtime. Marie unfolded a TV tray in front of her mother and carefully centered her meal on it. Claire didn't even look away from the TV. Marie figured she could let the

TV babysit her mother for an hour or two. She changed her mind about that glass of Scotch and poured herself a double shot, neat. Then she headed to the basement.

Seven

ROMÉO HAD BEEN hoping to interview them both, but Madame Lachance was away on a long-planned visit to her sister in Chicoutimi and wouldn't be back for another two days. Roméo glanced around the living room while Louis was in the kitchen fetching him a glass of juice. It was meticulously clean and cared for. Delicate lace doilies clung to the back of the sofa and matching armchairs were placed around a coffee-table with a full bowl of mixed nuts on it. On the wall by the front door was a faded painting of a very pretty, blue-eyed Jesus, pointing to his bleeding red heart with one holy finger, the other hand raised in greeting, or blessing. On the longest wall in the room facing the sofa was an enormous flat-screen television. On almost every surface—on every side table and on the mantel over the fireplace—were photographs of what Roméo figured were their children, grandchildren, and possibly great-grandchildren. One picture was set aside from the others, framed by tiny plastic flowers. A teenage boy, about sixteen years old, Roméo guessed, wearing a hunting camouflage jacket, a bright orange *toque*, and a huge grin. Roméo picked up the photo to look more closely but returned it quickly as he heard Louis behind him, grumbling a little to himself.

"I hope orange juice is okay with you," Louis muttered. "Me, I prefer the cranberry, but it's all gone."

Roméo accepted the glass, took a sip, and placed it gently on the coffee table. Louis opened a small drawer in the sideboard, pulled out a coaster, and placed it under Roméo's glass. "My wife can be a bit *tatillonne*." Louis settled himself on the edge of the armchair and looked at Roméo expectantly.

"What can you tell me about Madame Newman?"

Louis shook his head. It was clear he was having difficulty talking about her.

"How long have you worked for her?"

Louis looked into the distance and squinted. "About eighteen years. On and off."

Roméo was about to ask another question when Louis continued. "I had the cancer eleven years ago and had to take some time off for chemo."

"What kind of work did you do for her? What did she need you for?"

Louis almost smiled.

"She didn't need *me*, not really. She didn't need nobody, Madame Newman. She was the most...*autonome* lady I know."

"Well, what did she hire you to do then?"

"Little stuff—like sometimes I helped her harvest her garden if the weather was turning bad and there was no time before the frost. I changed her toilet once—it was so old and completely finished."

"Did she tell you anything about her family, her friends—"

Louis almost smiled. “No. Never. We talked about…” Louis let out a brief sigh. “What we were doing in that moment, you know? Just the moment we were living in. Sometimes we talked about the weather, or, or the birds. We talked about the birds a lot. She knew a lot about animals and trees and…*la nature*. She showed me what mushrooms we could pick in the forest and eat, and how to make salad from so many plants around here, and…” Louis trailed off.

“Did you ever see anyone at her house? In eighteen years someone must have dropped by when you were working—or more recently?”

Louis gave it some thought. “No. Not that I can remember. She was like a hermit, you know? A recluse. But she was very nice, not…” He hesitated. “Not a misanthrope, you know?”

Roméo scribbled down *Not misanthrope*. This interview was going nowhere. He thought about the call he got that morning—a more junior detective had offered to take this “dog of a case” off his hands. None of his fellow officers seemed to feel any urgency about solving the murder of the old woman—an old woman with no family who'd come forward to claim her or grieve for her or demand that her killer be found. Roméo was starting to feel an obligation to Anna Newman. He would stay on this case.

“You are certain you've seen no one visiting here?”

Louis twisted his wedding ring in his gnarly, arthritic finger. “Yes. I am certain. Well, except…maybe two weeks ago? Maybe longer than that, I'm not sure. Just as I was leaving her house, I saw a car in my rearview mirror slow down, and then turn into Madame Newman's road.”

Roméo looked up from his notes. “What kind of car? Did you recognize it?”

Louis frowned. "I didn't know the owner of the car, but it was silver-grayish and had the...the rings on the front—like the Olympics—what's that car?"

"An Audi?"

"*Oui!* That's it. A very fancy car, I think."

Roméo swallowed the last of his juice. "You didn't happen to see the license plate number, did you? Or any part of it?"

Louis shook his head again. "No. Not at all. I think the plates were from Quebec, though. I would say I am 95 percent certain of that. I remember the *Je me souviens* written on them."

Roméo smiled and wrote that down. "Monsieur Lachance, do you have any idea why someone would want to kill Anna Newman? Did people think she had money hidden in her house? If so, why would they think that?"

"If she had money, she certainly didn't spend it." Louis looked out the window as though the answer was outside in his tidy backyard. "Maybe it's because of that guy—what was his name? Welsh? Walsh? The one who stole all that money, and the RCMP never found it?" Louis looked directly at Roméo. "Remember him?"

Roméo certainly did. David Walsh was the biggest white-collar criminal in Canadian history, who'd stolen millions in savings from regular tax-paying Canadians through a mining investment scam. His elderly mother had a little country cabin not too far from Ste. Lucie, and when he died suddenly of a stroke in Nassau before the RCMP could recover the money he stole, locals were convinced the cash was stuffed in the walls of his mother's house. Many still believed that today, although the house was boarded up and derelict.

Roméo was almost done, for now. "Do you know if she was in some dispute with anyone? Did you hear any rumors? Did she have any enemies?"

Louis took his glass of juice in shaking hands and sipped delicately. "No. I don't know anyone who would want to hurt Madame Newman." When he said her name, Louis's voice caught and quavered. Roméo started to get to his feet, but Louis stopped him with a quiet hand on his sleeve.

"When my. When my...grandson, Charles-Etienne... died," Louis lifted his hand toward the photograph Roméo had noted earlier, "I went to the funeral in Ste. Agathe, at the big church. Many people came for him—he was very popular, had many friends." Roméo waited while Louis tried to continue. "But after, I could not go to the...wake at his mother's house...my daughter. I could not. I could not stand there and eat sandwiches and drink beer and pretend that I did not want to die myself. I never told the others, but Charles-Etienne was my favorite, the youngest of them all. He had depression, but no one knew that because he never talked about that. He was always happy, always the party boy, the one who everyone liked."

Roméo suddenly remembered where he had seen the face of the boy before. In the newspaper, maybe two years ago. The boy had shot himself in the mouth with his hunting rifle.

"The family, Michelle my wife. They were all mad at me for leaving after the funeral. They asked the priest to get me, to bring me back. But I could not. I went to..." Louis took a deep breath, "Madame Newman's house. I just needed to see her. I told her that I had forgotten to finish something. She knew what had happened with Charles-Etienne. But she asked me no questions, she didn't try to comfort me, she didn't tell me to go to my daughter's and be with my family. She made me a fresh coffee and just listened to me."

Louis removed his hand from Roméo's arm. "She was a lady of great *sagesse.* And grace. I know in my heart, that she earned it in a very hard way."

Roméo patted his breast pocket and removed his card.

"I am so sorry for your loss. Please keep this, and if you think of anything else about Madame Newman, please call me. Any time. Any day, okay?"

Louis accepted the card and followed Roméo to the front door.

"The last time I saw Madame Newman, there were dozens of crows hanging around her yard. I said to her I'd never seen so many as this year. It was like they were holding a big crow convention. I don't like crows." Roméo wondered where this was going. "She told me that in English, a big gang of crows was called a 'murder.' *Un meurtre de corbeaux.*"

Roméo shook Louis' bony hand and then headed toward his car. Louis watched him, turned to close his door, and then called after him.

"She also told me that crows can mean a big change is coming."

"She was right about that," Roméo said out loud to himself as he started the engine and wondered about to whom the mysterious silver car belonged.

Eight

ENNIS JAMIESON SAT at his enormous eat-in kitchen table and watched his three children eat their breakfast. Or rather, watched his three children frantically playing on their tablets and phones, never once looking up to acknowledge the bacon, eggs, and toast their mother placed before them. He thought about saying something to them about this but chose to remain silent. He was always on their case about their addiction to their technology, and he hated to be the hopelessly old guy who just doesn't get it. He could not face the eye-rolling and deep sighing that separating themselves from their devices triggered. Instead, Ennis decided to be cheerful and informative. He had just gotten the good news himself that very morning.

"So, guess what?"

No acknowledgment from anyone, including his wife, Bridget, who was now peering and poking at her own phone.

"Hey! Family. I have news!"

Bridget looked up at him in that unfocused, sleepy way that he used to find very sexy, and now found a little irritating.

"What's the news, hon?"

Ennis didn't really care if Brandon acknowledged his news because Ennis saw Brandon as a lost cause where he was concerned. It had been ten years since Ennis married Bridget and tried to become a father to Brandon. He had failed in every way except financial. Brandon still seemed to regard Ennis as some weird uncle who'd moved in with him and his mum and just wouldn't leave. Except that this was Ennis's house. Ennis's son, Liam, looked away from his iPad for a nano-second and then panicked. He smiled wanly at Ennis and tried bravely to not look at the screen. His daughter, Katie, put her phone down and beamed at him.

"What is it, Daddy?"

Ennis could hardly even look at her she was so beautiful. Ten years old, green eyes, auburn hair, and a scattering of freckles across her nose and cheeks. Already tall for her age. Smart as hell. Already a Queen Bee at her school, already a leader. And she worshipped Ennis. He had his daddy's girl.

"Well. I'm going to be...this year's..." He did a little drum roll on the counter. "Grand Marshal in the Montreal St. Patrick's Day parade!"

The response was underwhelming. Brandon looked confused. Liam started to clap, but he had no idea why. Bridget gave him a hug but dodged the kiss he was leaning in for. Only Katie got it. She leaped out of her chair and hurled herself at him.

"That is *so* fantastic, Daddy! Grand Marshal? Can I walk at the front of the parade with you? Can I?"

Ennis inhaled the fresh shampoo of her hair, felt the boniness of her frame under her school uniform. The love.

"I don't see why not. I mean, maybe there's rules about

that, but I will have you there right by me, pumpkin, if they allow it."

Katie pretend-pouted. "But you're the *Grand* Marshal. You could *order* it."

Ennis winked at Bridget, who was now applying too red lipstick to her own pouty lips.

"We'll see. It's a great honor. I hope you're all proud of your dad."

Katie and Liam danced around the table, chanting, "We are! We are! We are!"

Brandon slid off his chair, grabbed his knapsack and skateboard, and in one seamless move escaped out the kitchen door. Bridget followed him. Ennis watched her extract one cheek peck from him and send him on his way.

Ennis had married Bridget Burke when he was forty-nine years old and certain he would remain a bachelor for the remainder of his days. He had been a serial monogamist—ending intense, tumultuous relationships at the two-year mark over a twenty-year span. In his late thirties, he decided marriage and the whole family thing wasn't for him. Until ten years later, when he met Bridget. She was the receptionist at his proctologist's office (true story) and he fell in love at first sight. She was an adult version of his daughter—thick and real auburn hair, green eyes, and an astoundingly perfect figure. All genuine parts. Bridget was just not someone you ran into every day. Ennis did not usually flirt with his doctors' receptionists, but it was clear that Bridget had a fierce intelligence and an irreverent wit that left him making up excuses to see his bum doctor more frequently. This was not easy, as Ennis had always been blessed with extraordinarily good health.

On their first date, Ennis learned many things about Bridget Burke. She was twenty-two years younger than he but had lived what was to Ennis an unimaginable life. She was raised a fundamentalist Christian in the Bible Belt in the Kawarthas outside Toronto, and she and her seven siblings were homeschooled by their mother as Ontario public schools were considered much too liberal. There were no books permitted in the house except the Bible. Her father worked at the Pickering nuclear plant and was a highly respected elder at their church—an authoritarian and bankrupt patriarch who periodically shoved her mother through a wall or gave one of the kids a good wallop to keep them in line. But he never touched Bridget, as her behavior, she made sure, was always beyond reproach. She earned straight As in the high school she was allowed to attend for grade 12 and volunteered on several do-gooder committees as well as being the soloist in the school choir. She was accepted to several top medical schools with full scholarships. In her senior year, however, Bridget made one false move.

She fell in love. Although her first-ever boyfriend was also raised a no-sex-before-marriage fundamentalist, he was less of a believer. Bridget resisted his pleas to have sex for months, but finally gave in when he threatened to break it off, and although they had used a condom, Bridget discovered she was as fertile as her mother. He stuck around long enough to give their son his name. Then he disappeared to the oil patch in Alberta, and Bridget never heard from him again. Of course, her fornication and public shame forced her estrangement from her family, so she was on her own with no money and nowhere to go. Bridget ended up in a home for pregnant teenagers (at nineteen she just made the cut).

She spent the next six years picking up whatever underpaid work she could, spending most of her wages on childcare, only to get home in time to feed and put Brandon to bed. Her unlikely move to Quebec was the result of an ill-fated romance that lasted exactly two weeks once Bridget crossed the border. It turned out he was going back to his wife. Bridget was left once again with no money and nowhere to go. But she was still a smart and capable worker and wept with joy when she got offered the receptionist job at the bum doctor's. Brandon was starting school, and maybe she could start to save a little. Maybe they could finally go on vacation somewhere. Or think about him playing hockey. The proctologist had come on to her only twice in the two years she had been there, but his patients did all the time. When Ennis started his flirtation with her, Bridget figured he was just like all the other losers who try to pick up receptionists. But over time, Ennis convinced her that he was worthy. That he was not an asshole. That he would take care of her and love Brandon and maybe they could build a life together. For the first time in her twenty-seven years, Bridget felt like she'd met a real man.

Now Ennis watched Bridget watch Brandon flag down a friend at the end of their driveway, hop in a monstrous SUV, and spin off down the road toward the nearby town of St. Lazare. She curled a bit of that glorious auburn hair behind her ear, now seamed with a few long strands of gray, and slowly returned to the house.

"Katie and Liam! Time to go. Got your lunches? Homework?" Bridget threw her phone in her purse, grabbed her keys, and slipped into her heels. "I've got a meeting and then lunch with Lidia. Then Brandon has a dentist appointment at three. Can you pick up the kids today?"

Ennis nodded. "Yup. Today, I can do that. Just for you."

"Not for me, Ennis. They're your kids too, remember?" Bridget corrected him. "But thank you just the same."

Liam and Katie hugged him on their way out, Katie lingering a little longer. "I am so proud of you, Daddy. You will be the best Grand Marshal ever."

Then, in an instant, they were out the door, and the huge house was so quiet, the only sound Ennis could hear was the humming of the fridge and the barking of a distant dog. He thought about Katie's boast. What was perhaps most remarkable was that Ennis would be the first Grand Marshal of the St. Patrick's Day parade who didn't have a drop of Irish blood in him.

Ennis took his coffee over to the bay window that offered the best view of his property. The weak autumn sun was just above the horizon, but there wasn't a cloud in the pinkish sky. His ten acres of fields were hardened and whitened with morning frost. His mind's eye saw the brand-new stable he would be building that spring, and the horses he would fill it with. Two Anglo-Arabians, equine perfection. He had promised Katie a Welsh pony, and Liam a goat. He would definitely have to rethink that last one. When he asked Brandon what pet he'd like for the new "farm," he'd looked at Ennis like he himself had grown horns. Then he announced he didn't see himself sticking around long enough to care. If Ennis was honest with himself, he knew he hoped that that was true. He couldn't wait for Brandon to graduate from high school so he could send him to college in the city. Get him a decent apartment. Enough money to get by, not enough to get into trouble. Bridget could visit all the time. She often complained about how isolated the new place was. This was a perfect opportunity for her to scratch that big-city itch. He glanced at the kitchen clock and realized he'd savored his morning a few minutes too long. He had a meeting downtown at Le Warwick Residence at 9:15, and with traffic he'd be hard pressed to make it on time. His clients could be quite cantankerous. The ladies didn't like it when he kept them waiting.

Ennis was backing out of his long driveway when he noticed the red flag was raised on their mailbox. They hadn't gotten any mail in a few days and were about to lose their home postal delivery service altogether. Ennis was not nostalgic for this service despite being born in 1957 and thought this change had been a long time coming. He hadn't noticed the flag up earlier that morning, and there was no way their mailman had driven out here before midafternoon. He felt a flutter in his stomach. There was a single envelope in the box, addressed to him. Just his name. No address, so the letter had been hand-delivered. He debated opening it. He hadn't received one of these in four weeks. He thought the whole weird and slightly unnerving business was over. He noticed his hand trembled as he tore at the seal. Ridiculous. And there it was. Typed in boldface, capital latters.

TELL THE TRUTH.

Ennis looked up and scanned the horizon as though he might see a car peeling off into the distance, carrying whoever had delivered the message. Of course, there was no one. Just a lumbering yellow school bus making its dusty way down the road to the local public school. He stuffed the letter into his breast pocket and returned to his car. He chided himself for refusing to beef up security around the house when his alarm company had proposed it. He was now going to install cameras and get to the bottom of this.

Nine

THEY WERE AT LEAST ten to a cage, clambering against the chicken wire or standing stock still, staring. One hurled himself against the fence repeatedly. Another cowered in the corner, probably hoping the nightmare would end soon. It was like the United Nations of dogs—every possible bark, breed, color, and character on sad display at the Ste. Agathe SPCA. The kind, very young assistant had chatted nonstop since he had arrived, explaining to him their policy of waiting a week at least before euthanizing. She touched his arm. In special cases, the ones they really grew fond of? They would keep for even a month or two sometimes. She pointed to an old orangey dog with one flattened ear and a deeply sorrowful expression. "See that one?" Louis nodded, barely able to look at him. "His owners moved to Ecuador to retire and just left him behind—*in the house* they sold. Just like that. Like he was a piece of furniture. He's been here five weeks. No one will take him because he's old and has to take injections for diabetes. He's due to be put down two days from now." Louis knew she was appealing to his obvious empathy for this dog—he too felt like a piece of furniture at times—but Louis was here for another dog, God help him. He walked past another full cage, and then he spotted him. Kutya. Way at the back of the cage, separated from the others, who became hysterical when they saw Louis. Kutya was lying down, his nose buried in his curled tail, but not at all asleep. He was watching Louis with a look of profound despondence. When the assistant went to retrieve him for Louis, he barely raised his head. "This one has not eaten at all since he arrived. Only water. I'm not sure, Monsieur, if he is the best choice for you." Louis removed the new collar and leash from his pocket. "He is the only one I want."

Louis was prepared to face the wrath of Michelle. He used to have a dog, a poodle mix that was as unlikely a dog as possible for someone like Louis, but he'd cherished her. When she died several years ago of old age, Louis cried for three days. It was then that Michelle forbid him to get a dog ever again. Well, this time he was putting his foot down. There was no need for Michelle to know who Kutya had belonged to. It would only complicate things. Louis would make up some story about his provenance that would break down Michelle's resistance. He realized he'd better get started on that right away. Kutya slipped into his collar without complaint and followed Louis out the door of the SPCA to the truck, where he got into the passenger seat and looked out the windshield like he was Louis's navigator. Louis scratched the top of the dog's head and started up the engine. They looked like they'd been together for years.

Ten

MARIE DESCENDED the basement stairs, careful by force of habit not to hit her head on a low-lying beam. It was legendarily dangerous to anyone over five foot eight. The basement was a shrine to the 1970s—everything preserved more or less intact since her parents finished it around 1975. There was a wet bar in the far corner, dry since her father went dry as well, a few years before he died in a car accident when Marie was still in college. Over the wet bar was a mounted fish, a brook trout made to look ferocious. Marie could not remember where it came from; her father abhorred fishing, and Claire would've found it tacky. A few faded pennants from the original six NHL hockey teams were still pinned up, as well as an old Montreal Canadiens Stanley Cup Champions banner. There were three stools at the bar, as though waiting for someone to fill them and order a drink. Marie remembers her father behind that bar, dropping ice into glasses, already "lit" as they said back then, and gripping the edge of the bar to steady himself. Their guests would be in various stages of drunkenness, and Marie's mother would be watching Edward for signs of trouble to come, as predictable as her father claiming he would have only one that night. Only one.

On the wall next to the bar hung three black-and-white portraits of the three Russell girls. The photos were clearly taken in a studio, and each girl was wearing what was then called a party dress—all frills and buttons and poofy cap sleeves. All three were posing with their chins propped on clasped hands, like they were praying or pretending to be Shirley Temple. All three had stiff bows in their hair, which was pulled back severely from their faces. There was Madeleine, about thirteen years old, smiling and earnest, trying to please the photographer most of all. Then Louise (about eleven) slightly cross-eyed and looking confused by what was expected of her. Then Marie (about eight). Her curly mop had escaped the constraints of the bow, so she was the only one of the three who looked messy and unkempt. She was looking hopefully up at the photographer, as though she was about to get a treat, like a dog. Marie thought about what they all witnessed in the years of her father's drinking. What stories those pictures could tell. She also wondered why on earth her mother would hang those here, of all places. Were they meant to remind Edward every time he drank who he was hurting? Marie took in the rest of the room. It wasn't so bad. Maybe a day or two of more packing before it was all wrapped up.

A guitar with two strings left leaned against another corner of the room, next to a filing cabinet that Marie had yet to clean out. An ancient card table with six or so folding chairs was stacked up against another wall. A shag carpet (twin to the one in her old bedroom) had survived the 70s and still claimed the basement floor. Another survivor, a fluorescent orange bean bag chair, slumped by the guitar. Beside this were boxes. Many, many boxes, stacked right up to the ceiling. All packed up by Marie in a frenzy a few weeks earlier and labeled "Clothes/Goodwill." "Books/Library." "Useless Shit/Garbage."

The rest of the stuff was the problem; it didn't fit into boxes, literal or symbolic. How do you pack up a house filled with so many lives and fit it into two small rooms in a rest home—or the euphemism they call it—an assisted living facility? The *things* weren't the issue. Old wooden tennis rackets, dented golf clubs, beaten up Tack leather skates, a Mr. Coffee machine missing its pot, a green trunk covered in stickers from all over the world: Neuschwanstein, Germany; Paris; Il Collosseo, Roma; Vienna; and oddly, Milwaukee, USA. Marie had dragged that out of the furnace room but hadn't the heart to open it yet. Then there was the collection of World Book Encyclopedia, 1961. Published when Marie was two years old. They were probably bought for Madeleine, who would have been just the right age to start using them. But it was Marie who used to pore over these as a child, read them through every single suppertime. Her mother would order her to put the damn book away, but Marie was addicted. She loved *knowing* everything she could possibly know, especially about the natural world. She knew that crickets listened through their knees, and bats bounced sound waves off the walls to see, and that bees have 12,000 eyes. She knew the Masai were fearsome warriors, and that as children, the Japanese are taught to control their feelings.

Marie lifted one of the heavy tomes off its custom-made shelf. Start with Letter A, like she had as a kid. Marie flipped through the book randomly. Anaconda. Airplane. Algebra.

Afghanistan. *Almost all of the people of Afghanistan are tough, independent tribesmen. The women in the cities often wear heavy veils over their faces, in accordance with Moslem tradition.* Nineteen sixty-one. Her mind reeled with the knowledge of what had not happened yet. The Berlin wall up and down. African independence and failure. The moon landing. The Pill. Woodstock. Vietnam. Kennedy hadn't been assassinated yet. Martin Luther King. Test-tube babies. Women's Liberation Movement. The Parti Québécois. Expo 67. Tiananmen Square. The fall of the Soviet empire.

Mandela imprisoned and released. Climate change. School shootings. 9/11. Then there were the *Star Trek* fantasies now come true: the Internet. Cell phones. Only the transporter was waiting to be invented. Marie put "A" back on its shelf, reached for another letter but instead ran her fingers over its embossed green and gold spine. Now, you couldn't even give away these books. They were worthless now.

One thing Marie hadn't decided about yet stood against the wall: a Chatty Cathy doll that Marie had found buried and filthy behind the furnace. Marie was keeping it for Louise, whose doll it was. But Louise said she didn't want it. Louise didn't want anything that reminded her of her childhood. Marie remembers Louise being presented with the doll—she was about two feet tall, wore a red gingham dress, and had black hair and blue eyes, just like Louise—who clearly had received that Black Irish gene down through the generations from Donegal. Claire had made such a fuss about it, as *Daddy,* she kept insisting, had chosen it himself for his special blue-eyed girl. (Madeleine and Marie had brown eyes and almost black hair.) Like all mothers, Claire signed both parents' names on birthday, Christmas, and special occasion gifts, so Edward often was as surprised as the girls when it was opened. But the Chatty Cathy? This was the prize of the year, possibly a lifetime. Marie was intensely, seethingly jealous. She could barely look at her sister or her father for weeks.

And there Chatty Cathy sat. One blue eye permanently closed. Her string half-pulled out and hanging from the back of her neck, silenced forever. After Louise got the doll, Marie would sneak into Louise's room and pull the string, thrilled that she could talk, that she was so pretty, that she was almost as big as Marie herself. *Hi! Let's play house.* Or *Please change my dress.* Or *I love you.* Or *Tell me a story.* After a few weeks, though, Marie wanted Chatty Cathy to say other things. But it was always the same. She realized that it wasn't the doll she envied, but the idea that their father had actually gone by himself and bought something. And it wasn't for her.

Marie decided to bite the bullet and dragged the green trunk to the middle of the room. She flipped open the lid, which was coming off at one of its hinges and fell off at an angle. The trunk was full of paper. For a second, Marie thought she'd toss the whole thing in the garbage. Fuck it. The sheer volume of random paper here was overwhelming. But upon closer inspection, one significant part of it was very old, very delicate tissue paper, which when Marie pulled back its folds revealed a piece of lace. No, it was a dress of some kind. She lifted it out of the tissue paper. A tiny, long, lacy dress, for a baby. A christening dress. It was her maternal grandmother's. Marie had a vague memory of Claire showing her this once, when her daughter, Ruby, was born. But Daniel was Jewish, so there would be no christening in any church. Marie laid the dress gently aside and dived into the papers. There were recipes written in her mother's neat but flowery hand, a reminder of another century altogether. Madeleine's report cards from elementary school (all As of course), bills of sale from old appliances, warranties Claire dutifully kept, some dating to the 1960s. Her father's track and field award from high school. Her mother's appointment books from 1983 to 2001. There were birth announcements and party invitations. There were brittle clippings from old *Life* magazines and yellowing obituaries of their friends and her father's business associates.

Marie picked up a manila envelope and hundreds of old photographs fell out. There they are. Edward and Claire Russell. Or maybe not married yet, still Claire Lapierre. At a ski chalet in the Laurentians, toasting each other with steaming mugs of hot cocoa (his definitely spiked with rye. Or Scotch. Or vodka. It didn't matter). They are both gorgeously in love. Her mother looking at her father with adoration, he at the camera, winking. They had no idea yet what they were going to do to each other. Another of her paternal grandmother sitting miserably in a beach chair in Old Orchard, Maine, between her mother and father. She was horrified that her son was dating a French Canadian, and worse, a Catholic. But Edward had finally stood up to her and married Claire. As family legend had it, her grandmother had thrown a fit at the wedding and had to be taken home and given a sedative. That set the tone for the rest of their marriage, although in the end, it was Claire who took care of Nana when she got sick, as Edward was too sick himself to do it. It was Claire who found the nursing home for Nana, it was Claire who visited twice a week, who washed her underthings that she was too ashamed to have washed by strangers. It was Claire who combed what was left of her white hair, and plucked the hairs on her chin, and stroked her dry hands and who was with her in the end, perhaps praying for her soul to be taken to a better place than the one she had created on earth.

There were so many photographs that Marie figured she'd just bring the trunk home and sort through them at her leisure. As she began to dump everything back into the trunk, she noticed an old-fashioned birthday card: *Happy Birthday to the World's Best Wife! To my life, my love, my precious one, so fair to see, so slim, from the guy who's quick to say these things, if he knows what's good for him!* It was signed *xoxo Edward.* Inside the card, strangely, was another obituary:

> CATHERINE ANN KELLY 1957–1974
> Died tragically on June 16. She is deeply mourned by her parents, Robert and Eloise, her dear sister Susan, her adoring grandparents, loving aunts, uncles, and cousins, and her many school friends. Cathy was a gentle soul who was admired and loved by all. The funeral service will be held at St. Edmund of Canterbury Church on June 7, at 2:00. The family will receive condolences at 89 Angell Avenue in Beaurepaire from 5–7 p.m.

Marie stared at the faded school photograph of Cathy, who was much livelier and prettier than the picture suggested. She remembered the funeral, attended by practically their entire school. She remembered Mrs. Kelly howling for her child and collapsing in Mr. Kelly's arms as they were leaving the church. She remembered how everyone talked about nothing else for a few weeks, and then Cathy and the memory of her short, unremarkable life faded. One day a moving truck appeared at the Kelly house two streets over, and they just disappeared. Marie had been sort of friends with their younger daughter, who was a year behind Marie at school. She vaguely remembered Susie Kelly looking out at her through the rear window of their station wagon, not smiling, not waving. Just looking right at her as the car pulled away. Why had her mother kept this obituary tucked away in a birthday card from Edward? She slipped the paper and card back in the trunk and started to drag it up the basement stairs when she thought she heard a sound from upstairs, and paused to listen for it again. Marie could hear Claire's muffled voice, yelling "Louise. Louise!" Marie dropped the trunk and raced up the stairs and into the TV room, where Claire stood, her stretchy sweat pants around her ankles, half-laughing, half-crying. The TV dinner and tray had toppled to the floor, and there was a stain where Claire had been sitting. She just stared at Marie, clearly trying to recognize her. Had she had a stroke?

"Mum? What happened? Mum? Mum!"

The home caregiver had told Marie to buy diapers weeks ago, but until now, they hadn't seemed necessary. Marie lowered her mother's pants and unrolled them from her legs. Claire fell back into her chair, sitting in her pee. She had retrieved a piece of bread from the floor and was chewing it thoughtfully. Marie left her there and bounded up the stairs to fetch clean underwear and her nightgown. She paused on the landing to catch her breath. She suddenly felt like she was going to throw up and held on to the banister to steady herself. Growing old is not for the faint of heart.

Eleven

ROMÉO RAN DOWN the highway, trying to catch up with a line of cars that were crawling along in the dense fog. He reached for his gun, but the holster was empty. Instead, he pulled out his flashlight and shone it directly into the first car he caught up with. He tried to catch his breath as he ordered the driver to roll down the window, but the driver ignored him. He smashed the window of the car and felt something in his hand tear away. He reached past the driver and grabbed at the girl in the passenger seat. He was looking for Sophie—someone had taken her, and she was in one of these cars—he just had to find the right one before it was too late. When he pulled at her arm, it came off in his hand, but the girl didn't react. She just started laughing and laughing at him. She wasn't Sophie at all, and all her teeth were gone. The empty, gaping mouth of the young woman guffawed even louder at him, and Roméo staggered away from the car in horror. His hand was spouting blood like a fountain, and he realized he was stark naked and had nothing to stop the bleeding. All the cars started honking at him to get off the road, but he couldn't. He hadn't found Sophie yet.

Roméo opened his eyes and immediately felt a wave of relief. It was just another nicotine-patch nightmare. And a fairly "normal" one at that, compared to what Roméo's imagination had concocted over the last week. The night before he had found himself at a party at his ex-wife's house, and all the guests were dressed in tuxedos and cocktail dresses, but everyone had a bushy squirrel tail and was nursing a blue drink. When Roméo had entered the party, each guest went to a pile of stones in the middle of the room and selected one. Then one by one, they hurled their rock at Roméo. He protected his head as best he could, but his hands kept falling off. Every single night Roméo dredged up the worst his brain could conceive of, and then added a twist of nicotine-induced paranoia and psychosis.

Roméo woke up exhausted and deeply disoriented, a feeling that often lasted for hours, even days. He got up from the sofa and took himself to the bathroom, where he began to peel the patch off his arm. He was going to do this cold turkey. Anything was better than this. But this was Roméo's third attempt to quit smoking. He pressed the patch back on, leaned into the sink, and splashed some water on his face. He would give it one more try. Roméo returned to the living room, where he had left the television on mute, and his unfinished Scotch on the coffee table. CNN's breaking news was another stabbing attack in Jerusalem, the victim this time a young mother of three. Roméo switched off the TV and picked up the file he'd been reading when he fell asleep. He took it to the kitchen table, found his glasses, and promised himself he would focus for at least one more hour before he went back to his Scotch, and inevitably to his bed, alone.

Anna Newman was eighty-two years old and had died sometime between 4 and 11 p.m. on October 27. She had received a trauma to the right side of her skull, resulting in a hairline fracture. This had probably been caused by the fall from the ladder onto a protruding rock in her garden. The abrasion from the injury was consistent with this. But Roméo was right in thinking this was not what had killed her. There were marks on her neck consistent with strangulation by throttling. There were no ligature marks; she was choked to death by hand and had died from vagal inhibition. She had a fractured hyoid bone, strongly consistent with manual strangulation. None of this was surprising so far. The bruising Roméo had noted on her neck when he first examined her body suggested as much. Roméo thought of her last few minutes alive, after surviving almost eighty-three years of this world. Once her killer had firmly grasped her neck, she would have lost consciousness. Brain death would have occurred in two minutes. Before lapsing into unconsciousness, a strangulation victim will usually resist violently, but there was no evidence at the scene or on Anna Newman's body to suggest this. These defensive injuries may not be present if the victim is physically or chemically restrained before the assault. Or is already unconscious from a head wound, Roméo thought.

Fingernail scrapings from the victim produced no tissue, no DNA evidence. Anna Newman had *not* struggled with her killer. Roméo wondered if she'd even had time to feel terror. He suddenly found himself feeling very light-headed and nauseous, and had to put his head between his knees and breathe. A clear picture of a little boy, about eight years old, floated into his head and lingered. A man's huge hand on his neck, pressing so hard he lifted Roméo off his feet. Roméo could not fight back, could not even move. He was paralyzed with pain and shock. Just as suddenly, his father let him go, and he collapsed to the floor.

"You tell your mother about this, you little shit, and you're dead." For many years, Roméo had never told anyone, least of all his mother. He could actually smell his father's aftershave—Old Spice—which he had bought for him with his own saved-up money for Father's Day. Did quitting smoking restore his sense of smell to such a degree that he could actually smell a memory forty years old? Roméo shook that idea from his head and returned to the autopsy report. To Roméo's relief, the vaginal swab and pubic hair combing revealed that Anna Newman had not been sexually assaulted. This was an important piece of evidence with regard to the killer's profile. He may have known Anna Newman and possibly had not intended to kill her, although throttling someone to death often implies overwhelming rage. This anger often results in the desire to overpower the victim sexually, but that was not the case here. Was this an argument that had gotten out of hand? Was this killer trying to persuade her? To do what?

Roméo reread the social history of Anna Newman that had been compiled by one of the junior detectives. So far, they knew remarkably little about her. She was born in 1932 in Vienna, baptized in a Catholic church on November 26, and was the daughter of Kristof and Maria Hanning. She trained as a school teacher and worked for several years before emigrating to Canada in 1957. Then there seemed to be very little record of her until 1985. From what Roméo could see, this is when she became Anna Newman, living in Whitby, Ontario, and for many years, working as an art teacher in an elementary school.

There was no marital history, so Newman, presumably, was her chosen name. There was no history of any other family on record, and no record of any children, but the autopsy indicated she had had at least one child. She had no recent employment history, but for the past twenty-two years had identified herself for tax purposes as a self-employed artist. Anna Newman had a savings account at the Caisse Populaire in Ste. Agathe, with over $50,000 in it. She had purchased her little cabin in 1997, and there was no mortgage. She had lived there for almost twenty years, but very few people knew her or could offer any useful information about her. She did not have the Internet, so a social media footprint was out. She got a small Quebec pension and paid her taxes in full and on time. She had no criminal history and, amazingly, no credit rating as she did not own a credit card. Her neighbors, bank manager, local dépanneur owner—everyone she may have come into daily, weekly, or even annual contact with were being interviewed. Her habits, hobbies, and unusual behavior patterns would be flagged if possible. Roméo had also ordered a much more intensive search into her past. She was baptized Catholic but may have worn a necklace suggesting she was Jewish. One thing was clear, Roméo thought. Anna Newman was trying to hide something or hide *from* something.

Roméo swallowed the last of the Scotch and considered fetching another. Newman. New-Man. She was never married—or had she been and taken her husband's name? Now in Quebec it was the law that all women must keep their maiden names after they marry. You had to apply to change it to your husband's. Roméo wondered how it had taken so long for this to be law, and why every country hadn't adopted it by now. He had to admit, though, that he'd liked to have changed his name to his mother's, which was Limoges—like the fine china. She was like it, too. Fine and delicate but tough when she had to be.

But Roméo, of course, took his father's name. Leduc. He was long dead now, but his face could still come into painful focus. In retrospect, Roméo knew his father was probably bipolar. He would seesaw unpredictably from crushing depression, when he wouldn't get off the couch for days and weeks, to fits of explosive activity, to raging tantrums. All of which he self-medicated with alcohol. Roméo remembered the relief of escaping the house when his father was in one of his "moods"; relief for Roméo was hockey practice, every day after school. All Canadian boys were supposed to play hockey. It was something that was never questioned. It was like baseball to Americans. Soccer to Latin Americans. Cricket to Indians. Roméo's shameful secret was that he never liked hockey. He didn't see the point of chasing a puck for hours and hours on end. He didn't like the hyper-masculine bravado of the coaches and the desperation of the fathers for their sons to be the best. Every Québécois boy was supposed to dream of playing for the Montreal Canadiens, and every father seemed to think it was a possibility. It was a toxic combination of ambition, testosterone, and vicarious living. And he hated arriving at hockey practice after one of his father's brutal outbursts, still sniffling from his own stifled rage. The irony was that Roméo was good—really good. He was an intelligent and skillful player, deft with his hands and light on his feet. He had talent, and that made the other fathers very jealous and vindictive.

One day, Roméo's father actually came to watch a practice. Roméo had no idea why—to his credit, Claude had no hockey ambition for his son whatsoever, and he had never attended a practice before. Roméo was outstanding, and his coach told Roméo's father that he should send him to an elite hockey camp that summer, one he could not remotely afford. The coach mentioned there were scholarships, and Roméo was very likely to get one. Suddenly, Claude ordered Roméo to get off the ice and get home. Roméo refused. Claude skittered out onto the the ice and walloped him across the face, sending his helmet flying. Everyone just stood and watched like it was a movie, all the players, all the fathers, and the coach. Roméo skated off to the dressing room holding his cheek, crying.

No one said anything, and no one did anything. Several years later, Roméo's mother finally got the courage to leave Claude Leduc, but the damage was done. She was like a dog who'd been beaten too many times—mistrustful, terrified, but a survivor. What was this continuing stroll down bad memory lane? He had long ago declared amnesty for his mother's neglect, his father's brutality, and all the people who were too afraid or embarrassed to intervene. Roméo refocused his tired eyes on the words in front of him. Maybe Anna Newman had done something unforgivable. Maybe her killer did not feel that she deserved amnesty.

Twelve

"DID ANYONE EVER tell you you look like Paul Newman?"

"Well, now, Mrs. O'Rourke. No. No one has ever told me that. But I am immensely flattered that you would think so."

"Well, you do so. Oh, he was a lovely man. A *lovely* man. Married to Joanne Woodward for…goodness, fifty years or so. And he never cheated on her. Never. So they say. And he gave so much money away—with his spaghetti sauce and, and, salad. Salad…"

"Dressing?" Ennis offered.

"They don't make 'em like that anymore."

"No, they don't. That's for sure."

"There's no more real *movie stars* now. Just boys who can't be bothered to shave, or who look like women, and getting caught with their you-know-what in the wrong place all the time." She peeked at Ennis to see if she had shocked him.

Ennis had heard this particular observation many times. Despite her declared contempt for them all, Mrs. O'Rourke watched celebrity gossip TV religiously, and she knew everything about them—who they were currently dating, cheating on or with, their battles with drugs, their battles with weight, the challenges of being a star, the challenges of no longer being a star. Ennis made sure to bring her at least one magazine a visit, along with a small, and forbidden, Toblerone chocolate bar, her favorite.

"Now Mrs. O'Rourke, I could sit here all day listening to you telling me how much I look like Paul Newman, but I've got to get going—"

"You've got lots of other old ladies to visit?"

He leaned in closer. "You're the only one for me."

"Nonsense. I know you've got at least two others at the Warwick alone. But despite my cranky children, they tell me you're very good. Very trustworthy and kind. Now don't forget to send the check to the SPCA and one to Barbara. She needs that check."

"It's already done, Mrs. O."

Ennis gathered up the signed papers and slipped them neatly into a black file case, which he then tucked under his arm. He had long ago dispensed with the briefcase. It made his clients nervous. "If I can help you in any way, I'm here for you. Just give me a call."

"I'll see you next week, then? Next Tuesday?" Ennis smiled and gave Mrs. O'Rourke a very light peck on her desiccated cheek. "You bet."

Marie and her mother had a long-standing joke, or routine, that they shared. Whenever Claire asked Marie to help her out—eaves troughs that needed cleaning out, the lawn mowed, a doctor's visit to witness—Marie would threaten to put her mother in a nursing home in Shawinigan, a town two and a half hours' drive northwest of Montreal, but a backwater, remote town known for its pulp and paper industry and the humble birthplace of a recent prime minister. Marie would remind Claire that she would visit her only once a year and otherwise do what had become popular for overworked people in Japan with parents in elderly care—send surrogate children to spend "quality" time with their parents. Marie tried to imagine these fake children reminiscing with elderly, complete strangers. She and Claire would laugh about this, and Marie promised it would never come to pass. But here she was pulling up to the Residence Le Warwick about to sign the final papers that would have her mother living here in a few days.

Claire would be taken from everything she still recognized and loved and stuck in the purgatory of institutional life. Marie took a deep breath and closed her eyes for a second before she turned the car off. She wondered if she should quickly call the house—she had left her mother in the care of an unsettlingly young woman with so much orthodontic hardware in her mouth it was a wonder she could speak at all. But she was cheerfully talkative and appeared competent. Marie had really had no other option, although Claire had actually been in fine fettle that morning. She woke up early and dressed herself, got her own breakfast, and was sitting at the kitchen table pretending to read the morning paper when Marie stumbled in, mildly hungover from one basement Scotch too many and a restless sleep in her new old room. Of course, Claire knew she was going to the home, but she had been more lucid this morning than she had in months. Was it a sign? A test of Marie's resolve?

Marie reminded herself of her mother's increasing forgetfulness, her now regular incontinence, the wandering that had gotten her lost for an entire afternoon. The police had picked her up wading in the shallow waters of Lac St. Louis at Memorial Beach, almost two miles from her home. The in-home care that Marie had managed for months with her mother's pension and her own savings was simply not an affordable or safe option anymore. Claire's house had to be sold. She had to be placed. It had to be done. They had, at last, arrived in Shawinigan.

Le Warwick was a former post office converted tastefully into a middle-range assisted living facility. It stood at the end of a cul-de-sac in Notre-Dame-de-Grâce, a leafy, placid neighborhood on the western edge of Montreal. One of the reasons Marie had chosen this one was its convenience; it would take Marie sixty-five minutes door to door to drive from her little house in Ste. Lucie if she avoided rush hour and the city of Montreal was not committing its usual traffic-snarling atrocities. There was a rumor that they were going to actually close Decarie Boulevard, the main artery between north and south Montreal, but no one would believe it. Marie knew better. She knew that when an idea was floated by city hall, it almost always came to pass.

Marie pressed the automatic door button to the foyer of the building, passing a young black woman sitting silently with an elderly woman, who breathed through a plastic tube in each nostril, an oxygen canister hanging off her wheelchair. Another woman was asleep in her chair, her head slumped onto her chest where her breasts had once been. A middle-aged nurse saw Marie and hastily stubbed out her cigarette, waving away the smoke. Marie approached the front desk, where a young woman with very heavy makeup covering what looked like adult acne was on the phone. She raised a red-tipped index finger asking Marie to wait. The foyer of the building was functional and attractive, with several huge potted plants and, oddly, an enormous cage filled with at least a dozen gabbling lovebirds. The lobby gave way to an enormous living room, full of *faux* Victorian furniture—wing-backed chairs and matching ottomans, heavy drapery, and gilded edges to everything. It was entirely devoid of human life today. The last time Marie had visited, a very old man sat at the upright piano, playing out-of-tune songs and singing courageously in an aging tremolo. She was informed by the manager that he came once a week to delight their clients. Marie wondered what other delights her mother had in store for her.

Beyond this, Marie knew, was the library, the games room—full of puzzles with missing pieces, older versions of Clue and Monopoly, and a least five boxes of Scrabble. Beyond that was a small chapel where a Virgin Mary welcomed with outstretched hands and an enormous, bleeding red heart on the outside of her breast. One floor down was a fitness room where Claire could take at least a dozen different classes, and the indoor pool, so heavily chlorinated Marie had been unable to visit for more than a few minutes. Must be all that peeing in the water, she thought.

"*Bonjour.* Hi. *Comment est-ce que je peux vous aider?* How can I help you?" The classic bilingual Montreal greeting.

"I'm here to see Mme. Purdy—"

"Oh, yes." She peered into her computer. "Madame... Russell?" She pronounced it *Roosell.* "She's expecting you." She pressed the phone with another blood-red fingertip and announced Marie. Then her face entirely transformed itself as a very good-looking man approached her desk, tapped it, and wished her a cheery "Have a great day!" She beamed at his receding back. "*À la prochaine*, Monsieur Jamieson!" Marie could have sworn she heard the woman sigh, like a smitten girl in an old beach blanket movie. It was unusual to see any man, let alone one who looked like Paul Newman, in the residence. Marie had noticed that caregiving, pretty much everywhere in the world, was almost entirely a female occupation. Husbands or sons were sometimes seen flipping through magazines or gazing absently at a muted TV on a Sunday visit, while their wife or mother stared at them gratefully. Marie wondered what lucky woman Paul Newman was visiting.

Mme. Purdy was suddenly beside her, taking her elbow, guiding Marie down the faux-Persian-carpeted corridor and into her spacious office. Mme. Purdy looked like a casting agent's idea of someone who ran an old folks' home. She was in her early forties, Marie guessed, had pretty, even features, wore subtle makeup, a flattering pencil skirt, sensible heels, and a well-tailored blouse. Marie figured she had at least seven variations on this sartorial theme in her closet that she rotated for each day of the week. She also never, ever stopped smiling. No matter what. She could be telling you members of a satanic cult had just eaten your first-born child with a smile on her face. It was very disconcerting, and at first Marie was certain it was a deal-breaker. But everyone she had asked confirmed that Le Warwick was the best place in its price range on the entire island of Montreal. So, she sat across Mme. Purdy's desk and let her bare her teeth another time.

"How *is* Mme. Russell?" She pronounced it Russell, the anglo way.

"She ate her supper sitting in her own pee last night and thinks I'm my sister, Louise, who hasn't bothered to visit in eleven years."

Mme. Purdy smiled. "That is why Mme. Russell is ready for Le Warwick. And we are ready for her. Her room has been vacant for three days now, and we are just repainting and freshening everything up for her."

Get the lingering odor of death out of it, Marie thought.

"So, we are expecting her on November 3, which I understand is her birthday!" Her smile grew even bigger.

"Yes. She'll be turning eighty-four. But I'm not sure she knows it's her birthday—or she does but then she forgets—"

"The short-term memory goes, but those old memories remain and provide such a solace for so many of them." Marie figured Claire would sooner live in perpetual short-term happiness than be "comforted" by her past. She shrugged her shoulders and reached for her purse. Mme. Purdy never took her eyes off her. Still smiling. Marie handed over the last of the four checks. This was it. What Claire Russell did not know was that her modest house, which had been her home for over sixty years, which carried her secrets and heartaches and joys and tragedies, was going to be demolished to make room for a much larger one. The new owners had confided their plans to Marie, displaying almost no sensitivity to her feelings. The house was going to be enormous and—as far as she could tell from the plans that they excitedly unrolled on the hood of her car—ostentatious and kitschy. There were turrets. Statues of Roman gods surrounding the swimming pool. A gazebo with mini-gargoyles. Marie saw that her old room was now where the four-car garage would go. The plans also suggested that almost every old tree would be cut down, including the blue spruce. Marie had fought the urge to punch this woman squarely in the face, perhaps knocking out a perfect tooth or two. Instead, she'd mumbled something about being *happy in the new* and fled to her car. That was a week ago. They were dying for her mother to abandon the house so they could be satisfied nothing would threaten the rapidly approaching closing date. Mme. Purdy was getting up to shake Marie's hand. "You are doing the right thing, Mme. Russell. Please know that I understand how you feel, and that we will take the best care of your mother possible. She may still have several good years left. We, like you, will treasure them." Her handshake was barely a gentle pressure, the kind that suggested passive aggression. Marie squeezed her hand back, hard. Then she got the hell out of there before she changed her mind.

Thirteen

TI-COUNE COUSINEAU had just settled down to watch the "Last Rose" episode with Jo-Jo as *The Bachelorette*. He had been looking forward to this all day. He got himself a fresh beer, opened a bag of chips, grabbed his dog Pitoune, and sat her on his lap. He knew he was in for three solid hours of uninterrupted viewing, especially satisfying after a day's work flagging cars in and out of a construction zone. Eight hours of annoyed drivers glaring at him as they drove past. One or two lifted an index finger off the steering wheel at him in recognition. One or two lifted a different finger at him. The sun had come out and burned the top of his scalp, which he now touched tenderly. He felt exhausted, like his blood had been slowly draining from him all day. Maybe he had sunstroke.

Pitoune looked up at him, hopeful that a chip might fall from his mouth and into hers. His eyes never left the TV screen. The Bachelorette was pretty, but nothing like his sister, Hélène, had been. But that was thirty years ago. The last time Ti-Coune saw Hélène was two years earlier. He hadn't even heard from her in almost seven years, and suddenly she'd appeared at his front door. She had just come in from Edmonton, where she'd been living. Since she was a little girl, Hélène was convinced she was part Indian—or *Native*. Or *First Nations*, you were supposed to say now. In their school history books, Ti-Coune remembered the Mohawks described as *les sauvages*, who drank the blood of Jesuit priests and routinely scalped French settlers. He knew a few of the Mohawks from down the road at the reserve. They were tough, for sure. But they seemed like decent guys if you didn't do something too ignorant.

Hélène had gone out west to find her people. The basis of this belief of hers was a family rumor that some great-grandmother was one-quarter Stony Indian, part of the Sioux nation. There were no family records and no family left to back any of this up. Hélène ended up working as a cocktail waitress in the oil boom town of Fort McMurray, then migrated to Edmonton. She neglected to mention what she did for a living there. Ti-Coune thought she'd looked pretty rough. Her once thick, almost black hair was now two colors too many and was thin and frizzy. She slipped a cigarette every ten minutes between two brown, skinny fingers with nails bitten to the quick. Ti-Coune could still see the beauty that was once there, but she looked like she'd been around the track a few times too many. They chatted about old times, laughed hysterically about their biker clubhouse years, and drank beer into the early morning. Ti-Coune left her on his sofa, her mouth wide open, snoring. He had covered her in the blanket he still kept from their apartment in Outremont—a pink and green afghan their grandmother had knitted.

When he woke up the next day, hungover but happy

to continue the conversation, Hélène was gone. She left no address, no phone number. Just a photograph of the two of them, taken at the Granby zoo, when they were little kids. They were both scowling at the camera, because they had no money for cotton candy and the stuff regular kids got. Ti-Coune remembered an elephant tethered by a chain rocking back and forth behind them. He couldn't even remember who took them there or who took the picture. He slipped the photo into the frame of the mirror in his bedroom. Hélène was all he had.

The Bachelorette was preparing to introduce one of the finalists to her parents. The father looked like a dwarf, and the mother was very overweight. How was the daughter so gorgeous? He wondered if the Bachelor would take one look at the parents and run for the hills. Suddenly, Ti-Coune's outdoor dogs started barking hysterically. He struggled to his feet to see what had gotten them going, dropping Pitoune into his chair. His door smashed open. Two men who looked like they'd planned their outfits to match stood in the door frame. They were almost as wide as they were tall, big *bedaines* hanging over their jeans. One had long, stringy gray hair held back by a leather headband. The other was bald, the fat in his enormous neck folding over itself. They wore black leather jackets but no death-head logo. Not full patch. Not even associates. Just wannabes. Ti-Coune felt his testicles shrivel.

"It's not Halloween yet. You guys are a bit early."

Baldy stepped into the house and pointed to the TV. "You like that show? Me too." Then he shoved Ti-Coune back into his La-Z-Boy, almost on top of Pitoune. The other one opened Ti-Coune's fridge and took out two beers. He opened both with his teeth and passed one to his colleague. Ti-Coune wondered why his dogs weren't barking anymore.

The two men took in his house. Looked at the pictures on the walls. One grabbed the bag of chips and shoved a mouthful in. "Ketchup chips? Who the fuck eats ketchup chips?" He emptied the bag on the floor. Pitoune growled and trembled visibly on Ti-Coune's lap. He was really hoping she wouldn't pee on him.

"To what do I owe the pleasure of this visit?"

"What was the cop doing here?"

"What cop?"

Stringy Hair plucked Pitoune from Ti-Coune's lap and threw her across the living room. She howled in pain and limped off into a corner. Ti-Coune tried to go to her, but Baldy pulled him back in his chair hard enough to dislocate his shoulder. Ti-Coune felt like crying. It was a bad habit that he'd thought he'd overcome.

"Why were you talking to Leduc?"

"He was asking about the old lady who died—"

"The crazy old *Jew*?"

"Y…yes. He thought I knew something about that—but. I know nothing and I told him nothing—"

"'I told him nothing.'" Baldy leaned in to Ti-Coune's face. His breath smelled like beer and stale puke.

"You got nothing to do with that? That's right. And *we* got nothing to do with that." He slapped Ti-Coune's face hard.

"I know. I know. *Lâche-moi!*"

Stringy Hair flicked the top of Ti-Coune's head. Then he took a swig of beer and gestured to the TV with the beer bottle.

"Who do you think will win? That faggy cocksucker? Or his cocksucking little friend? I'd like to do that bitch, though." He sat his bulk down on Ti-Coune's sofa, which nearly collapsed under the weight.

Baldy strode over to the television and smashed his bottle against the screen. Nothing happened, so he put his foot through it. Stringy Hair pulled Ti-Coune to his feet. The last thing he remembered was the man's huge hand around his throat. Once Ti-Coune's body crumpled to the filthy carpet, Baldy added a few kicks to his kidneys and ribs. Stringy Hair stomped on his knee. On the way out, they grabbed the rest of the beer, a jar of peanut butter, and the remainder of a loaf of bread. Then they both unzipped themselves and peed all over the kitchen. Unbeknownst to Ti-Coune, the Bachelorette had made her choice and given her final rose.

Fourteen

THERE IT WAS again. Another ping from her phone insisting she respond to the text message. She started to get up to check it and caught herself. No. She would not read it, would not answer. She turned up the volume on the TV and forced herself to refocus on the documentary about global warming. They were interviewing a British anthropologist who claimed it was already too late for the planet, that the damage from carbon emissions was irreversible. He was very persuasive. And depressing. Or, she thought, maybe that was the new optimism? It's all over anyway, so stop worrying and just enjoy every minute of the here and now. Screw the future. Screw everything. She had no children to worry about, no family, really, to fret over. She was wonderfully, exuberantly alone. She could do whatever she wanted, whenever she wanted, with whomever she wanted. *For me the world was created but I am nothing. The world was created for nothing. I am me. Nothing was created for me. I am the world. I created me. The world was for nothing. I created me. The world was for nothing. I created me. The world was for nothing. I created me I created me I created*—the phone pinged again. She struggled to stay on the sofa, grabbed another handful of popcorn, and stuffed it into her mouth. She had already had two bowls of the stuff and was emptying a third. Popcorn was her Achilles heel. Popcorn was healthy though, wasn't it? Not the extra-buttery kind that she liked. That was bad, full of transfats that blocked your arteries like concrete, so you had a heart attack. Now the phone was ringing. She was sure it was him. He was really very nice in a mamma's boy kind of way, not like the last one, who had sent her pictures of his privates after one coffee date. They kept popping up on her computer at work, and the girl in the cubicle next to her whom she considered to be her best office friend had wandered over for a chat and seen them. She looked at Susie as though she had just grown a tail or a set of horns, snorted into her coffee mug, and returned to her desk. For weeks afterwards, everyone in the office had giggled whenever she joined them for lunch or poured herself a coffee. She overheard one say she probably gave great blow jobs, because "she's old enough to have no teeth." It was beyond mortifying. Despite that, they all insisted on calling her *Susie*, even though she'd requested for years they refer to her as *Susan*.

She had asked for a transfer from that department to another, and with her seniority they had to give it to her. She packed her coffee mug, her Rubic's cube, and the picture of her and Cathy at Expo 67 and her desk was cleared. The phone rang again. She snatched it off the coffee-table. She had three messages. *Call me.* Then *Call me please.* And the last one: *I need to see you. I'm coming over.* Susie smiled at that last one. He had no idea where she lived, she'd made sure of that. After their last date, when they had done sex and he insisted that he drive her home, she had him drop her off at some random apartment building in St. Henri, when she lived in Lachine. So-named because when Jacques Cartier, the Frenchman who had discovered Canada, saw the rapids of the St. Lawrence River he thought he had discovered China—*La Chine*. Susie had always found that hilarious. Lachine was far from China in every way imaginable. She'd got out of the car and walked into the unlocked lobby, waving him away with a flirty kiss. Then she walked the three blocks to where she'd parked her car and headed home. She thought of him looking for her name on the mailboxes in that building, wondering why it wasn't there.

Of course, she didn't use her real name with her dates. That would take all the fun out of it. But he wasn't honest, either. When he went to the toilet, she had checked his wallet and saw the two kids—an older girl and younger boy—and wife. The apartment was obviously not his. He tried to hide the fact, but he didn't know where the bottle opener was or the wine glasses. He knew her as Daphne, the forest nymph who had been turned into a tree so Apollo couldn't have her. He *had* been quite sweet, though. He always paid for dinner, put his arm gently around her shoulder when they watched the movies, and looked at her like everything she had to say really mattered to him. But of course, he eventually was like all the others. He lay himself on top of her one night when they were just watching TV together and opened a condom package with a questioning look on his face. She was appalled to think that perhaps he expected her to put it on for him, but he fumbled it over his thing, and then put himself inside her. He seemed to really like it, but she never understood what all the fuss was about.

He'd moaned her name over and over. Of course, not her real name. Susie erased the message with a sigh. She would have to change her cell number again. He would never *have* her. Besides, right now, she had much bigger fish to fry.

Fifteen

"ARE YOU SURE?"

"We talked to everyone we could think of so far. It's all in the report." She paused. "Did you read it?"

"I'll look at it later on today. No red flags, no nothing?"

"That's what I said, boss."

That last word, a gentle knife twist. Roméo and Sergeant Nicole LaFramboise had had awkward sex one night seven months earlier when she was reeling from a recently broken heart. She'd asked him out for a beer at a local watering hole in St. Jerome, and they had talked for hours, their intense conversation punctuated with a Scotch and a beer chaser every forty-five minutes or so. They had later staggered up the stairs to her little apartment, where they had drunken sex that was frantic, furious, and ultimately embarrassing to both of them. There had been awkwardness in the office, but it had passed as all things eventually do, and they were now just colleagues again. Roméo recalled that she had very large breasts that she tried to disguise in sexless cop clothes. Those breasts were the *objets de désir* of almost every male cop in the precinct office, and a few women as well. They plotted ways to get a glimpse of them, invited her to pool parties, openly ogled them when she was busy not noticing. She was a nice woman who deserved a nice man. Certainly not the assholes in her precinct. And certainly not him.

"Keep me posted if *anything* stands out, got it? I'm heading up there now."

"Yes, Chief Inspector Leduc."

"Merci." He hesitated. "Nicole?"

"Oui?" She sounded hopeful. Too hopeful. "Call me immediately if there is anything that turns up. I mean it. Anything that ties her to anyone or any thing. There is *someone* out there who knows her."

Her voice returned to professional flatness. "Of course, chief inspector." There was an awkward pause, and then Roméo ended the call. He reached for his coffee mug nestled in the dashboard and started his car. He needed to take another look at Madame Newman's house. There had to be something there they'd overlooked, something that tied her to a past. The team he'd put on this case was known to be thorough, but there was always the possibility of human error. As chief inspector, Roméo was supposed to spend his time behind his enormous desk, leading his investigative team, inspiring them to think outside the box. Not the easiest thing to get a bunch of cops to do. Thinking *inside* the box is why they're attracted to the idea of being a cop in the first place. But Roméo preferred being on the road, being a hands-on detective. He didn't feel a crime scene had really been examined unless he'd gone over it himself with the proverbial fine-toothed comb.

Roméo pulled out of the Sûreté du Québec headquarters on Parthenais Street and headed north toward Highway

15. He needed to get ahead of the traffic out of Montreal and into the many bedroom communities lining the highway—Ste. Therese, Ste. Rose, St. Jerome—practically every town in Quebec was named after a bloody saint. It was especially ironic now, given how staunchly secular the province was. Roméo had once spent a gloomy post-divorce weekend looking up how each saint had been martyred. Saint Lawrence, after whom the massive river that encircled Montreal was named, had been roasted alive. Sainte Agathe had refused the advances of a Roman prefect, and for that had had her breasts cut off. Saint Hippolyte had been torn apart by horses. Roméo's gruesome reverie was interrupted by the ping of his phone. It was a text from Sophie. Christ, he'd almost forgotten to check on her.

He reached for the phone and held it up to read. Of course, he should pull over, but he was in an unmarked car. *we're in roatan in honduras! pple r amazing & so nice!* Honduras? She was supposed to be in Costa Rica. San Pedro Sula, once a small Honduran backwater, was now because of the drug trade the murder capital of the western hemisphere. It was not so far from Roatan. What was she doing there? Roméo read the rest: *raining a lot but safe & happy xxoo*. He knew Roatan was a scuba-diving mecca, populated by old hippies and evangelical back-to-nature Christian types. Strange bedfellows. He had to message her right away to warn her off the rest of the country. He punched her number into his dashboard display. The phone rang once and went straight to voice mail, which was full, of course. Roméo put on his turn indicator to pull off the highway then changed his mind. It could wait another half hour. He reread the text message. Sophie wasn't his anymore. He remembered the way she would play with his hair when they read a book together, twirling it in her tiny fingers, for reassurance. For comfort. His or hers? He thought he would die with the joy of it, the *completeness* of his life with Sophie and his wife, Elyse. And then two miscarriages. Then he went for detective. Then William Fyfe. Then his wife in bed with Guy Provencher. The exit to the 329 North appeared suddenly. Roméo turned onto it in the direction of Ste. Lucie. He wondered how *she* had been tortured. Maybe she had a daughter who would never listen to her, too.

Roméo pulled into Anna Newman's driveway. Her little house seemed forlorn, like it knew its mistress was never coming back. Roméo thought of her dog—what was its name again? Someone had mentioned it was taken to the SPCA. He hoped it had been adopted, or at least euthanized and put out of its misery quickly, then. Madame Newman's small and orderly garden was dotted with numbered orange flags marking where the forensic team had discovered possible evidence. So far nothing conclusive as to the identity of the killer, or even a hint at something conclusive had been found. Except that he or she was most probably right-handed. Roméo looked at where the body had been found and reexamined the ground. It had been completely frozen—so they could take no footprint casts. According to the coroner's report, there was no DNA under her fingernails, no fibers, no hair, nothing. It was like some ghost had come and throttled her to death. Or her killer had been wearing a forensic hazmat suit himself. Or herself. Roméo closed his eyes and tried to recreate what had happened here, but nothing came to him. He looked up at the gray midmorning sky. Big fat snowflakes were swirling wildly in every direction, like the wind couldn't decide which way to blow.

Roméo turned up the collar of his jacket and reminded himself to get his heavier coat out of storage in the basement. They were predicting a very long and snowy winter. He stepped over the yellow police tape and turned the key in Madame Newman's front door. He took in the kitchen and living room. Most of her personal possessions had been identified, packed up, and sent to police storage while they were still trying to locate next of kin. No will or any legal papers had as yet been found, either. Some odd items, however, were still left—a pair of rubber boots with caked mud still on them stood by her back door, as if they were waiting for her feet to claim them. A plastic Tim Hortons coffee mug had been left in the sink. Roméo frowned and thought he'd have a word with someone about that. He walked into her studio and saw that perhaps twenty of her charcoal sketches were leaning up against a wall, waiting to be wrapped in plastic. He understood that someone from the Artists' Co-op was coming to deal with them. Roméo looked through them and stopped at one he'd noticed before. It was a drawing of a horse's bowed head—so accurate and lifelike a portrait that he could feel its breathing, warm body. He could see a sentient being in those eyes, so fine in detail it could have been a photograph. But much better. She was an extraordinarily skilled illustrator.

Roméo wandered back to the bedroom and scanned what was left. Her bed had been stripped for DNA evidence. Her small chest of drawers opened and emptied, her closet now abandoned to a few metal hangers. The carpet was rolled up and leaning against the wall. He recalled that there were virtually no personal items to be found. Except for the necklace with the broken chain they had found in the garden. With the chai pendant. It was probably hers. Was this some kind of hate crime? They could not overlook that.

Quebec had a long and sordid flirtation with anti-Semitism. Even as recently as 1995, the then premier of Quebec had blamed the narrow defeat of the referendum for independence on "money" and the "ethnic vote." Everyone knew who he meant: all anglos, all non-francophone immigrants, and the Jews of Montreal. Roméo had been deeply ashamed at that moment and realized then and there that he could not afford to turn a blind eye to the sometimes uglier side of Quebec nationalism. His own father used to rage at the "doughnut-heads" of Outremont, Hasidic Jews who had a lively community there. Up here in the Laurentians, there were also well-established summer communities of Orthodox Jews. They drove up from New York in convoys of vans and settled in very plain dormitory-style houses. The men walked in pairs up and down the country roads, in their prayer shawls, black fedoras, and *peyiss*, the sidelocks they never cut. The women also went on daily constitutional walks, but in larger groups, probably to get away from the several children each seemed to have by the time they were out of their teens. They walked with purpose in sensible sneakers under their long skirts, cell phones in hand, their shaved heads covered in turbans. There had been no trouble between their community and the locals in years, but recently some hateful graffiti had been sprayed on their houses, and there had been a scuffle in one of the stores in town. Could Anna Newman have been part of some backlash? Was she even Jewish?

Roméo glanced around her bedroom one more time. Just as he turned to the door, something caught his eye. Well, not some *thing* exactly, but a part of the bedroom floor that wasn't quite right. In the grain of the polished pine floor, now grimy with the boot marks of strangers in her house, was an anomaly. Roméo squatted to the floor, his knees cracking with the strain. There was definitely a break here. He took out his penknife and poked at it. Although it was nailed shut and clearly had not been altered in some time, the floorboard came up in Roméo's hands. And there it was. Stuck with duct tape to the underside of the wood was a small key. Roméo removed it and turned it over in his hands. Was it a post-office box key? Locker? It was too small for an apartment or house. He examined the numbers engraved on it: 765. Why would she have hidden this?

He slipped the key into his pocket and practically skipped out the door to his car. There was a sudden, loud, hysterical honking. Roméo looked up to see a flock of Canada geese create a near-perfect V in the bruised gray-blue sky the snow squall had left behind. He let himself appreciate them for a moment. Experts in aerodynamics, Canada geese rely on the updraft from each bird to reduce the energy expended in flight. They each took turns doing the hardest job—flying at the head, the apex of the V.

It was very late for their migration, Roméo thought. These must be the last few stragglers. He watched them disappear into a cloud with the same bittersweet feeling most Canadians felt at that familiar sight: winter was almost here. Roméo turned the car out of the driveway and set out on the twenty-minute drive to the Artists' Co-op in Val David, where whatever friends Anna Newman had were to be found. He had been dragged to their studios by his ex-wife a few times. There were *many* potters, a few weavers, and a handful of painters. The vast majority were what Roméo would call "artsy" types. They had no discernible talent but a burning desire to have one. The investigative team had interviewed each of them, but so far, as Detective LaFramboise had reminded him, nothing had turned up. He understood they had started a collection to place an obituary in the Montreal and local papers for their friend. Maybe that would shake a few apples from the tree.

Roméo turned onto the dirt-road shortcut to Val David. He went by a shack passing itself off as a house and wondered again whether some low-life Hells Angels wannabes were involved. Was robbing and killing Anna Newman some kind of initiation? There'd always been a connection between motorcycle gangs and white supremacy. None of the five major American gangs—Hells Angels, Bandidos, Outlaws, Mongols, and Pagans—allowed Black people to become members, as far as Roméo knew. Then there was the Nazi paraphernalia. They loved it—swastikas, iron crosses, death-head logo, German-style steel helmets. Roméo wasn't sure how many were true white supremacists. They just wanted to piss people off, and this was the most effective way to do that. At least superficially. Roméo had recently heard from his people in Vice that the Hells Angels, largely wiped out by 2009 in a massive sting by the SQ called Operation SharQC, were making a comeback, especially in the Laurentians. They were no longer "keeping a low profile," as one of his colleagues had euphemistically put it. And so, it starts all over again, Roméo thought.

He suddenly remembered he had meant to try to call Sophie again. As he reached for his phone, he was forced to swerve wildly to avoid squishing a small dog that torpedoed itself across the road. He braked to a stop on the soft shoulder, the gravel screeching under his tires. The dog had run into the bushes and then stopped, glaring and yapping at him as he got out of the car. He grabbed the dog and looked into its ratlike face. He recognized it. This was one of Ti-Coune's dogs. Roméo placed the animal in the backseat and considered what to do. He turned the car around and headed back down the dirt road to Ti-Coune's house. He was expected at the co-op, and the key was burning a hole in his pocket, but he had a bad feeling about this little lost dog. Ti-Coune doted on her. There is no way she'd be out wandering the back roads of Ste. Lucie unless something was wrong.

Roméo left the exhausted little dog in his car and headed down the overgrown "path" to Ti-Coune's front door. It was ajar. Roméo eased his gun from his shoulder holster and removed the safety. He gently pushed the door wide open and peeked inside. He could see a smashed TV set. Overturned chairs. Where were the other dogs? He stepped across the threshold and saw Ti-Coune's slumped body. He felt for a pulse. Ti-Coune was still alive, but barely. Roméo went to call for help, but it would take an ambulance at least seventeen minutes to get here, even if they left the Ste. Agathe General right away. Roméo hoisted him gently into his arms and carried him out to the car. Ti-Coune mumbled something he couldn't make out. He put Pitoune back in the house and closed the door. As he ran back to the car, he noticed one of Ti-Coune's two guard dogs stagger in his direction, then sit down, panting. He looked like he'd been poisoned. The other one was still passed out or maybe dead. Roméo covered Ti-Coune in a dirty car blanket and ran around to the driver's door. Who would do this to Ti-Coune? Had he broken into Anna Newman's house on his own and pissed someone off? Had he killed Anna Newman? He glanced back at the two guard dogs. One was still not moving, but the other was more awake now. She watched Roméo, her only shot at supper, drive off. Then she began to howl.

Sixteen

EVERYTHING WAS DONE. Packed. Boxes categorized, labeled, and stacked into neat piles. Furniture sold, in storage, or moving to Marie's house. Her grand-mère's fine china wrapped in tissue paper and saved for what Marie laughingly called Ruby's hope chest. (Ruby referred to her small breasts as her Hopeless Chest.) She went through her mother's closets and pulled out at least half of her clothes to give away. The women's shelter downtown would be thrilled. Much of it was in excellent shape, as Claire was of the generation that bought quality over cheap quantity sewed by young children in sweatshops. One thing about quality, Marie mused. It never really goes out of fashion. She recognized at least two Burberry coats from the 1970s that would be very hip today. There were sumptuous cocktail dresses in taffeta and satin, and designer dresses that Claire must have snapped up at a super sale. Claire had remained quite petite, so many of these had fit her well into her old age.

Moving day was three days away, and already Marie felt exhausted. She had hoped Ruby and Ben would help out more, but Ruby had just split with her boyfriend, the one they all thought she would marry, and was too stressed to be useful. Ruby would often text Marie ten times a day, but had been silent now for about a week. Ben was pulling double shifts at his job. He was saving up to buy a house with the new girlfriend, which Marie found to be insanely premature—she had been buying his underwear for him until quite recently. She wished they could both be here to go through each item, each memory, and also be clear about what they wanted to keep for themselves. She had set aside some special items for each of them, but she felt resentful that she was left to do this all alone. At least Ben had called several times to check in—and Marie could hear what seemed like sincere regret in his voice.

Marie took her coffee and stepped outside onto the patio. She had thrown an old jacket of her mother's over her shoulders to keep the morning chill away. Snow was definitely coming. The little cabin that her father had built for Marie and her sisters was still standing across the driveway. She turned the doorknob. Not locked. As soon as Marie breathed in the moldy, stuffy smells trapped within those pine walls for so many years, she had to submit to the memories that overran her. She had shared that old double bed with Lucy Atwood for years. It was so concave that both sleepers ended up squished together in the middle. The cabin was only about twenty feet from her house, but Marie and Lucy were so terrified of spiders and monsters and psychopathic killers that they never lasted an entire night in there. They would come creeping back into the house, trembling flashlights on, and climb into Marie's bed. There were just too many scary things out there. By the time they were old enough and brave enough to spend the night, they were also too old to not be self-conscious about enjoying it. What did they think could happen twenty feet from their house, from their sleeping parents? She looked to where she and Lucy had carved their names in the wall—Lucy and Marie inside a heart—*together 4 ever*.

Lucy had been in Toronto for over thirty years now. She'd been a spin doctor for a PR firm, and a very good one. She'd recently handled the crack-smoking mayor's public image, followed by a prominent late-night talk show host accused of sexually assaulting young women interning at his television network. Then after a heart attack that nearly made her husband of thirty-four years a widower, they moved to a small town and started an organic farmette. She had goats. Ponies. Ducks. She had two gorgeous daughters, a great husband, and a new grandson. Lucy and Marie were still close, but distance kept them from having that intimacy of proximity—the daily exchange of indignities, joys, and grievances. Marie traced their names with her finger and resolved to call Lucy that night. It had really been too long.

Marie closed the cabin door behind her. There wasn't anything she wanted to keep in there. Still, she was saddened by the loss of it, by the passing of a such a specific time and place. Soon the whole thing would be crushed by a bulldozer. Marie watched as her mother's neighbor pulled into his driveway in a monstrously large SUV. It looked like it should be at the head of an armed convoy in Afghanistan. He stepped out, his phone stuck to his ear, too busy to notice Marie. Suddenly, she could see her father's first Buick, the day he drove it home from the car dealership. A Buick Le Sabre, a new one every three years. Robin's egg blue, leather seats, power steering and power windows. The three Russell girls piling in, touching all the consoles, the new radio, the thrilling smell of pristine new car. They would drive down Woodgrove Avenue to the lake, along the lakeshore, past the yacht club and Christmas park, then past their school, to Campbell Farm. It had once been an actual farm where Marie remembers Mr. Campbell circling the front meadow in a horse and buggy. Now it was an upscale community of enormous houses, each with a matching pool. They continued up St. Charles Road and then stopped at their destination: the new McDonald's that had opened its first franchise in Quebec. If that was too busy, the A&W, where they'd obediently order a Papa, Mama, 2 Teens, and Baby Burger. Marie remembers Louise complaining that Marie wasn't old enough for a teen burger—and Marie bursting into tears. Stupid sister crap. Siblings can fight over anything at all. All day. All night. Their entire lives. On the way home, they'd all three pile into the rear window space and beg their father to slam on the brakes so they could all go pitching forward onto the back seat in a tangle of arms and legs. There were seat belts then, but no one would think of putting them on. They were dutifully buckled and slipped back into the seat upholstery.

Marie looked down their long driveway, lined with once neatly trimmed bushes, now an inpenetrable thatch of dying evergreen. It had once promised a much grander house than the Russells' modest ranch-style. That would all change very soon when the latter-day Marie Antoinette moved in. Marie looked down the driveway and remembered a different picture. It is probably late March, early April. Marie, Louise, and Madeleine are standing on the patio, watching their sobbing mother, in her bathrobe, stagger down the driveway. She is reaching into those same bushes, now sagging under the weight of melting, dripping snow. She is pulling out bottle after bottle of vodka and tucking them into her bathrobe. She drops one. When she goes to pick it up, two more fall out of her. Edward must have planned on going back for them before the snow melted. Of course he forgot about them altogether. The three girls are crying because their mother is. She has to retrieve them all before the spring melts the snow completely away, and the shameful evidence is there for all the neighbors to see.

"Is Daniel coming by today?" Claire was suddenly standing right beside her.

"Mum! You scared me! You're up." Marie hesitated and then said gently, "Daniel and I divorced eight years ago, remember?" Claire looked right at her. For a moment, Marie saw the beautiful woman she once was. Then Claire pointed to the hedge with a shaky hand.

"He promised he'd clean up that. That…that green thing …for me. He's such a good boy. Is he coming by today?"

"No, Mum. Daniel can't come by today. He's busy. But I could help you. You want me to do it?"

Claire didn't answer. She wandered down the driveway and started deadheading the desiccated October flowers. Her garden had once been her pride and, especially, her joy. Her sanity, as well. It hadn't been properly tended to in well over two years.

Just after Marie and Daniel were married, Daniel had taken over his father's *shmata* business, which was thriving and very lucrative. Within twenty years, he had driven it into the ground. It wasn't entirely his fault. Everything had been outsourced to China, or India, or Bangladesh. It was hard to compete, especially if you were a hippie turned businessman with a penchant for good dope and a three-day work week. He left Marie for a life that did not involve navigating his kids' adolescence, her peri-menopause, and his new girlfriend. He'd told Marie he just couldn't do it anymore. What hurt the most was he didn't even want to try to save their marriage. He refused therapy and counselling. Marie had begged him, and he conceded once, but it was clear that he considered the marriage over. After twenty-one years.

Ruby blamed her for driving him away, for always nagging him about something. For always being the Fun Police—that was Marie's official name in the household. Ben understood more of what had happened between them—he was more able to see his father for who he really was. Ruby adored her father the way she never could her mother. Marie feared she would never find a man because he could never *be* her father. This latest one had actually called Marie to weep on her shoulder. He said he had given his all, and it wasn't enough. *Join the club,* Marie thought. Marie had become a hermit when Daniel left. All those people they socialized with—with very few exceptions—didn't mean anything to her. Her in-laws were kind but had lost interest since she wasn't attached to Daniel and his happiness anymore. She remembers being told once that Jewish men made great husbands—that they were loyal and committed to marriage. She had found the exception.

"Edward used to like sex. He used to like sex very much." Claire offered this nugget to Marie as she tried to snap stray branches off the hedge.

"Okay! That's too much information before coffee, Mum—"

"But then he couldn't do it anymore." She looked right at Marie and mimed drinking from a bottle. "Too bad. Because sometimes I liked it." Claire dropped the bent branch in her hand and walked over to Marie. "Not like Mrs. Donergan," she whispered. "Did you know Mr. Donergan pays her fifteen dollars to have sex with him? Once a week. On Fridays."

Marie started to laugh. Mr. Donergan was long dead. "And how do you know this?"

"Everyone knows. It's the only way she can afford to get her hair done, because Mr. Donergan is such a cheap. Cheap. Skate."

In those days most women were given allowances by their husbands to manage the households. If there was anything left over, they'd treat themselves to a new outfit or some trifle for the house. Those were also the days, Marie remembered, when suburban housewives got their hair washed and set once a week. They all cut their hair pretty short by the time they were forty. Many got those poodle perms by fifty that made them look twenty years older. A woman could go from an attractive middle age to old age overnight with just one treatment.

"I wouldn't mind if someone paid me fifteen dollars to have sex with them," Marie said. She hadn't had sex with anyone besides herself in four years. Claire stared at her blankly, then bent over to remove a dead leaf from her path. Marie noticed with shock she was wearing no underwear.

"Mum, let's go inside and get you into some clothes, okay?"

Marie guided Claire back inside, down the stairs, and into the kitchen. She sat Claire at the table and put on the kettle for her tea. The *Montreal Gazette* was neatly folded in a clear plastic bag. Marie opened it and placed it before Claire—what was left of the paper, anyway. It had been decimated by the forced retirement of a slew of local journalists, and all but a few stories were being written in Winnipeg. They tried to make it look fuller by having many sections, but each was about six pages long. It typically took Marie less than ten minutes to read it.

"Anything good in the paper, Mum?"

Claire stared at it. Then she started turning the pages, but nothing registered, Marie knew.

"So today, I thought we could go get your hair done. What do you think of that? Go to Yvon's Salon and let him make you gorgeous? Maybe get a little manicure?"

"Edward doesn't like my hair short! But I told him it's much easier to. To. To. To—"

"But your hair is short, Mum. And it's beautiful. But it could use a little styling."

"Edward doesn't like it. He likes it long." She ran her hands through her frizzy gray hair. "I am not cutting it."

Marie was pretty sure Claire had only ever slept with her father. She tried to imagine sleeping with only one man your whole life. Imagine getting married at twenty-one or twenty-two years old and knowing that was it. What if the sex was terrible? She thought of all those women, the world over, imprisoned by marriage, by the Catholic Church, by misogynist double standards. How had her mother's generation not collectively lost their minds? She poured the boiled water into Claire's favorite mug and left it on the counter to cool a bit. Claire often guzzled her tea now and had once burned her mouth badly. Marie turned to put some bread in the toaster and noticed her mother staring at the newspaper with her mouth open. She was pointing to something. Her hand trembled quite severely, Marie was disappointed to see. Probably the new meds they had her on, trying to slow down the disease.

"Something interesting, Mum?"

Claire was peering at something. "Why is Mrs. Kovak in the newspaper? Is she getting married?"

"Who?"

Claire pointed in exasperation. "Mrs. Kovak!" Marie took a sip of her coffee and leaned over her to the paper. At the very bottom of a page of the local news was a short article and a very grainy photograph of an elderly woman. A woman identified as Anna Newman.

> Police are investigating a suspected homicide in Ste. Lucie des Laurentides, a small community northeast of Montreal. The 82-year-old woman was found dead at her home on Wednesday. Chief Inspector Roméo Leduc of St. Jerome says the woman's body was discovered shortly before nine in the morning. "The call came through a neighbor who visits the victim on a regular basis to help her with some maintenance work," Leduc says. The cause of death has not yet been confirmed. He does say that there were no signs of forced entry, or of a violent struggle. Police are trying to locate her family and are looking for the public's assistance with any information they can offer.

A phone number was provided in bold print at the end of the article.

"Mum, this is *not* Mrs. Kovak." And she is definitely *not* getting married, Marie thought. "I think it *is* a lady who lives down the road from me. I drove right past her house when it must have just happened. I thought it was an accident—but. God, I wonder what happened."

"Is she getting married?" Claire repeated.

Marie looked at the photograph more closely. The woman in the picture looked to be in her sixties. Must be an older photo, she thought. Marie didn't recognize this woman at all. "Mum, what makes you think this is Mrs. Kovak? You mean our old neighbor? The one who came here from Hungary?"

Claire looked at Marie and nodded emphatically. "I am very hungry."

Marie dropped the peanut-buttered toast before her mother and reread the article. Then she grabbed her cell phone from her purse and punched in the number.

"Yes. I'd like to speak to...Chief Inspector Roméo Leduc." Marie watched her mother shove a huge piece of toast in her mouth that she was now trying to chew. Marie looked away from this sight, and out the kitchen window.

"Yes! Hello—?" Marie sighed. "Yes. I'll hold."

Seventeen

ENNIS JAMIESON PULLED into his driveway with that electric sense of excitement he got when things went his way. It had been an exhausting but tremendous week of work. Two more clients had passed and had named him as estate executor. He also signed on two more—twin sisters who were both diagnosed with the same untreatable cancer. What were the odds of that? They had some RRSPs and mom and pop investments that he could do much more with. It was always shocking to him that the estate planners most people hired were so incompetent and lacking any vision. He dropped his keys on the kitchen island and went to pour himself a Scotch from the bottle of twenty-two-year-old single malt that he'd discovered on a whisky tour with Bridget last year. He smiled at how far he'd come since the bad old days, when he'd go cap in hand to anyone who'd give him the time of day. He'd had to earn *their* trust, *their* confidence. But no more. Now they had to gain *his* confidence. They had to cajole, seduce, and finally beg him to take them on. At the top of his game, Bernie Madoff wouldn't even take a lunch with someone unless they had three million to invest—three *million*. Yes, it had been a good week. Now it was Friday and he couldn't wait to tell Katie and Liam the news.

Ennis grabbed his glass and wandered into the enormous living room. A fire was burning in the wood stove, and there were traces of his kids here and there—a plastic cup with a bit of juice left, a pencil case and *cahier d'exercises*, a pair of dirty socks. Liam's, of course. He picked them up and then dropped them again. Not his job. Ennis could hear muffled noises upstairs. He knew Bridget was out on one of her extended late lunches with her girlfriends. She would roll in around six o'clock, flushed from one glass of wine too many, full of rich food and even richer gossip. They hardly ever saw Brandon anymore since he'd started his last year of high school. He came home just to stock up on food, money, and sleep. Ennis felt grateful for this. Suddenly the kids came skittering down the staircase, followed by their babysitter. They hurled themselves at Ennis, Katie into his arms, and Liam wrapped himself around his knees. Emma, the babysitter (or was it Emily, or Amanda?), followed behind more languidly.

"Hey, Mr. Jamieson."

"Hi. Kids done their homework?"

"Yup. And they tidied their rooms and had a snack." She gathered her long, thick blond hair in her elegant fingers and tied it into a topknot. Despite the cool weather, she was wearing a little tank top that bared her stomach. Ennis noticed the ring in her belly button and a small tattoo on her hip. Why was Brandon not home to tap into this possibility? She caught Ennis's eye and smiled.

"Is Mrs. Jamieson not home yet? Would you like me to stay and get supper on?"

"Thank you so much for the offer, but I think I can manage. And Mrs. Jamieson should be home shortly. Do you have your car? Or do you want to wait until Mrs. Jamieson gets home and I can drive you—or she can," Ennis said, too quickly.

"My brother has my car." After Ennis said nothing, she added, "I guess I could call my mum to come and get me." She didn't make that sound too appealing.

"Why don't you do that, then. Is that okay?"

Emma/Emily/Amanda pulled her phone out and sent a message. "It may take her awhile."

Ennis smiled at her. "No problem. You can hear the news, too, then."

Katie removed her head from her father's shoulder and wiggled out of his arms. She and Liam started shrieking, "What news? What news!"

Ennis carried a kid under each arm and dropped them on the sofa. The babysitter joined them.

"Well. Today. Daddy bought. For you. Two...*ponies*!" Katie started to squeal in ecstasy, and Liam copied her. "Two Welsh ponies, not too big, not too small. Just right, for you and Liam—and they are rescue ponies—"

"What does that mean?" Katie asked, dancing from foot to foot.

"That means nobody could take care of them, and now we are. We are rescuing them."

"From what?" Liam asked.

"From...a place that couldn't take care of them. So *we* get to. Are you happy?"

"Yesyesyesyesyes!" Katie shrieked. Then she stopped just as quickly and regarded Liam.

"Liam wanted a goat. He didn't really want a pony."

"Don't worry, my love. Liam will get what he wants, too."

"And Brandon?" Katie looked at him with those green eyes that made him want to die of love.

"Brandon, too." He kissed the top of her head as she wrapped her arms around him. "I don't play favorites." Katie knew this wasn't true but played along.

"You and Liam have to think of names for them—"

"Don't they already have names?"

"Well. Yes, but they need new names now for their new home. Names that you like. You'll have to meet them first to choose what suits them, don't you think?"

"But won't they be confused? When we call them their new name and they don't know it?"

"You can call them whatever you like. If you prefer their old names, that's fine, sweetheart."

"I like Pegasus. If it's a girl pony, we can shorten it to Peggy."

"I think they're both boys."

"What could the name be for the other one?"

"Maybe you should let Liam choose?"

She shook her head vehemently. "He'll pick something like 'Pony' or 'Little Horse.'" When people asked Liam what he wanted to be when he grew up, he often responded with household objects, like a washing machine or a lawn mower.

Ennis picked them both up under each arm again and carried them upside down to the kitchen. The babysitter followed and sat on a stool close to Ennis.

"Let's wait to meet them. Then Liam can choose a name. He might get inspired!"

Ennis noticed the two lunch boxes by the kitchen sink, still unemptied.

"I thought I told you two to wash out your lunch boxes after school!"

"I am sorry, Mr. Jamieson. I forgot." The babysitter slid off the stool and moved very close to him at the kitchen sink. He felt her hip brush his thigh. Ennis carried both lunch boxes to the other counter and opened them. Katie's lunch box always pristine, her plastic wrap folded into a neat square, her Tupperware rinsed out and resealed, her apple eaten, her veggies, too. Liam's was often covered in red stains from some former gastronomic atrocity, fruit never touched. Usually a juice box spilled all over his schoolwork. Katie was the kind of kid who neatly folded the wrapping paper after she opened a gift. Liam tore through it without even looking at the carefully chosen illustrations on it. Liam liked to eat a chocolate bar in about three bites. Then he'd ask Katie to share some of hers. She would refuse, of course. She would patiently watch him devour his, then slowly, tantalizingly eat hers. One square at a time.

"Oh, Daddy? A lady came by my school. She asked me to give you this letter."

Ennis felt his skin prickle along his neck. It was a plain white envelope. No name. Like the last one. He tried to control his voice.

"What lady, honey?"

"She was in the schoolyard after school—at the fence. Just before the school bus arrived." The look on her father's face startled her. Ennis grabbed her shoulders. "What did she look like? How old was she?"

"Daddy, that hurts. Let me go!"

"I told you not to *ever ever* talk to strangers like that—"

"She was just a lady—"

"How old?"

"I don't know!"

"Gray hair? Brown hair?"

"Kind of brown and gray—"

"Tall, short, fat—"

"Mummy said not to call people fat—"

"How old was she, Katie?"

Katie was about to cry. "Maybe…thirty?"

"Was she as old as Mrs. Glover?" Katie hesitated for only a second as she considered her school principal.

"Yes! About her age!" Mrs. Glover was sixty-five years old and months from retirement. "But she was taller. And prettier."

Ennis was trying to picture her. A taller, prettier Mrs. Glover. Nothing was coming.

"Go get started on your homework. And tell Liam to start his, too."

"Daddy, don't you know anything? Liam always *says* he never has homework. But he does. And we already finished it with—"

"Can you go watch a little TV, then?" He kissed the top of Katie's head. He looked at Emma/Emily/Amanda. "Can you just give me fifteen minutes?" Katie went running out of the kitchen to the TV room, and then raced right back.

"When do the ponies get here, Daddy? This week?"

"They're arriving Saturday. So be a good girl and do what Daddy says, okay?"

Katie cantered off with pony dreams in her head, and Liam followed behind, whinnying. Ennis tore open the plain white envelope. Inside was one sheet of paper, and typed in boldface:

NICE KID. HOW DID THAT HAPPEN?

Eighteen

ROMÉO LOOKED at his speedometer and noted that he was driving way too fast, even for a cop. He was on his way to see Ti-Coune at the hospital—he'd been transferred to the Labelle Medical Centre north of Ste. Agathe, where he could get more specialized care. He had just regained consciousness that morning, but the doctor on duty had warned Roméo that it was too early to question him. He had a broken eye socket, a hairline skull fracture, a collapsed lung, and a shattered elbow, as well as deep bruising on his knee and contusions covering most of his body. Poor Ti-Coune, he thought. He never really had a shot at life. Ti-Coune had made some pretty bad choices, but it's like his entire life was mapped out for him before he even had a say.

Roméo knew a lot of cops who felt this way—they saw so many human casualties over the course of their careers. You couldn't help but think that if they had had a mother who'd driven them to soccer, or taken them to a museum, or hadn't abandoned them to the rages of drunken fathers, things might have been different. Roméo was still hoping he could ask Ti-Coune a few questions. He had no real expectation of an honest answer, but what Ti-Coune did *not* say could be very informative. His house was being examined for DNA evidence as well. Maybe something would turn up that connected the attack on Ti-Coune to Madame Newman's killer. Maybe the goons who beat him up had something to do with Anna Newman. But why would they almost beat the life out of Ti-Coune?

The key Roméo had discovered at Madame Newman's house was being investigated by Nicole and her team. They still hadn't found what it opened, but Roméo felt certain they would, and soon. He glanced out the windshield at a mass of gray-black cloud that unfolded along the horizon. Was this the first big storm of the year? That's what the weather channel had been going on about for two days now, like a snowstorm was *news* in Quebec. Roméo slowed down as the first flakes began to fall; it was as though someone had just turned on the snow-machine switch. He noted lots of For Sale signs along the highway—many local businesses that were struggling, their clients sucked up by the powerhouse of Mont Tremblant, a huge resort conglomerate the locals could not begin to compete with. Its presence had entirely altered the local economy, and not for the better, despite the promises of politicians, both the crooked and the naïve ones. Even the old and well-established local golf course was closing, unable to compete with the much bigger and sexier resort course. Roméo had heard, though, that golf just isn't a thing people do anymore—especially young people. No loss there, he thought.

A small car packed with large middle-aged men in camouflage jackets and caps accelerated past him. Roméo briefly considered pulling them over but let them go.

Hunting season was in full swing. Roméo had gone once. With about half a dozen of his colleagues from St. Jerome. The best part had been standing around their cars with that first cup of coffee, steaming hot in the chill morning air. The quiet conversation. The unspoken acknowledgment of a common, manly purpose. Then they tramped around the woods for two hours or so and sat in a deer blind for another six. Cold. Bored. Hoping to hell a deer never showed its face, but of course it did. They offered Roméo the first shot as their senior officer. He lifted the rifle to his shoulder and through the scope watched this delicate creature, its legs so thin, so elegant it was a wonder any of them survived a Quebec winter—and deliberately missed. The deer startled, got its bearings, and vanished into the forest with one jump. They all knew Roméo had missed on purpose—he was the marksman of their department—but no one said anything. At least to his face. He suspected there was lots of water cooler gossip back at the precinct. Roméo was not sentimental about animals. He just did not take life when it was not necessary. Of course, he wore leather boots and still had his old raccoon-fur coat that had been so popular in the early 1980s, but Roméo had been a vegetarian since Sophie converted him when she was around twelve years old. Somehow, he had kept that a secret from his colleagues as well.

He had not heard back from Sophie. He struggled with whether to call Elyse and Guy and alert them to his concerns, but in the end chose not to. He'd had another nicotine nightmare last night that had been very unsettling: Sophie was getting married to a man he didn't know (not the current dude) and Guy was walking her down the aisle. All his former friends from his marriage to Elyse were there. Roméo called out to Sophie, asking if he could walk her himself, and all the guests looked at him and pointed. He was completely naked and for some reason could no longer speak French. He could speak fluent Russian, though, and was trying to make people understand him. Then his father, who was dressed in an orange spandex cycling suit, gave him a hockey stick and asked Roméo, in Russian, to join him in skipping around the wedding with it between his legs. Roméo followed him, laughing and waving at Sophie and her groom's guests each time they circled them.

Suddenly, through the dazzle of snow that was coming down harder now, Roméo saw two people running across the highway. At first, he thought they were children. Then he realized they were two *deer*. They cleared the southbound Highway 15 in two jumps, cars swerving and skidding to avoid them, their horns screaming. It was a miracle they made it. They hesitated in the median, then made a leap for it across the northbound lanes, where Roméo was going seventy miles an hour. He couldn't hit the brakes in time, and he couldn't avoid them—so in that dangerous second, he just hoped their timing was right—which it was. They danced over the lanes and onto the shoulder of the highway. Roméo turned to see if they'd made it—and they had. In all his years driving up and down this highway, he'd seen a lot of deer—dead deer, live deer—but never two crossing the entire highway in unison. Never.

Roméo's phone buzzed. When he saw the caller, he decided to pull over. It was Nicole LaFramboise. He picked up his phone and got out of the car. The snow was coming down harder now and coated the sleeve of his jacket in seconds. He realized he still felt like a kid, sometimes, with that first snowfall—that same delight and wonder.

"Where are you?"

"Almost at exit 122. Why?"

"Not sure I should bother you with this right now. But there's been another break-in around the Ste. Lucie area."

"Anyone hurt?"

"No. There was nobody home. Could be the Jumeaux Thibodeau, could be our guy. Or guys. You're pretty close. Do you want to go there now?"

Roméo hesitated. He was eager to get to Ti-Coune, but maybe a few more hours of rest would do him good. "Yes. I'll call you from there. What's the address?"

Nicole told him, and he punched it into his GPS. He wasn't familiar with that particular road, which surprised him. Roméo thought he knew most of this area pretty well.

"Roméo—Chief Inspector?"

"Yes?"

"I would very much like to talk to you in private in the near future."

"Is it of a personal nature?"

A slight hesitation. "Yes."

Roméo sighed inwardly. He'd had impulsive sex once in the last three years, and he felt he was going to have to answer for it in ways disproportionate to the act.

"Of course, Detective LaFramboise. We could meet early next week. In Montreal, perhaps?"

Mistake. Montreal? She'd think he was asking her out—but it was too late. He could hear the elation in her voice.

"Yes! I'll check your schedule and get back to you."

There was another awkward pause. Roméo ended the

call and returned to his car. As he opened the driver door, he noticed the two deer, not a hundred feet away, staring at him. Then with a flick of their white tails, they disappeared down the embankment and into the thicket beyond the highway. They made it this time, he thought. A miracle.

He put his flasher on the top of his unmarked car and pulled a U-turn at the earliest opportunity. On his way back south, he passed one of the favorite local casse-croutes, the imaginatively named 100% Boeuf/Beef. They made the best hamburgers in the Laurentians, possibly all of Quebec. The owner, Jean-Paul, knew everyone and everything within a sixty-mile radius. Roméo resolved to stop in soon for a veggie burger and a poutine when he had the time.

Nineteen

MARIE SAT AT the kitchen table, trying to work on her book, which was now six weeks off schedule. She looked out the window at two squirrels spiraling up and down the big maple in the backyard, chasing each other. After an explosion of energy, each would pause and remain completely still, as though figuring out what the other's next move would be. Then they would circle crazily around the trunk again, in what seemed like a frenetic game of hide and seek. I could write an entire book about squirrels alone, Marie thought. *They run very quickly—up to twenty miles an hour. Like beavers, they have front teeth that keep growing, so they must gnaw—constantly—to wear them down. Otherwise, the teeth would grow into their necks. When they are frightened, they dart back and forth to confuse enemies.* This doesn't work with cars though, kids, so most city squirrels don't live very long.

Although considered granivores (animals that eat grains and nuts), they will eat almost anything—Marie had seen one two days earlier trying to cross the street with a baguette in its mouth. It kept having to stop to readjust its position, as the bread was twice its body length. But it managed to get it up a tree and cached somewhere. Marie imagined that little family of squirrels wearing berets and eating their baguette with a glass of wine.

Marie always found it odd that humans are often so contemptuous of urban animals—when they are such survivors, she thought, and could probably teach us a lot about how to manage the upcoming climate change cataclysm. Marie loved the raccoons in her mother's neighborhood, who would amble down the long driveway to the side of the house, unlatch the "animal-proof" lid of the garbage can, and proceed to their buffet dinner. Marie didn't like how obnoxious gulls could be, but she respected them. The pelagic ones—the ones that always lived at sea except when they were nesting—were amazing, but even the urban ones, the ones you see gorging on abandoned french fries outside strip malls were impressive. They navigated a city full of the most rapacious and destructive species on the planet with unflappable *élan*. Marie liked the pun there. She would keep that for the book. And crows. They were so damn smart. Marie had seen a crow actually take a giant maple leaf and use it to cover up a piece of bread she had thrown out. It watched and waited for the other birds to fly off and then it retrieved its prize. Marie was starting to get excited about this book and really wanted her publisher to find her an exceptional illustrator. *Mature males are philanderers. This is a big word that means they fuck anything that moves and leave the girl squirrel holding the bag—or nest full of oldoo! If they suspect they are being watched, squirrels will pretend they are burying their food to prevent other creatures from finding it. They dig a hole as usual, pretend to place the food in it, and pretend to cover it over, all the time holding the food in their mouths!* She had written the words *food* and *pretend* too many times.

Marie finished off the crust of her toast and swallowed the last of her morning coffee as she watched the chickadees flutter around the old feeder that she had washed and filled up with niger seed. She marveled at them, so fragile and so strong—tiny little birds that can survive at minus 50 degrees. A nuthatch was dangling off the feeder as well, but every other bird had long since flown south. Marie remembered a study she'd read about migrating whooping cranes—the young cranes really depend on the oldest bird in the group, the one with the most experience. The older birds are just better navigators, better at spotting landmarks like rivers and mountains to guide them accurately. She imagined the map in the older birds' brains—passed on complete from one generation to the next. It showed them the topography of their collective journey.

If only the map in Claire's brain could remap itself in mine, Marie thought. To have access to all those memories, to the experiences of the most tumultuous century in history. Her mother had lived through the Great Depression, the Second World War, Hiroshima, the landing on the moon, home computers, cell phones, Facebook. Actual reality to virtual reality. Marie felt a sharp pang of anxiety. Now there was so much she would never know about her mother. Her father. The door to that world was closing, and fast. Marie thought about her mother identifying her dead neighbor up north as her old neighbor from long ago. She felt relieved she hadn't heard back from the police yet, and now felt embarrassed for having made the call in the first place. When she had asked Claire about it again, she had no idea what Marie was talking about.

She glanced over at the clock on the stove—it was almost eleven o'clock and Claire was still sleeping. The caregiver from the community health center was coming over shortly, and Marie wanted to step out as soon as she arrived to go for a walk and pick up a few groceries.

Within two blocks, Marie wished she'd worn a hat and gloves. The day was blustery and hovering around freezing. It was the day after Halloween, so all the decorations were still up—witches flying into trees, skeletons swaying in the wind, plastic tombstones on people's lawns with hands crawling out of the frozen ground. There were overturned pumpkins everywhere, their insides chewed out by squirrels. Halloween, like everything else, had become a huge, expensive *thing*. When Marie was a kid, people used to just carve a pumpkin and stick a candle in it. Back then you'd throw a sheet over your kid, cut out two eyeholes, and call it a costume. The Mitchells across the street were particularly popular for a time because they made candy apples every Halloween, until those kids ate razor blades in theirs somewhere in Nebraska or somewhere and the whole candy apple thing came to an abrupt end. But Marie still loved Halloween. She had thought about giving out candy the night before, but Claire was being particularly difficult, and Marie couldn't run to answer the door every two minutes. Instead, she had turned out all the lights and watched an awful remake of *The Exorcist*.

Marie had especially loved Halloween when her kids were young. She couldn't sew, but she was game and handy with a glue gun, and was known for her eccentric costuming of her kids. She also enjoyed decorating their rambling, fixer-upper house in Montreal West and having all the kids from their block over to divvy up the loot, make trades, and supervise how much candy could be immediately consumed. Even now, she could see Ruby, a miniature Medusa, and Ben, a diminutive Darth Vader, holding hands and running across the neighbors' lawns, avoiding the paths to people's houses to save time and get more candy. Marie and Daniel would wait on the sidewalk, watching them, reminding them to say merci or thank you. She had no idea, back then, how happy she was.

Marie suddenly found herself outside what was once their corner store, Roger's Rexall Drug Store. She and her sisters used to race to it every Friday once they got their allowance to buy their weekly comic book—*Superman* for Marie, *Archie* for Louise, *Betty and Veronica* for Madeleine. Ten cents each. Twenty-five cents for a jumbo. They would sit on the floor and read as many as they could until Roger gently reminded them they had to pay for them or put them back. It was now a giant chain store, identical to thousands like it across the country.

Marie crossed the street to where the Posners' butcher shop used to be. Marie used to go there after school about once a week. Betty and Marie had become friends by grade 3, and Marie remembered how desperate the Posners were for their daughter to have a friend. The Posners always tried to feed Marie something—they thought she was too skinny—but most of the food in the store was too exotic for her. Mr. and Mrs. Posner had thick accents and kept a barrel of pickles in brine by the front door of their shop. Marie never saw a single taker for those pickles. Mrs. Posner suggested she try one once—and rolled up her sleeve to reach into the barrel. There Marie saw—blue numbers tattooed on the inside of her forearm. She thought to ask her about them, but something had stopped her. Marie accepted the pickle and pretended to like it, but in fact it tasted awful to her. Later, at supper when Marie had asked her father what the numbers meant, he told her to ask her mother. When she asked her mother, Marie was told she was too young to know the answer. It was only several years later, when Marie was in high school and watched a documentary on the liberation of Auschwitz, that she understood what those numbers meant.

"Can I help you?"

A young woman with a sweet, heart-shaped face and very blue eyes looked at her quizzically. Her cobalt blue hair was just a shade darker than her eyes, and very colorful tattoos covered every inch of her exposed arms and neck.

"No. Sorry. I was just thinking about this building. It used to be a butcher shop. Everything has changed so much. I grew up here."

Inexplicably, horrifyingly, Marie felt like she was going to cry. And not just cry. Blubber. The girl seemed to sense it.

"It must have really been beautiful here in the olden days. I mean. It's still nice, but I heard it was like, farms here. People came here on *vacation* from the city."

"That was a bit before my time. It was suburbs when I lived here too—newish suburbs, though. It was a lovely place to grow up. I played in that park right over there."

"So did my mum! She grew up here."

"What's your mother's name?"

"Maureen Manning? Do you know her?"

Marie rolodexed through her memory file. "Doesn't ring a bell—"

"Her maiden name was McMahon. Maureen McMahon. Did you know her? That would be amazing!"

Marie hesitated. "Was her father Mr. McMahon?"

"Um, yes?"

"Of course, he was. I mean, did they live on Cedar Crescent? Near the civic center?"

"Yes! My grandmother still lives there! She's like, eighty-six years old now. My mum lives with her. She takes care of her since my grandpa died. Did you know them?"

Marie knew them. Mr. McMahon drove his daughter Fiona and Marie to their high school on days they missed the bus. One morning, only Marie was late and missed the bus. Mr. McMahon saw her running after it and offered her a lift. About a mile from school, he pulled off the highway and headed north into a housing development rising up out of acres of rolling meadows.

"I just have to stop in at a house I'm selling. It'll only take five minutes."

Marie consented, of course.

They pulled up into a gravel driveway, alongside a half-constructed house. There were two dozen more exactly like it along the dirt road, all half built. Mr. McMahon turned off the engine, but he didn't get out of the car. He put his hand on her knee. Then he swept the back of his hand up towards her crotch. Then he stuck his hand up her skirt and put his fingers in her panties, in her vagina. She was so shocked she didn't react at first.

"Do you like this? Has your boyfriend done this to you?"

"I…I don't have a boyfriend."

Marie was frozen to the seat and hot at the same time. But she recovered enough to shove his hand away and jump out of the car. She ran down the makeshift driveway, but there was nowhere to go and no one around. Not a soul. He followed her in the car and told her to stop being silly and get back in the car. Marie refused at first, but when she realized she'd be very late for school and was stuck miles from anywhere, she finally got back in. She leaned as far away from him as she could and stared out the window, but she saw nothing. When he dropped her off outside her school, the bell had already rung. There was no apology. There was no begging for her not to tell anyone. They both knew she would never tell.

"I knew your mother's big sister, Fiona."

"My aunt Fiona? No way! She moved out to Vancouver a long time ago. We don't see her so much."

The girl took a last drag of her cigarette and crushed it into the asphalt with the toe of her boot. "I got to get back to work. It was nice talking to you."

"Where do you work?"

She pointed to where the Posners' butcher shop once stood. It was now a boutique veterinary clinic, which included, Marie noted, a massage therapist for pets, as well as a pet ophthalmology clinic. Marie felt a fit of giggles come over her. She imagined a bunch of dogs wearing glasses and getting a massage while reading a book. Like in one of her sister's tacky posters.

"I love animals. It's an amazing job. Some people are so nice. I mean, there's others, who are just. You wonder why they got a pet in the first place, you know? Hey what's your name? To tell my mum?"

But Marie's phone had buzzed and she was already turned away and looking at the screen. She had a text message from Shelley—a picture of Barney sprawled out on the sofa, watching TV with Joel. She texted back a smiley face emoji, despite the fact that she loathed them. Then she noticed that Louis Lachance, the local handyman, had called three times. She waved the girl away with a faint smile and returned his call. It was his home landline, and her call went straight to his answering machine. Marie figured he was the last person in North America to have a landline only. Louis rarely called Marie, and when he did, he never left a message. Marie was fairly certain he wasn't sure how. Or maybe he didn't believe in such a thing. So why would he be calling her now? Whatever the reason was, Marie thought, it probably isn't good.

Twenty

SHE PULLED UP about half a block away, merged in among the line of parents there for pickup, and turned off the engine. This was her favorite part—when the last bell goes and the kids explode out the school door, yelling and shoving and laughing down the stairs and out into the brief freedom of the schoolyard, and for a few of them, home. For the rest, another three hours of after-school prison. Still, she loved the anarchy of kids—the chaos of children let loose. She loved watching them and could already clearly observe the pecking order from her car window. There were the wall-huggers. The teacher-clingers. The gossipy queen bees and the sporty alpha males. The super-popular kid they all sucked up to, the weirdo off by herself, pretending to prefer it that way. But all of them, in their own way with that chaotic, instinctive, potent *energy*. Which then they try to medicate right out of them. Like they tried to do to her when they couldn't figure out whether she was depressed or bipolar or the latest—borderline personality. Or maybe she was a witch? Or just a hysterical woman? In the old days, they gave women like her hysterectomies and, for the very unlucky ones, lobotomies.

Now they gave you enough pills to medicate a small country. She remembered her last visit to her psychiatrist, seven months ago. He'd barely even spoken to her. Instead, he increased her medication to the point where she only ever felt numb. Flat. Even. When life was like that, there was nothing to look forward to, nothing to live for. It was a world drained of color and smell, a perpetual November. Just like today. Except today she was feeling good, like her whole body and mind were cooking on all four burners.

Halloween decorations still peered out from the classroom windows—and a bit of fake cobweb clung to the stair rails and the brick walls where some enterprising teacher must have stuck it. Today was the Day of the Dead. Or, more accurately, *día de los angelitos,* when it is believed that the souls of young children rise at midnight. She did a presentation in grade 8 on the Day of the Dead, the first Halloween after Cathy. Died. She wore a *muerta* costume, painted her face in a garish death mask, and really played the part. She was convinced that the souls of the children did rise at midnight—and that this would happen with Cathy. She even managed to gather a gang of her classmates after school and headed to the cemetery. She promised them that Cathy would appear.

It was frosty cold and they all huddled together by the gravestone. She had felt it was necessary to say something, so she did the witches' chant from Macbeth. *Double, double, toil and trouble, fire burn and cauldron bubble.* That was all she could remember. Then she summoned her sister. Some say she fell into a trance and then collapsed. The next thing she remembered was being told to report to the principal's office. Then to the guidance counsellor. According to them, she had frightened her entire class. That's when the whole thing started for her, when she was identified as the total weirdo who had to be pitied because of what happened but was mostly avoided or ignored. Not very long afterwards, Mum and Dad separated, and she found herself a prisoner in the so-called mental health care system—where you were sure to come out sicker than when you went in.

And suddenly, there they were. She ran down the steps ahead of him and into a gang of girls who all, she could tell, wanted to be her best friend. He straggled along behind her, sliding his body down the stair railing like he was drunk. She glanced into the back seat of the car to make sure she had everything. The boy would be easier. It was obvious to see he was more compliant, more of a people pleaser than the girl. She was like her father and would be difficult to handle. But she knew that he'd put up more of a fight for the girl. Oh yes, he most certainly would. He'll do anything for the girl.

As she unbuckled her seat belt and got out of the car, a huge SUV lurched alongside her and nipped into the parking spot right in front of her. A gorgeous woman in her late thirties or so jumped out and strode over to the schoolyard. She stood by the gate to the frost fence and waved, her car keys jangling in her fingers. She was like an adult version of the girl, or rather, the girl was the kid version of her. The boy saw her first and ran to her. He touched her fingers through the fence holes, grinning with what was obvious joy. The girl turned to her, and then back to her girlfriends. So this was the mother, she thought. Not surprising at all. Not at all. But shit. Shit. Shit. Shit. Shit. Shit. Shitshitshit. SHIT! She snapped her seat belt back on and turned her car down the street and away. She could not afford to be seen or recognized. It was time for Plan B.

Twenty-One

MARIE TURNED DOWN the narrow dirt road to her house and felt her car fishtail wildly in the heavy wet snow that had fallen. She was driving too fast, but her pounding heart would not let her slow down. She roared up the last curve before her house and saw three cars waiting for her—a Sûreté du Québec squad car, Louis Lachance's little truck, and a black sedan with a red light sitting asymmetrically on its roof, flashing. As she pulled up, she saw Louis emerge from the house and let a dog out of his truck. It followed him down to see her, stuck to his leg like a small child. Louis didn't even say hello before he launched into his report, and chastisement.

"I noticed the door was off its hinges. That didn't make sense. I *told* you to get that door fixed—"

"I know. I should have fixed it right way. But, excuse me, Monsieur Lachance, I need to speak to the police now."

He continued to talk and harangue her while he followed her to the house. Her front door had been kicked in and was hanging by one hinge. "The police took forever to get here. At least an hour. I been here now for almost two hours. Do you want me to stay with you? I could, but I have to call my wife. She'll have my lunch ready, and she'll be worried."

Marie stopped and looked at the old man. "Louis, I can't thank you enough. But please go home to your lunch. I'll call you in a bit, okay? And can you come back to fix the door?"

He patted her shoulder stiffly, and then his thigh for the dog to follow. He started back to his truck. Marie couldn't tell if he was angry with her.

"Louis? Where did you get the dog? What's his name?"

But Louis was already halfway down the driveway, and well out of range for his eighty-six-year-old ears.

As Marie stepped across the threshold past her broken door, she noticed a very young cop in her living room with a clipboard. The report he was waiting for her to help him fill in, she imagined. He looked like the teenage cop she'd seen the other day on the road—outside the house of the woman who was killed. Murdered. Marie suddenly felt breathless. She held on to the door frame and inhaled slowly. That had nothing to do with her. This was a break-in. Nothing more. A stupid, pointless break-in. She owned absolutely nothing worth stealing. Except. Marie ran up the stairs to her bedroom two at a time. They had ransacked her chest of drawers and thrown things from her closet. Her mirror lay shattered on her floor. But they had not found the only things she really cared about, beside her photographs and a few letters from her kids and friends. She dropped to her knees and felt under her bed. She had taped a little box between the box spring and the mattress. It was still there. Inside it was the bit of jewelry she treasured—her mother's pearls that would go to Ruby, her engagement ring she was keeping for Ben. When Marie crawled back out from under her bed, someone's feet in very black, thick-soled shoes were there, attached to a very tall man. He extended his hand to help her up. "Detective Inspector Roméo Leduc," he offered. She took his large hand and noticed his squared-off, clean nails. Her knees cracked loudly as she got to her feet.

"They didn't get my jewelry," she said, brandishing the box.

He nodded. "Is anything missing up here?"

Marie glanced around the small room. "I don't think so."

"Could we go over the house together then and determine what they did take?"

He followed her back downstairs into the living room. It too had been overturned, but in a half-hearted way, like the thieves knew as soon as they'd gotten in there was nothing worth their time here. That was if robbery was their motive, Roméo thought. The house was not expensively furnished but was eclectic and tasteful. There were books everywhere. Faded kelim rugs with exquisite patterns on every floor. A surprising collection of African masks on one wall, an Inuit print of a polar bear and a seal facing off on an ice floe that was astonishing in its power, on another. A few healthy plants. A compact woodstove bookended by neatly stacked wood, uniformly cut. A small, bright kitchen. Roméo picked up a photograph that had fallen to the floor. Marie Russell, her children, and her husband he guessed, taken about ten years earlier. They were all on a hike in some snow-capped mountains and looking splendidly outdoorsy and healthy. There were several more photos of Madame Russell taken in exotic parts of the world. A picture of her in a sea kayak, a killer whale breaching behind her. The photo was taken at such an angle that the whale appeared to be jumping over her head. Another of her in a wet suit, a dripping shark cage pulled out of the ocean behind her. Another on a boat somewhere tropical, many more years earlier. She was in a bikini, and a very Scandinavian-looking man had his arm tightly around her. On a small side table was another. Her parents, he presumed, lifting two martini glasses to the camera. It all suggested a person who had lived a peripatetic life, now contained and held within this small house deep in the Laurentian forest. He spoke to her but didn't look at her.

"Do you live here full time?"

"Yes."

"This is your primary residence?"

"Yes. I said that already." Why was *she* being asked questions? Marie disliked cops. She'd had too many run-ins with too many cops at the many protests she had marched in over the years. What *kind* of person actually became a *cop*?

"What do you do, Madame Russell?"

"What do I do with what?"

Roméo's neutral expression turned into a wry smile. "What is your occupation?"

"Oh! I—"

"Would you prefer that I speak to you in English, Madame Russell?"

"No, thank you." Marie's French was fluent, but years of working in English only had given her an accent. She hated when people noticed it.

"I'm a marine biologist—"

"In the...Laurentians?" They both glanced out the window at the same time. All the trees were now completely leafless, but the boughs of the balsam trees undulated gently in the wind. No ocean anywhere in sight.

"Well, I *was* one—a hundred years ago. Now I'm a biology tea…professor at a college, but I'm on sabbatical. I'm writing a nature book for kids, but—it's for all readers, really. Like a G-rated movie." What the hell was she saying?

"I'm sure your book will appeal to many people. Could you now look carefully and tell us what has been taken?"

Marie walked around the living room, picking up the books that had been thrown to the floor, straightening the chairs and rugs.

"As far as I can tell—nothing."

She went through a door into an adjoining room and returned right away.

"My TV is gone."

The teenage cop was standing in front of her now.

"Is anything else missing, Madame?"

Marie shook her head. "Just my stupid TV. It's maybe three years old. Forty-two-inch. Flat screen. An LG, I think. It's not even a good one."

"They were probably looking for electronics—things to sell quickly, like laptops. They were probably also looking for money—"

"Who keeps their money in their house?"

"You'd be surprised. Especially out here in the country." He held the clipboard out to her. "Could you check this and sign here, please?"

"Wait." She walked over to her kitchen cabinet, opened the door, and sighed. "They got all my booze, too."

"Teenagers for sure, then."

Marie took a long look at the uniformed cop. "Like you?"

Suddenly, Marie felt like she couldn't catch her breath. She leaned on the back of the armchair and tried to take some air into her lungs. Roméo pushed the chair closer to her. "Madame Russell, please sit down. You look a bit pale."

Marie perched on the edge of the chair and held her head in her hands. "I feel a bit dizzy."

Roméo went to the kitchen and filled a glass of water for her. Marie took it from him gratefully. "Just the *thought* of some assholes being in here, in *my* house, looking at my pictures, and touching my things…makes me…sick."

Roméo took the glass from her and placed it gently on the coffee-table.

"That is a very common reaction. It is a violation, Madame Russell. Of your space. Of your very life—"

"My friends don't think it's safe for me here—a house in the woods, miles from the nearest town. But then I remind them about how safe the city was. I lived in Montreal for many years, and I've had five…or maybe six?…bikes stolen, a car stolen, two laptops, one mugging, and one—" Marie stopped. *Attempted rape. And more than one.* Why had she just said all that to him? What was wrong with her?

Roméo nodded, but she could see he wasn't really listening. He was checking her place out. Intensely.

"I have a question. I have also been broken in to before—"

Roméo turned sharply. "Here?"

"No, not here. In my house in the city. But I've *never* had a detective inspector come to…file a report. So why are you here? Do they usually send *you* to investigate a break-in?"

He glanced over at the teenage cop.

"There have been two…incidents in the area. We are looking into whatever connections there might be. To two robberies and a home invasion in the last two weeks."

Marie touched his arm very softly. "Do you mean that woman? On the Fourth Range Road?"

Roméo hesitated. "Yes. She was one of them."

"Was she murdered?"

"We suspect there was foul play."

Marie felt another wave of nausea. "Who would kill an old woman? And what do you mean by a 'connection'? Am I in danger? Is there a fucking killer on the loose?"

Roméo pulled up the other chair and sat closer to her. He looked straight at her. He had dark green eyes—with long, black, very thick eyelashes. It was disconcerting.

"No, Madame Russell. I do not believe you are in danger."

"What does that mean?"

"Is your husband coming up later?" Why did he ask her that? Irrelevant. He covered by returning to his notes.

"I don't have a husband."

Roméo did not look up.

"I'm divorced. And not remarried."

Why did she just say that? He was at least ten years younger than she was. Really good-looking in a rugged. Not rugged. Lived-in. A lived-in way. And his voice. His voice was a rich baritone. Masculine. Male. Gregory Peck as Atticus Finch, Marie's first great love.

"Is there someone who could come and stay with you for a few days? It might be a good idea—"

Just as Marie was about to answer, Roméo's phone buzzed. He frowned and ignored it.

"No. I—I don't think so. And I have to get back to the city. Like, today—"

His phone buzzed again. This time he checked the

caller and excused himself. Marie heard his muted voice just outside on her screened porch.

"Sophie? Is everything all right?"

So, he is married. Of course. And his wife's name is Sophie.

"Sophie? Can you hear me?"

"Daddy? I'm okay. Well, I'm okay, but Trevor—well, he's okay but.... Oh, Daddy." She started to cry.

"Take a breath. Breathe. That's it. Now. Just tell me."

"We were out at a cantina, in, in Roatan. In the resort—nowhere dangerous. And these two guys just grabbed my bag and ran for it. It had all my money, my cards, my glasses. My phone was in my pocket, so they didn't get it, thank *God*."

"Do you have your return ticket?"

"Trevor chased them and got my bag back, but he got beaten up. He was so brave, Daddy! I told him to let them go, but he wouldn't. He's in the hospital here—he's okay, they're just keeping him for observation. But we need money—"

"Can he travel? Come home."

"No, Daddy. We want to stay. Two bad apples don't ruin the country. And you have to ask yourself. Why would two kids steal from two other kids who obviously have no money?"

"Because compared to them you're very rich."

"It's just. There's something very wrong in the world, Dad. People are so poor here."

"A thief is a thief is a thief," Roméo said. But he didn't really believe it. "Sophie? I'll send the money. Text me the details. I need the bank, the Swift number—be sure to ask—and Sophie? I need a text every other day, do you understand me?"

Marie watched as information was exchanged. She was beginning to think this wasn't the wife. She watched him pocket his phone and take a second or two before he returned.

"Is everything all right? I guess that's a stupid question to ask a co—police officer."

The next thing she knew, she was saying, "Would you like a coffee? Or, or a cup of tea?" What was this? A Doris Day movie?

"I have to leave immediately. I apologize. I will leave my colleague here, and follow up with you later. A forensic team will come in shortly—"

"What? Why?"

"I would like fingerprints taken, and some basic evidential work done."

"So, this *is* about the woman who was killed—"

"Anna Newman."

Marie stood up suddenly and briefly covered her mouth with both hands.

"Oh my God! Shit. I completely forgot. My mother. My mother has Alzheimer's disease. She's moving into a home. The day after tomorrow." Roméo looked at her. He didn't say anything.

"That's not important. It's just a fact." Roméo still watched her. "But she said something very strange the other day. I called your office, I think, or the number in the paper, but I was put on hold, and then I rethought the whole thing—she has Alzheimer's and can't really be trusted." Roméo still didn't say anything. "The woman down the road. The one who was…attacked?"

"Yes?"

"My mother saw her photograph in the paper, in the *Gazette*, and identified her as—this is weird, but she said she was Mrs. Kovak—a woman who lived up the street from us in the West Island. A long time ago."

Roméo took out his pen and paper. "Can you write the name down, please? And could you also write your cell number, please."

Marie did so. "Listen, seriously. Should I be worried about this? Should I be staying someplace else?"

"I think you should have your door fixed. And think about getting an alarm system put in. It doesn't stop them, but it does slow them down."

"I'll call today. Now."

"My colleague will give you some numbers." He pulled a business card out of his wallet. "I will be in touch very shortly, Madame Russell."

Their fingers touched for a half-second as she accepted his card. Despite the circumstances, it was thrilling. Marie hadn't felt anything like that in a very, very long time.

Twenty-Two

"LOOK AT HER TAIL! It's so long! And silver!"

Ennis watched as their new pony was backed out of the horse trailer. Katie was squealing with excitement as the second one came out. The ponies had arrived. One was a dapple gray with a silver mane and tail that hadn't been brushed in a very long time. The other was reddish brown, with a darker mane and tail. They both looked cruelly neglected—Ennis had found them through a rescue website that informed him they'd been left to forage in a small pasture the entire summer, but the grass had all been consumed, and they were starving. The only reason they were still alive was the drinking water they'd been able to sip from a little stream that the summer rains had managed to keep running just long enough. Ennis watched as Bridget gently held the gray one's filthy halter and led it into the paddock. Once inside, it paced for a few seconds noisily sniffing the dirt. Then it fell to its knees, onto its side, and rolled with such sheer pleasure that Ennis had to smile. The other pony did exactly the same thing. Then they both hauled themselves up to their feet and shook most of the sand and dirt off.

"They haven't been groomed in months," Bridget said, shaking her head. "What a terrible shame. And they're so skinny." She looked straight into Ennis's eyes. "Thanks for this. You're a good man, Ennis Jamieson."

"I want to feed them!" Liam yelled. Overtaken with excitement, Liam had been yelling all morning. He ran to the side of the driveway and pulled up bits of yellowy grass. Then he ran over to the smaller pony.

"Make your hand flat, Liam! Hold your hand out flat!" Bridget warned. Liam held his hand flat, and of course the grass fell away before the pony could eat it. Ennis didn't know much about horses—but he did have a dog once, and he figured horses were just big dogs. Bridget went over and joined the kids. She was totally in love with them and, by extension, Ennis all over again. He watched her scratching the smaller pony's ears, showing Liam how to be gentle and make no sudden moves. Bridget knew horses—she had worked summers on a horse farm near the bible-thumping town where she grew up. Bridget looked to the manor born—an aristocrat if ever he saw one, Ennis thought. She looked like she should have owned the horse farm, not mucking out horse shit all day.

Bridget lifted Katie onto the gray pony's back.

"Hey! Is that safe? You got a good hold of that thing?" Bridget waved at him and smiled. Katie clutched the pony's mane and looked like she was ready to take it for a spin. Liam was on his back rolling in the dust now, his arms and legs waving in the air. He was probably hoping the ponies would do it again. Katie leaned down from the pony's back and hugged its neck. "This one is mine!"

Ennis reminded them that the hay would be arriving

shortly, and everyone had to pitch in unloading and stacking the bales. Of course, that meant him. And Brandon. If he ever got up.

As if on cue, Brandon emerged from the house, sipping from a steaming mug of coffee. He watched the scene unfold before him, then ambled over to the paddock and leaned on the railing. Liam came running over to him. "Bran, Katie gets a whole pony to herself, but I'll share my pony with you. He doesn't have a name yet, though. I call him Pony."

Ennis draped an arm over Brandon's shoulders. He smelled like teenage boy. "I didn't forget you, don't worry."

"I'm not worried," he answered, too quickly.

"Come here. I wanna show you something." Ennis gestured toward the garage.

Brandon sighed loudly. He swallowed the rest of his coffee, dropped the mug by the paddock fence, and followed Ennis.

"Your brother and sister get the ponies, but you get the real thing." Ennis was pointing proudly to a powder-blue vintage Ford Mustang.

"So? What do you think?" Brandon looked at the car, then at Ennis. His expression had not changed.

"I don't know. What am I supposed to think?"

"It's for you—I picked it up from an old buddy—had it driven all the way here from Thunder Bay. The V-8 engine's completely rebuilt. All leather interior. Had it repainted. It's brand new—except it's not. That's the point. It's a car you can work on, if you feel like it. Get your hands dirty." Ennis slid into the passenger seat.

Brandon nodded. "Thanks. I guess."

Ennis stopped admiring the car. "Any guy your age

would think this was a very sweet ride. You'll drive the girls crazy."

"I'm not like most guys my age."

"What? You don't care for girls? Come to think of it, I've never seen you with one."

Brandon sighed again. "No, Ennis. I'm not gay if that's what you're implying. I'm just not into cars. Like, thanks and everything—but I think something like this is wasted on me."

Ennis felt a kind of anger—not anger—humiliation. It made him want to slap the boy.

"Suit yourself, then."

He got out of the passenger seat and slammed the door.

"It's just that you seem to appreciate borrowing your mother's car. A lot—and I thought you'd like a car that's for a guy—not the family car." Ennis reached for the keys in his pocket and felt the note that had been given to Katie. *Nice kid. How did that happen?* For a few hours he'd forgotten all about it. But suddenly, a conversation came back to him. One of his clients—who'd died about two months ago—had a family who did not fully appreciate his work. The son lived in Toronto and after a few weeks stopped harassing him. But the daughter—she was about sixty years old and in fact *did* look like Mrs. Glover—had been relentless. She had told Ennis to stay away from her mother or she would call the police. She said she knew he wouldn't be happy until he got everything her mother had, even the old family car. Why would they be harassing him again?

Ennis threw the keys onto the driver's seat. "It's yours if you want it. If not, let me know and I'll give it to some kid who'd give his left nut for a car like this."

Ennis felt the note in his pocket again. What was the daughter's damn name?

He left Brandon still standing in the garage without another word. Bridget was in the paddock with the kids, just watching the ponies. Her face was luminous.

"I'll be back in a few hours. I have to go see a client. There's a bit of an emergency."

"You're *leaving*? But the ponies just got here. And we're going to move them to the stable. I'd really appreciate your help here—"

Ennis kissed the top of Bridget's head. She smelled delicious, as usual. "They're in good hands, I know. Just let them sniff around and get used to their new home. I'll be back before you know it."

He noticed Brandon had left the garage and was watching the kids watch the ponies. "Brandon, help your mother."

"What? With what?"

Bridget pulled away from Ennis's embrace.

"Please don't do this. Tell them *you* have a family emergency—"

"I tried that. I can't get out of this one, my love."

Ennis turned back to the house to retrieve his keys and wallet. It'd take him two hours tops to get to the Warwick and back if traffic went his way and the right girl was working today. Ennis was pretty sure she worked Saturdays. He could easily be back before dinner.

As he drove down the long driveway, he glanced at his family. Against the bleached and muted colors of the early November landscape, Bridget and the kids were like brilliant flowers in their bright jackets and hats. They looked like a postcard of what a happy, active family should look like.

Ennis waved at them as he pulled onto the main road, but none of them were looking his way, except Brandon, who did not wave back.

Twenty-Three

MARIE SAT IN her father's old den, drinking the dregs of the last bottle of single malt. She was so exhausted it felt like someone had drained her blood. She'd spent the day cleaning up her little cabin and listening to Louis Lachance lecture her on living alone *dans le bois* when there were such nice apartments in the village. He was not making things better. Marie had arranged for Louis to supervise the locksmith and the alarm company, if she could not be back up north in time. There was really nothing left to steal, anyway. Marie noticed a tremor in Louis's hands as he worked the screwdriver into the old lock he was repairing. She didn't remember seeing that before. Normally, Louis was a man from whom conversation had to be extracted, but today he had actually offered up information. Marie learned that Kutya was Madame Newman's dog. That Madame Newman was a very gracious and kind person. Always respectful, always thoughtful. "If Madame Newman is not safe in her bed at night, then no one is," he claimed. He explained how the shock only hit him two days after he'd found her. Marie continued to sweep up and listen.

"My wife, Michelle, is so scared at night now that she made me buy a baseball bat at Canadian Tire—it's not easy to find this time of year—and keep it by our bed."

He stopped tinkering with the lock and straightened up his back, which had gone stiff. "I have an old hunting rifle, but I haven't fired it in years." Louis trailed off. Marie was reminded of the tragedy with his grandson. They had never spoken about it beyond the usual condolences, and they were not going to now. Louis returned his attention to her door. When each of them had fixed and restored what they could of her house, Marie announced she had to get back to the city. The traditional Québécois greeting or farewell is a kiss on each cheek. This would be unthinkable with Louis Lachance. Marie extended her hand for him to shake, but he pulled her to him and hugged her, their faces uncomfortably close. He smelled like wood smoke and coffee.

"Everything has gone to hell around here. I wish you would think about moving into the village. I don't think it's safe out here for you." They separated abruptly. Louis was obviously embarrassed by this display of affection. Marie was too surprised to know how to feel.

When Marie finally got back to her mother's house in Montreal, Ruby was sitting in the kitchen, waiting for her impatiently. She had her coat on, a small backpack and her car keys on the table next to her. Marie kissed the top of her head.

"Thanks so much, sweetheart. Sorry I'm late—"

"Is everything okay at the cabin?"

"Well, it's a long story and you look like you're in a hurry—"

"Yeah, I got something on in the city and I'm late already."

Marie pointed up with her index finger.

"Is she all right?"

Ruby stood up and slung her bag over her shoulder.

"Grand-mère was fine. I mean, really okay. She's sleeping now."

Marie perched on a chair opposite Ruby. "Oh, thank God. I was terrified she'd still be up and…I don't know… needing me."

Marie watched her daughter tuck her long auburn hair into her hat, pull on her old boots that needed replacing. Ruby did not like to spend money.

"Mum? Are you sure this is the right thing to do?"

"Are you kidding me? Am I *sure* this is the right thing to do? Of course not. I just don't know what *else* to do, Ruby—"

"I was thinking—maybe we could all take turns caring for her. You, me, and Ben."

Marie barked out a laugh. "Right. You both do such a good job of that already!" That was not what she *wanted* to say. When it came to Ruby, she couldn't help herself. It's just that she always felt judged by her—always felt like she didn't measure up to some standard she never quite understood. And, Marie had to admit, Ruby probably felt the same way about her.

"Well, thanks for that. I can always count on you to be reminded of my character flaws and general inadequacy—"

"Ruby. I didn't mean that—"

"Yes, you did. Look, Ben and I are trying to help out. But he's working like, sixty hours a week, and…I'm…"

"You're…what?"

Ruby grabbed her backpack, heading for the front door, and stopped. "I'm studying for my LSATs. Thinking I'll maybe go to law school next fall."

"Ruby, wait! What?"

Ruby turned to her mother and dramatically dropped her head in defeat.

"I did *so* not mean to tell you that. Look at you. You're all dewy-eyed with excitement—"

Marie tried to keep her delight and exhilaration in check. She'd never been good at hiding her feelings. Her mother used to say every emotion she'd ever had was written on her face. "I always told you you'd make a great lawyer—"

"It is so *not* a done deal. If I get in, and that's a big if, I have to sort out student loans, probably change apartments, maybe move out of Montreal if I get accepted out of province—"

"Your father and I will help you. We've put money aside—"

Ruby sighed. "I know. I know. Let me get into law school first, and we'll see. Okay?"

Marie nodded. "I know you'll get in. I just know it."

Ruby groaned and headed back to the door. "This is why I try not to tell you *anything*. Good night, Mother!"

Marie heard the front door slam. "Good night, Daughter. I love you, too."

Marie swallowed the rest of the Scotch, left the den, and slowly climbed the stairs to her parents' old bedroom. Her mother's bed was leaning up against the wall, under a sheet of thick plastic. That would be given to the women's shelter in the city. She looked at the near empty room. She could see both her parents in their old bed. It was huge. Marie had always thought it was a king-size bed, but it was actually two twin beds pushed together. She remembers one early and cold morning crawling into it, and burrowing under the blankets between them. Her father was still sleeping and snoring lightly, but her mother woke up, pulled Marie into her arms, and fell back to sleep. Marie had tucked her head into her mother's shoulder and breathed in her scent. She always wore *Je Reviens* perfume, which Marie was allowed to dab on her wrists sometimes if she asked especially sweetly.

Another scene appeared before Marie, one that happened every few months. Marie and her two sisters are all on their bellies on that same bed, their feet crossed at the ankles behind them, peering into a two-tiered jewelry box that their mother had. They were trying on all her jewelry and play-fighting over which piece was theirs. Louise was going to get the charm bracelet that Claire had added to over the years, one charm at a time. Madeleine loved the pearl necklace. She thought that pearls were the most precious, because they were formed when the oyster was trying to protect itself from an invading grain of sand. Maybe Madeleine always felt like a pearl before swine, Marie thought. Before she became a drunk, Madeleine had often asked Claire if she was adopted, because she felt so different from the rest of them. Claire always laughed and said, "I'm afraid not, honey. We're blood. *Tant pis pour toi!*" Marie's favorite piece was a gold bracelet studded in emeralds (fake of course) that would fall off her wrist unless she held her arm aloft, as it was much too big. She wanted so badly to grow into it.

Marie walked into her old bedroom—now the beige room. Her old bed was long gone, the guest bed still there. She still had one night left to sleep in it. She looked out the window. The trees were mostly all bare now, their branches silhouetted and outstretched to the cobalt sky, like they were asking it a question. How did life disappear so quickly like this? Where does it go?

Another memory. Marie's sisters were asleep in the room they shared and she was alone in her bed. Their babysitter was a boy about seventeen years old who lived five houses down their street. He was the one her mother called when no one else was available. Marie was about four or five years old. After she was supposed to be asleep, he would come and wake her up. Sometimes he thought she'd be asleep but she often wasn't. She was too anxious. He would stand her up on her bed, pull her nightie up and her panties down. And he would just look at her. Sometimes he would touch himself, pulling on his penis and panting like a dog until Marie could see something come out of it. One time he kissed her there. Right on her hairless mound. She knew it was wrong. Or maybe she didn't. She knew it was something he was not supposed to be doing, but Marie wasn't sure she could apply the word "wrong" to it. If he had done more than that to her, Marie had no conscious memory of it. Marie never told her sisters, and they never reported to her that he was anything but the quiet and polite boy from down the street. Years later, when Marie was about Ruby's age, she finally told her mother what had happened. Claire looked at her oddly. "I don't even remember who you're talking about. I never hired a boy to babysit you and your sisters. Are you sure you're not making this up?" What was Marie supposed to say to that? She understood that no mother wanted to believe such a thing could happen to her child, and better to deny its very possibility than acknowledge the truth of the memory. She had never brought it up again.

Marie sat on the beige bed and half-heartedly committed to folding up the clothes that had spilled out of her suitcase. Her bra, underwear, a few rolled-up socks. It was the only mess left in the entire house. Her mother's well-worn leather purse leaned against a chair. Marie kept it in her room, as Claire would sometimes decide she had somewhere to go and head out the door, clutching it like a shield. Marie remembered how as a little girl, she liked to go through her mother's purse. Smelling her lipstick, looking at the portrait photos in her wallet, touching the embroidered lacy handkerchiefs her mother always carried. The purse now looked empty, deflated with underuse. It was their last night in this house. It was almost as though her mother was already dead.

Marie wasn't sure if it was that last Scotch or sheer exhaustion, but she suddenly felt very weird and disconnected. She thought she might faint, so she put her head between her knees and breathed deeply several times. Maybe she needed to call someone—someone whose voice would ground her, moor her. Marie made her way back down the stairs and retrieved her phone from her purse. Many of her friends had become bitter and lonely over failed marriages and disappointing children. Some tried to heal this by devoting their lives to saving animals—they are so much easier to deal with than the human kind. Some tried to outrun the clock and became workout fanatics, ruining every girls'-night-out dinner by loudly declaring how fat they were. Or they'd gone for liposuction and Botox. A few had face-lifts, boob jobs, and butt lifts. Forget gray hair—most of Marie's friends were now blonds. Marie had shoulder-length, dark brown corkscrew curls that she had always loathed. Going blond was out of the question. Some had buried themselves in their work and were so busy they couldn't even talk on the phone—all conversation had to be by text or e-mail. Some were still hopeful that love would come their way, and spent days, months, and years online looking for Mr. Right. Or at least Mr. Not Completely Wrong. One had gone off men completely and was now in love with a much younger woman. Marie tried an online site once. The nice man she'd corresponded with a few times sent her a photo of his penis before they'd agreed to meet for coffee. Old-fashioned dating had also been a disaster. She just didn't see the point of sitting somewhere with a total stranger who obviously just wanted to get laid. Or worse, be her *boyfriend.* Like Marie, a few of her friends had completely given up on the possibility of romance and announced they were so happy being single way too loudly and too often to be convincing. Marie needed to talk to someone who knew her. Who knew her and this house. Who knew Marie *in* this house. There was only one person, besides her sister, in the entire world who fit that description. She punched the numbers in her cell phone. It rang six times. Marie was just going to hang up when she answered.

"Marie! How *are* you?" She didn't wait for a response. "Is everything okay?"

"Yeah, everything's. Okay. I just felt like hearing your voice. And I have a question to ask you." Marie could hear at least one child shrieking and a TV on in the background.

"Hang on, I'll go in the bedroom. The grandkids are here for a few days—I love them, but they are *exhausting.* Hey, is Ben or Ruby having one soon?"

"No! But Ben's moved in with his girlfriend. And Ruby's going to law school maybe—"

"*Law* school? Ruby? Has she given up on acting? She is so talented—and there's too many damn lawyers already! Oh, but you're happy about this, right?"

Marie thought of the years of auditions Ruby had gone to, after graduating from a very prestigious acting school. Every time she got rejected for a role, it was like a little piece of her heart broke—and she never really got it back. Marie felt relieved.

"I think it's a good Plan B for her. I think she'll make a great—"

"Of course, she will. Ruby is good at everything. She'll make you proud for sure."

There was a pause. Marie knew what was coming next.

"And you, my dear friend? How's the love life?"

Lucy's life had turned out the way they say it's supposed to: she'd had a long career of rewarding and meaningful work. She had a marriage that had lasted, two lovely kids, and two even lovelier grandkids.

"Are you seeing anyone?"

Marie hesitated before committing to her answer. "No."

"You've got to *try*, Marie. You're not *old.* Do you want your vagina to dry up and fall out—that's what happens! It can atrophy."

"I didn't say I wasn't having sex. I said I wasn't seeing anyone—"

"*What*? *Who* are you having sex with? Tell me *now*."

"No."

"So, there is someone."

"No. There's no one."

Marie had disappointed her again. Lucy was one of those people who spent most of her life being pretty happy. It wasn't her fault—she'd got the "happy" gene. Part of being like that was Lucy wanted her friends to be happy too, especially her oldest and dearest friend. Lucy understood that people got depressed. She just didn't understand why a vigorous walk on a beautiful day didn't fix it. Marie needed to change the subject.

"How are the grandkids?" It was funny, Marie thought, how I don't ask about the kids anymore. There's a cut-off age or something. You just go directly to grandkids.

"Delicious. I mean, literally. Except Rosie has the chicken pox—what do you call that in Quebec? *Poulet pox*?"

"I thought kids didn't get that anymore—"

"Zara and Matt don't believe in vaccinations—so they just took her to play with a kid who had it and voilà! But she's feeling pretty crappy, poor lamb. I've been watching *Frozen* over and over for two days."

"And how is Graham?"

"He's over his obsession with farming edible insects. Now he wants to get some sheep to add to the menagerie we have here already. Did I tell you we have six beehives? I told him I'm allergic to bees, but it's not true. Don't ever tell him you're interested because he'll convert your whole backyard into a bee colony." Lucy's husband, Graham, was a former tax lawyer turned professional fundraiser. He made very good money persuading people to give theirs away. Now he was also a gentleman farmer and life coach guru.

"Lucy, I'm actually calling to ask you about something—"

Lucy's voice dropped. "What's wrong?"

"Nothing—"

"Oh my God, have you already moved your mother to the nursing home—residence?"

"Tomorrow."

"Oh, Marie. I am so sorry. I totally forgot. Do you want me to come? I could drive up tomorrow morning. No, wait, not tomorrow morning but tomorrow afternoon. I could ask Graham to stay with the kids and I could be there in six hours—"

"It's okay, Lucy. I thought I wanted to reminisce with you—it's our last night in this house—but I actually don't think I'm up for it now."

"I completely understand. You're exhausted. Emotionally, physically—"

"I actually wanted to ask you about the Kovaks…our old neighbors on Woodgrove?"

"The Kovaks."

"Yeah. Our old neighbors? What do you remember about them?"

"Oh. The *Kovaks.* I didn't really know them so well. I mean, I remember Maggie a bit. And the older brother sort of."

Marie didn't know the Kovaks well either, even though Maggie, the daughter, was just a grade ahead of her. She knew they'd built some kind of bunker below their house—in case of nuclear war with Russia—but she'd never seen it. Her sister Louise had when the Kovak boy had invited her over. Louise had reported that there were two huge water tanks and an escape hatch to a storage shed. She said she'd love to live there—food, books, and her own private escape from all of her family for a while.

"Do you remember the pool accident?"

"The drowning? Of course. But I don't really remember much detail about it. I know it totally destroyed the Kellys. They moved away, but I heard they divorced soon after and the sister had problems. What the hell was her name? Stacy…? Or maybe Nancy?"

"What about the Kovaks? It must've been rough for them, too."

"I'm sure it was, but I don't remember. We didn't really know them. Everyone kinda kept their distance after that—"

There was a sudden shriek in the background. "Shit! Just a second. Be right back!" The phone dropped.

Marie could hear a lot of crying, then Lucy patiently asking one kid to give the other back his toy. More crying. Then Lucy's soothing voice.

"Sorry. I'm here. I don't know how I ever had kids. How did we do it?"

"We were young. And we didn't know any better."

"They're just exhausting. I mean, they *flatten* me."

Marie didn't want to listen to how tired Lucy was.

"Do you remember anything else? It's just that my mother said this really weird thing about Mrs. Kovak—the other day, which is not that surprising except that—"

Lucy cut her off. "Shit, I almost forgot! You *do* know what they found out about Mr. Kovak?"

"No."

"Come on, Marie."

"No. What?"

"Remember how we always thought the Schlondorfs were escaped Nazis?"

"Yeah. Sort of."

"Well, *they* weren't the Nazis."

"What?"

"Mr. Kovak. *He* was."

"What are you talking about?"

"Mr. Kovak was a Nazi. In Hungary. Oh my God, this all came out—maybe ten, maybe fifteen years ago? How do you *not* know this?"

"What? I never heard any of this—" Marie was shaking her head although Lucy couldn't see her, of course.

"I told you years ago—"

"You most certainly did not—"

"I saw it on the news. Betty Posner was being interviewed—"

"Betty? From school?"

"Yes. Her name was different because I think she was using her married name. Her mother had been sent to Auschwitz, and Kovak—that's not his real name by the way—was part of the operation to deport Hungarian Jews or something. Little Betty Posner—she still had that lisp—and there she was on TV, saying a Nazi was living in her old neighborhood—hiding in plain sight! It was Mr. Kovak. But like I said, *not* his real name—"

"Was his real name Newman?"

"No. It was way more…Hungarian sounding. Like Laszlo or something. Laszlo…Goulash—I don't know. It's easy enough to look up—"

"Where is he now?"

"Well, I imagine he's long dead, now. I *did* tell you this—in God, I don't know…1997? 1998? I find as I get older time gets compressed, you know? Like I think something happened two years ago, but it was actually like, ten years ago—"

Marie heard a sudden loud crashing sound, then the piercing scream of a toddler.

"Marie? I have to go. Graham's at his book club, and I'm on my own here with the babies—Zara and Matt have gone to see a movie in Cobourg—oh shit, I got to go." Marie heard two kids howling now. "I'll call you tomorrow. Tomorrow!"

Lucy hung up.

Marie's head was spinning. The day had already been so intense, so emotionally charged. She went to the window and looked at Lucy's old house, now almost unrecognizable, but there it was. And seven, or was it eight houses away, the Kovaks' house. Did Marie's mother know this? How had Marie not found out? She had read about Nazis in the United States—there was one living in Ohio, she seemed to remember, who was found out and went to trial. But Mr. Kovak?

Marie had expected to spend the rest of the night strolling, or maybe staggering, down memory lane. Instead, she went to her laptop, opened it, and googled "former Nazis living in Canada."

Twenty-Four

ROMÉO SAT WITH his long legs crossed on his cluttered desk, sipping crappy coffee from the machine. He had just gotten back from his bank in St. Jerome, where he transferred money to Sophie and what was his name? *Trevor.* Trevor? A very anglo name—no chance of that translating well into French. At least he had proven he had guts, if not smarts. She could be traveling with worse. Roméo had called her back and read her the riot act about being aware of her surroundings, taking no unnecessary risks, trying to act less like a *gringo*. She had been a bit dismissive of his concerns, which Roméo took as a good sign: Sophie was back to her old self.

For the last half hour, Roméo had been staring at his wall of suspects in the Newman homicide without really processing anything. The autopsy report was pinned next to the DNA evidence—or lack of it—and beside that was a grainy mug shot of Ti-Coune Cousineau. Roméo had not yet spoken to him, but it was too late in the day for that now. He planned to go to the hospital first thing in the morning. Was Ti-Coune somehow involved in this? Had he gone to threaten Anna Newman out of her money and things got out of hand? Then why was he beaten up? Did his gangster cronies not appreciate him going solo? Or did the local Hells wannabes beat up Ti-Coune because he did it with them and then was seen talking to Roméo? What about the Thibodeau twins? Their family had been committed to thieving for three generations now and counting. But homicide? They had been brought in for questioning, along with an older brother and an uncle. But after several hours of grilling them, Detective LaFramboise was convinced that although the entire Thibodeau clan was missing the gene that gave them any sense of moral obligation to another human being, they had nothing to do with this. Roméo looked at the photograph of the broken necklace with the chai. It was the only indication that Madame Newman was Jewish, or at least liked Jewish symbolism, if in fact the necklace was hers. Her birth certificate said she was baptized Roman Catholic. Yet Ti-Coune had thought she was Jewish and suspected she had money hidden in that house. He wondered again if this was some kind of hate crime.

Roméo continued to stare at the wall as though it would suddenly reveal something to him. His speculation was interrupted by a buzzing on his desk—it was his ex-wife, Elyse, calling about Sophie, he was sure. He decided not to answer—which was cruel, but he didn't care. Let her sweat it out for once. He felt satisfied and pleased that Sophie called him, not her mother or her stepfather. He was a cop, that's true. But still…she still needed *him*. Roméo looked out his window at the blue wash of twilight in November that was really quite beautiful. In Quebec, the time when day is just slipping into night, which comes around five in the afternoon in November, is called *la brunante.* Roméo felt this was a misnomer, because everything is really bathed in deep, dark blue. They also call it *entre chien et loup*—when the light is so dim you can't distinguish a dog from a wolf. But it also expresses that time between the safely familiar and the unknown and dangerous. The threshold between hope and fear. What did the English call it? *Dusk*? It didn't begin to carry the poetry of the French version.

Roméo took another sip of the vile coffee. He really would have preferred a single malt right now and used to keep a bottle in his desk drawer, like the hard-boiled detectives do on TV. But after the horrors of the William Fyfe case, Roméo recognized that booze at work was a dangerous temptation. He knew very well how easily you could run away from yourself into a bottle. Roméo pulled his feet off his desk, not quite as nimbly as he used to. He went to the garbage can and poured out the rest of his coffee. On the wall was pinned his business card where Marie Russell had written *Mrs. Kovak.* Underneath, she had also written her cell phone number. Roméo was struggling not to think about Marie Russell. She was very pretty. But *pretty* was too small, too insipid a word. She was very alive. Lit up. Like there was a light behind those brown eyes. And she had beautiful hands—not elegant, feminine hands, but long, muscular fingers with perfect symmetry. He couldn't really see the rest of her under the coat she'd kept on, as her house had been very cold, what with her smashed-in front door. He would stop this now. She had said that her mother identified Anna Newman as this Kovak woman. But her mother had—was it dementia? Was Marie Russell's break-in related to all this? If so, why and how? But that name Kovak rang a bell. An old bell. He had done a quick search on the SQ database, but nothing had come up. Then he googled the name, but nothing relevant had surfaced there either. He would assign one of the officers to that file as soon as one was available. Right now, everything was chaotic at the Sûreté du Québec. A huge case involving several SQ officers accused of sexually assaulting First Nations women in Val d'Or had just been investigated, and the officers involved had gotten off with basically a reprimand. There would be another official inquiry that would produce the usual sanctimonious platitudes. It was an ongoing disgrace. In every marginalized community it was always the women who got the worst of it, he concluded.

But Roméo also had a brand-new case to find manpower for: a terrible road-rage incident. A woman in a Dodge Caravan with her two small children had pissed off some guys in a BMW. They tailgated her at high speed and then chased her into a parking lot, where she tried to defend herself with a hockey stick. They took it from her and beat her up, right in front of her own kids sitting in their car seats. Roméo would like to lock those guys up for a very long time, too.

The truth was, no one was knocking himself out on this one—an old lady with no next of kin that anyone could locate, whose only friends were a bunch of old hippies at the co-op. The only person who was still pretty broken up was Louis Lachance—Roméo had seen him get quite teary at Marie Russell's house when he spoke of Madame Newman. He had pulled out a huge, well-used handkerchief and blown his nose very loudly. Roméo's phone buzzed again. It was Elyse calling for the third time, but just as he decided to put her out of her misery and answer her call, Nicole

LaFramboise came bustling into the office. She was beaming with satisfaction.

"Okay. So, we called all the local banks to see if Anna Newman had a box with them. The answer was no. We widened our search to this radius," she indicated a larger circle on the map, "and the answer was no."

"The key could be to any box anywhere in the world," Roméo answered, "so that's not surprising."

"We also visited three locksmiths in the area to see if they could identify the bank or anyplace that used that particular key. They had no idea. Not one recognized it."

Nicole unbuttoned her coat and shook out her hair from her SQ-issue coyote fur hat. She sat down in a chair opposite Roméo.

"Then I thought, the key looks pretty old-fashioned. And I was supposed to go check in on my grandfather at the old folks' home he lives in, so I took the key to show him."

Roméo thought this was going on a bit too long, but just as he was about to tell her to cut to the chase, she continued.

"I get to the home, and there he is line-dancing with about twenty old women. He was one of two men in that whole gang. It's like heaven for those old geezers. Anyway, I had to wait till the dance was over, and then I showed him the key. He knew nothing about it. Then, one of his 'girlfriends' from the home comes over to pull him back into the dance, and she sees the key in my hand. Okay, so get this—she recognized the key as belonging to the old Caisse Populaire in—are you ready? *Joliette*! She had a safety deposit box there and said the key looked the same. Can you believe that?" Roméo did not seem to think that this was as crazy as Nicole did. If she'd said the woman recognized it from a bank in Timbuktu, he might share her astonishment. Joliette was less than an hour's drive away.

"I would have gone to the bank right away, but of course, it was closed. I thought it could wait till tomorrow." Nicole took in Roméo's expression. "I'll go myself."

"Well done, sergeant. That was a bit serendipitous."

"The *key* could well be the *key* to the whole case." Nicole grinned. "Sorry, I couldn't help myself."

Roméo wrote on a piece of paper and handed it to her.

"I also need you to get Villeneuve on the name Kovak. Get him to do a search of databases from Montreal, circa 1960. I will get you more information on that when I speak to Madame Russell. It is probably nothing, but we need to be sure."

"Will do that right away."

The conversation was over, but Nicole didn't move. In fact, she moved her chair closer to his desk and abruptly put her hand over his. "I know we're supposed to have a supper together to…talk. But. I wanted to tell you something."

Roméo held his breath.

"You know that I'm almost forty now."

"Are you? You look much younger than that." Empty thing to say.

"And I have wanted to have a baby for a long time now. You know that, I think."

Roméo thought, Please, no. Where was this going?

"And you and me. It was…very necessary, I think. We needed each other, I think you could—"

"Nicole, I need to stop you—"

"Let me finish. I want you to know that I've been seeing someone—no one in the office knows—I've been very discreet."

Roméo exhaled.

"I wanted you to hear it from me, so your feelings wouldn't be hurt."

"Th...thank you," he stammered.

"I'm pregnant. Four months. You can't tell because of this attractive outfit."

Roméo said nothing.

"I met him at a Tim Hortons—we were both in line for coffee—I know—a big cliché, cops at the doughnut shop—and we just started talking. It was a *coup de foudre*. Never felt like that in my whole life. You don't believe in that, do you? Love at first sight? Even with that name of yours?"

Roméo's hand remained frozen under hers. "This is wonderful news, Nicole."

Nicole released his hand and got to her feet. Roméo could see the small bump where her belly was straining at her shirt.

"I wish you only the best. You deserve it. *Bonne chance*, Nicole."

"Merci, boss." Nicole hovered in the doorway. "I'll get to the bank first thing in the morning." She retucked her hair into her hat, turned, and left his office without another word or a glance back. Roméo watched as the other officers followed her progress down the hall. They were all trying desperately to hear what had been said between Nicole and Roméo, and he could see the anticipation of a good story on their faces. He closed the blinds on his window, ensuring himself a bit of privacy. Should have done that a bit earlier, he thought. Roméo looked again at the card where Marie Russell had written *Mrs. Kovak*.

He punched her cell number on his phone. After one ring, it went directly to her voice mail. Roméo waited for the message to end and said, "Madame Russell, it is Roméo Leduc, the investigating officer on the Newman case. I would like to ask you what you know about Madame Kovak. Please call me back." He hesitated, and added in English, "And thank you."

Twenty-Five

MARIE WAS SITTING in the foyer of the Warwick, trying to regain her composure. She had just left her mother in her room with a caregiver. Together, they had unpacked and carefully folded her clothes into a small dresser. Marie remembered that Claire liked little bars of soap placed among her underthings, so she discreetly tucked in a few. Then she found the right place for all her mother's favorite things: on the bed the teal mohair throw from Scotland that Edward had bought her; on her dresser, framed photographs of her three daughters and her grandchildren, her wedding photo, and a music box that played *À la claire fontaine*. A few beloved books—Alice Munro's *Dear Life, Les Fleurs du mal* by Baudelaire, an illustrated *Le Petit Prince* were placed on her bedside table. Books that Claire will never again read. Marie made a mental note to replace the ugly lamp that threw off a box-store light. When she had fussed and done all that was possible, she knelt by her mother in her rocking chair to say good-bye and promised to return the next day. Madame Purdy stood in the doorway and suggested that Marie not linger too long. The Social Animator, a very pregnant young woman with braces on her teeth, kindly reminded Marie that it was "easier for them" if you made a clean break of it. She also suggested that Marie try not to visit for a few days, so Claire could adjust to her new surroundings and "reality." Marie got to her feet and after a few moments tried to extricate her hand from her mother's. Claire gripped it even harder and looked up at her. "What do I do now, Marie? What do I do now?"

She seemed so diminished, even in that small room. Like Alice in Wonderland, she was shrinking before Marie's eyes. She remembered her mother being so alive, so vital—throwing the three girls into a car and driving to the Maine coast one weekend when Edward had gone off on a drinking binge. Marie remembered her mother singing funny songs and treating them to all the ice cream they wanted. She remembers her counting out the cash to pay for their motel room, the few last dollars paid in coins. She remembers her mother sobbing in a phone booth, then returning to them and all four cozied up in the bed, watching *Bonanza* on the motel's black-and-white TV. She remembers her mother looking for work when her dad was in hospital drying out. Claire knew shorthand and was a masterful multitasker. She remembers how jubilant her mother was when she got a job working for a local construction company and, later, for the City of Montreal in the public works department, the makeup covering her puffy eyes in the morning when Edward had kept her up all night. Her mother took a second job as a bookkeeper to keep making their house payments. Hers was a small life—one foot in front of the other, day in and day out. Marie understood only years later, when her own marriage had failed, and her own life seemed so diminished, what a hero her mother really was.

Marie wasn't sure exactly what she was feeling—guilt for sure. And relief, which made her feel even more guilty. But also, such a loss. Marie remembers spending so much time when she was younger wishing Claire wouldn't worry about her so much. Her mother had driven her crazy all those years, checking up on her with late-night calls to see if she was safe. Happy. Unhappy. Then when Marie got older, she worried about her mother's worrying, so she withheld things from Claire that could cause concern. Now, Marie missed her mother's worrying. Now, there was no one else on the entire planet who would worry about Marie the way her mother did. And that's the hole a mother leaves when she dies, Marie thought. Or in my mother's case, checks out prematurely.

Marie watched Madame Purdy make her way down the hall, glance at Marie, and keep going. She had clearly already given Marie her allotted ten minutes of solicitous smiling for the day. Marie began to gather her things and checked her phone. There had been a call from Roméo Leduc. She stared at the name for a few seconds before she remembered who he was. Maybe he'd found her TV. Or the *perps*, she thought. That's how they said it on TV. She should call him back right away, of course, but instead she looked up from her phone to a bit of commotion at the front desk. It was that gorgeous man again. The one who looked like Paul Newman. He seemed to be in a hurry, but he had a bouquet of flowers and a Toblerone bar. Very thoughtful. He was leaning over the counter, quite close to the receptionist, who smiled conspiratorially. He whispered something into her ear, and she shooed him away, but not very convincingly. As he passed Marie on his way to the elevators, he looked right at her. For a second she thought he'd stop to whisper something in her ear too, but he smiled—no, it was more of a smirk—and hustled past her. Marie watched him step into the elevator and could hear him chatting up its occupant. She waited until the doors closed and wandered over to the receptionist.

"Good morning."

"Good morning, Madame…Russell." She looked at Marie expectantly.

"This might…seem a little strange. But I'm wondering if you would tell me who that man was?"

The red-tipped hands crossed at her chin like she was praying. "What man?"

Marie nodded toward the elevator. Of course, he wasn't there. "The very handsome man who you were just talking to. Maybe fifty to fifty-five years old? Very blue eyes and dimples?" The woman said nothing. "The man? Who was just here—with the chocolate and the flowers?"

"Oh. Yes?" Her eyes were teasing Marie.

"He looks like someone I knew a long time ago, way before you were born. I'm wondering…if it's him, I'll say hello. I think he'd get a real kick out of it."

The receptionist—Marie had dubbed her Red Fingers—looked carefully at Marie, as if gauging the truth of that last remark.

"His name is Jamieson. Mr. Ennis Jamieson. Is that who you're thinking of?"

Marie hesitated. She had felt there was something so familiar about him, but the name didn't register.

"No, it's not him, then." For a second, she'd been so sure she knew him from somewhere. "Thank you anyway."

Marie stood awkwardly at the front desk. Red Fingers

had returned to her computer with buds in her ears, clicking away. A decrepit old woman rolled past with her walker, her two grandchildren skipping around her and regaling her with stories about a mean teacher at school. Marie heard a few tinny notes. Piano Man had installed himself at the old piano and was playing a few arpeggios with flourish. Then he launched into "I'm Dreaming of a White Christmas," and no one objected. It's early *November,* for God's sake, Marie thought. There ought to be a law.

The Social Animator was working the room, trying to get the few residents to gather around Piano Man for a singalong. Only one took her up on the offer. Marie watched as the room started to fill with all these people who had once been so active and alive, now clinging with varying degrees of determination to what life had left to offer. Marie realized that just like that, her mother had been absorbed into this new world, this final chapter, and Marie suspected there were very few pages left to write. She wondered if Ruby and Ben would stick her in a place like this one day—but then realized they could never afford it. Suddenly, she very much wanted Ruby to get into law school.

Marie returned to the sofa where she'd left a bag with a few extraneous items her mother really didn't need—or more accurately would not fit into her already overstuffed dresser. There were half a dozen diapers as well that she'd stupidly brought, but of course, if there was one thing Le Warwick did not need it was more diapers. Marie figured she'd hang on to them—she might be wearing them herself one day soon.

She was just leaving the reception area when a woman about her age entered the foyer. She was a bit shorter and a bit thicker all around—one of those women with small hips and bum, but no waist. Her hair was a beautiful chocolate brown, and curly like her own, but Marie could see the line of gray in the part in her hair—so a very good dye job then. When did she start *noticing* this crap, and why? The woman approached the receptionist, who was now deep in conversation with someone on the phone. Red Fingers held up her index finger asking the woman to wait, then turned away from her. The woman's hands were very fine and very white, Marie observed, like they had never seen the outdoors or done a day's manual labor. They fidgeted with an envelope she had pulled from her purse, turning it over and over. Was she visiting her—who was it—mother? Father? But not bothering to look in on them? Paying a bill? The woman waited patiently while Red Fingers remained on the phone, but she scanned the foyer several times before she returned her gaze to the receptionist, who now had completely turned her back to her and continued talking. The woman stared at the back of Red Finger's head, as though the intensity of her gaze could will her to end the call and turn around. Then she quickly slid the envelope to the center of the desk where Red Fingers could not miss it and left it there. As the woman turned to leave, she caught Marie's eye. Marie smiled at her in solidarity, but the woman did not return the courtesy. She looked right through and past Marie like she was a window, and then as quickly as she had come in, she was out the door and into the cold and gray November morning.

Marie zipped up her down coat and slipped on her shoulder bag with the diapers in it. She was just passing the reception desk when Red Fingers finally got off the phone and returned to her duties. She spotted the envelope, read to whom it was addressed, and then slid it out of sight behind the enormous desk. She noticed Marie watching her, gave her a small smile, and nodded her head. Marie looked at Red Fingers as though there should be some parting acknowledgment, some admission that what Marie and her mother had just done was difficult and a moment to be marked in some ritualistic way. But Red Fingers had returned to her computer and didn't look up again. Marie realized there was nothing left to do. She decided to head home and call Roméo Leduc back.

His visit to Le Warwick had been a total waste of time. Earlier that morning, he felt pretty sure his stalker was Mrs. O'Rourke's daughter, who had threatened to call the police before. She had warned him to stay away from her mother. And he had. It was Mrs. O'Rourke herself who had asked him to come back, begged him really, to manage her affairs. His clients were all women of a certain age. Many were recently widowed. Some had never handled any of the finances in their marriages—had never so much as written a check. Ennis handled all the fussy paperwork, such as paying taxes and canceling credit cards. He did *everything* for them. The daughter had not intervened again. But the little chat he just had with Mrs. O'Rourke had yielded no information about her. Instead, he had to listen to the saga of Brangelina's breakup, proof of how phony their whole marriage and family life was. Bridget had sent three increasingly nasty texts demanding he return home, but once Mrs. O'Rourke had him trapped, she was unwilling to let him make a quick exit. When he finally extricated himself from her, he took a few minutes to look in on two other clients, but one was asleep and the other at aqua therapy. He felt quite certain their children were not involved, either. There had been three notes so far, one per month since September. Since *September.* What could have triggered this now? The first two were left in his mailbox. The last one, with Katie at her school. *At her school.* If she was after his kids, then he had to go to the police. But who was *she*? Or was she part of a *they*? And *why*? He racked his brain again trying to think who might want to threaten him. His family. There were always enemies—people who resented his success—who envied his lifestyle, his wife, his family. What they saw as his "easy" success. But none of it came easy. He had worked his butt off to get where he was and had eaten lots of shit from lots of people before he could stop going cap in hand like a beggar. Now he was a real person, a real man. A crackerjack of a man. A rainmaker. Someone who made things happen. Someone who could buy his family anything they needed. Or wanted. Someone who got what he finally deserved, what he had worked for all these years. He thought about his many clients in the several homes across the city. He had carefully nurtured his relationships with them for years. They needed him. They relied on him. They would be lost without him. And now, someone was trying to…what? End that? Scare him? He thought again about involving the police before… before what? It's too late? *He* was the victim here. She had gone to Katie and Liam's school! She could be a kidnapper—want ransom. But so far, nothing had been requested, nothing demanded. Except that Ennis *tell the truth.* About what? Ennis realized he had to sort this out, and fast.

He was just heading to the door when he remembered he hadn't said good-bye to Josianne at the front desk. It was very important that she remain on his side—she was an extra set of eyes and ears for him when he wasn't there.

"I'm taking off, my lovely. See you on Tuesday?"

"I'm not coming in on Tuesday, Mr. Jamieson."

Ennis frowned. "You always work on Tuesday."

She lowered her eyes and then her voice. "I'm taking a mental health day. This place can drive you crazy."

Ennis laughed. "No one deserves it more than you—you run this place. I just hope it doesn't all fall apart. One day without the efficient and charming Josianne might do it."

Ennis tightened his cashmere scarf and slid on his leather gloves.

"Tell me. Has Mrs. O'Rourke's daughter been in lately? Has there been any correspondence there?"

Josianne rolled her eyes. "Are you joking? No one has called for her in months! If it weren't for you, Mr. Jamieson—"

Ennis leaned in closer and swallowed all of her with his eyes. "Call me Ennis, please."

Josianne tilted her head coquettishly.

"If it weren't for you, Ennis, no one would ever come to see them. They just sit there day in and day out, sleeping, drooling, looking out the window, waiting for someone to come and change their diaper, or take them for a walk, or make them listen to that horny old guy." She gestured toward the man at the piano, who was now plonking at "I Saw Mommy Kissing Santa Claus."

Ennis raised an eyebrow.

"He's always trying to touch me. He pretends it's a hug, you know, Mr. Touchy Feely, but he always holds on too long and too hard. And he smells like cat pee."

"A guy's got to dream, Josianne." She didn't get it at first, then frowned at him. "But that is unacceptable behavior. You should report him. Do you want me to? I'll go speak to Madame Purdy right now."

She shook her head. "No. Thank you Mr.—Ennis. I think he performs here for free, and he's just lonely."

Ennis's pocket buzzed. He glanced down at his phone so Josianne wouldn't notice. It was Bridget again.

Ennis made a little bow to her. "Well, I for one will miss you terribly on Tuesday. Enjoy your day off. You deserve it. I hope you do something extravagant. Indulgent." He hesitated. "My good friend owns the Le Sybarite spa downtown. Tell him I sent you and it will be no charge."

"Really? That would be awesome. Thank you...*Ennis.*"

He touched his forehead with a finger and turned to go. If he went straight home he could be back before lunch. A late lunch.

"Oh Mr. Jami—Ennis!"

Ennis walked backwards from the door like a robot and turned to Josianne. She slid the envelope across her desk to him.

"I totally forgot—this was left for you."

It was like the others, a plain white business envelope, but this time *Ennis Jamieson* was written on the front. His heart began to pound.

"Are you okay, Ennis?"

"Who left this here?"

"It was this woman who was asking about you—she said she thought she knew you from before, from the past. She seemed surprised that you weren't who she thought you were."

Ennis slipped the envelope into his coat.

"Sorry—what the hell are you saying?"

Josianne's entire body language changed.

"A woman was here who thought you were someone else."

He tried to control the timbre of his voice, but it was hard.

"Who, Josianne? Do you have a name?"

"It was Madame Russell. *Marie* Russell. Her mother moved in today. She was just here—you just missed her. She wanted to surprise you, she said."

Ennis tried to breathe.

"What did she look like?"

Josianne tapped her lips with her red fingernails.

"Oh. She's quite old—older than you—maybe about fifty? Or maybe sixty? She has curlyish brown hair and she's quite tall. Taller than me, I think."

Ennis had already turned away from her. "Thanks. See you next week." He felt Josianne watching him head to the door. He tried not to run out to the parking lot before he tore open the envelope. In it was a single piece of paper, a photocopy from an old newspaper.

CATHERINE ANN KELLY 1957–1974
Died tragically on June 16. She is deeply mourned by her parents, Robert and Eloise, her dear sister Susan, her adoring grandparents, loving aunts, uncles, and cousins, and her many school friends. Cathy was a gentle soul who was admired and loved by all. The funeral service will be held at St. Edmund of Canterbury Church on June 21, at 2:00. The family will receive condolences at 89 Angell Avenue in Beaurepaire from 3–7 p.m.

Ennis stared at the paper for a good few seconds before he registered what it was. It was like a door that had been closed shut was now kicked wide open. This was not about what he did for a living. This was about the past—an old story that Ennis thought was long dead. But evidently, someone—this Marie Russell—did not think so. If that bitch wanted to dredge up that old story, then so be it. And if she was after his kids? His *children*? Ennis would find her. Face her. And deal with her.

Twenty-Six

ROMÉO WAS LYING on an examination table in a hospital gown, with his feet in the metal stirrups. His grade 4 teacher, Madame Faustin, was holding a small apple aloft and announcing that she was now going to insert it into Roméo to test for disease. He was desperately trying to get out of the stirrups, but his feet were strapped into them. He was trying to imagine where that apple was going. As he looked around the room for help, Nicole LaFramboise, Ti-Coune Cousineau, and his ex-wife's husband, Guy, were all watching and applauding. Roméo woke up before the medical procedure began. This time, Roméo swore, he would forgo the nicotine patch. Enough was enough, Roméo thought, as he pulled into the hospital parking lot, showed his badge to the guard, and was waved on in.

He was a big believer in socialized medicine, which had been the model for health care in Quebec since 1968. But sometimes, he had to admit, that faith was challenged, and today was one of those days. As he made his way to see Ti-Coune, he counted at least a dozen people in beds in the hallway, because no more rooms were available. Many were elderly chronic-care patients who could not afford a private nursing home. They were often stuck here in this hellish state for weeks and months at a time as they moved up the waiting list to get into a government-run home. There was no privacy. Their most intimate moments were exposed to anyone walking in off the street. And the sad thing was, most were too sick to care. It was almost enough to make him a convert to a privatized system—almost. Roméo had also seen what that was like when he had had a brief stint studying in the United States. He had witnessed parents who actually had to choose whether they could afford to take their very sick children to the hospital. It was barbaric. But in Quebec, despite all its many problems, someone like Ti-Coune who had no insurance, and certainly no reliable income except welfare, could get excellent care. As if to contradict Roméo, one of the ghosts lying on a gurney in the hall grabbed his arm with unexpected strength.

"*S'il vous plaît, Monsieur, aide-moi?*"

Roméo stopped and held the man's hand. "*Qu'est-ce qu'il y a, mon vieux?*"

The man had tubes attached to every part of his body, and an IV bag slowly draining into his stomach.

"Please. Can you drive me home? If I could get home, I would feel much better."

Roméo extricated his hand from the man's grip and placed it gently back on his chest.

"I'll go see if a nurse can come and take a look, okay?"

"Go fuck yourself, then." The man turned painfully over on his side. Roméo smiled and decided to give the nurse a pass.

Ti-Coune was sleeping in his plastic bed, the back elevated slightly to offer better drainage to his shattered nasal cavity. A tube disappearing up his nose was taped into place. One side of his face was sunken—a broken eye socket and fractured cheek bone. Between those two purplish-yellow spots were about forty stitches running like a road map. The other side of Ti-Coune's face was almost pristine. Roméo also knew that he had severely bruised kidneys, but luckily, no renal failure. His right kneecap had been kicked so hard it had dislocated to the back of his leg. That would take several surgeries to repair. His recovery would be long and torturous. Roméo sat down in the plastic chair beside his bed, glancing over at the other patient in the room. It was an old man. A very old man. He looked like he weighed about eighty pounds and was sleeping with his toothless mouth wide open. An emaciated, veiny hand gripped the stiff sheet tucked around him. No chance we'll be disturbing him today, Roméo thought. He leaned into Ti-Coune's bed and touched his arm. Roméo noted again the tattoo portrait of his sister, Hélène, and a small swastika by the elbow. Ti-Coune must have sensed his presence and slowly opened his eyes. It took several seconds for them to focus and process.

"*Hey! Comment vas-tu, mon grand?*" Roméo touched the small area of his arm that had no tubes in it. "*Peux tu me parler?*"

Ti-Coune closed his eyes but couldn't turn his body away from Roméo.

"*Chuis icit à cause de toi.* I'm here because of you, for Christ's sake." The words came out slurry and salival, the result of the broken cheek and the potent painkillers he was on.

"*Comment ça?* How is that?"

Ti-Coune licked his lips slowly, painfully.

"They saw me talking to you. That's enough for them."

"Who's they?"

Ti-Coune closed his eyes and tried to smile. "If I knew I wouldn't tell you."

"So, you didn't know these guys? Well, at least it wasn't your good buddies who did this to you."

The man in the next bed suddenly snorted loudly and startled both of them. Ti-Coune tried to laugh but couldn't. He tipped his head slightly in the man's direction.

"When he came in here he was six-foot-two and two hundred pounds. And that was just a few days ago. This place'll kill you."

"Do you know if these guys had anything to do with the murder of the old lady? Do you think they were involved? They got something against her?"

Ti-Coune looked away. "What could an old lady do to them?"

Roméo shook his head. "I don't know. Did they think she was Jewish? She wasn't, you know. Good old Roman Catholic, just like us. They got something against the Jews? I mean you got the swastika, and I know they love all that German death head stuff—Nazi stuff."

"That's just for show. They don't know nothing about that."

Roméo sat back into his chair and studied Ti-Coune. There was something he wasn't saying.

"Look, I have to go. When you're ready to tell me who those assholes were, tell the nurse and she'll give me a call. Okay?"

Roméo got up from the chair and turned to return it

to its spot between the two patients. Suddenly, Ti-Coune grabbed Roméo's hand, and with surprising strength, pulled Roméo closer.

"Roméo. Listen. Can you do something for me?"

Roméo didn't answer.

"My sister, Hélène. You remember her." He stopped to catch his breath. "Yes, you do. I remember the way you looked at her."

Roméo didn't say anything. He allowed Ti-Coune to hang onto his hand.

"Can you find her for me? She's in Edmonton, I think. Let her know that I'll be laid up awhile?"

Roméo pretended to consider the request.

"I don't know. What's in it for me?"

Ti-Coune took another labored breath through his clenched teeth.

"I don't know those guys. Honest. Never seen them before."

"Were they members of your little club?"

Ti-Coune nodded. "But not from here. Maybe Lachute? They weren't full patch but connected for sure."

Roméo gestured toward all the tubes attached to Ti-Coune.

"They weren't fooling around this time. What did you do to piss them off this badly? And don't give me the bullshit about talking to a cop."

Ti-Coune looked Roméo directly in the eye with the one that still could.

"They were pissed because...Okay." He hesitated. "Someone...maybe me...was supposed to go and give her a little scare."

"She was eighty-two years old. You in the business of scaring little old ladies, now?"

Ti-Coune took what passed for a deep breath.

"Someone wants her land, her stupid three acres—I don't know why. Something about it's…close to that rich guy's place—with the weird name—Batman or something? The guy who's selling his *chateau*? There's something on her land that they want, maybe? And I guess she wouldn't give it to them."

Roméo sat back down. "Do you mean Pierre Batmanian?"

Ti-Coune nodded. "I think so. I was just supposed to make her afraid, but they thought I did…that to her and took her money. But I didn't, Roméo. I never went near her." He squeezed Roméo's hand with surprising force. "I swear it."

"What does a man like that want with an old lady's little piece of the world? Did they discover oil there?"

Ti-Coune closed his eyes. "I don't know. It's just a bunch of trees and rock. Like everything else around here."

Roméo removed Ti-Coune's hand from his own and stood up.

"If you decide that you remember who these guys are, let me know."

"Roméo. You will find Hélène? Just let her know about me, okay?"

"I can't make any promises, but I'll make a few inquiries. But it is at the bottom of my to-do list."

Ti-Coune nodded and fell back against his pillow. Roméo leaned in.

"Some fuckhead strangled an old woman. And left her to freeze in her garden like she was an old shoe. If I find out you're involved in this, Ti-Coune? I will be coming for you, do you understand?"

Roméo strode quickly past the hall dwellers before another one grabbed him and begged for help. He realized he hadn't had breakfast that morning and briefly considered the hospital cafeteria. Not this time of year. Flu season was almost in full swing, and he was a sitting duck. He went to the antibacterial hand cream dispenser and vigorously rubbed some into his hands. He felt like rubbing it over his entire body. His phone buzzed in his pocket. For some reason, he was really hoping it was Marie Russell. But it wasn't.

"Boss! We did it. We found where the key fits!" Nicole was almost breathless with excitement.

"And?"

"The Caisse de Dépôt in Joliette. Just like my grand-papa's...um...friend said!"

"And?"

"It's nothing but letters. Many letters, and it looks like they're all to the same person."

"To who? Weren't they sent *to* Madame Newman?"

"No. They are all *from* her to someone named...Magda Mayer. But they all came back to her, it seems. Unread."

Roméo slipped into his car and put the cherry light on his roof.

"I'll be there in forty-five minutes. Read one to me right now."

He swung the car out of the hospital parking lot and put his phone on the car's speaker. Nicole hesitated.

"I'd love to, boss. But here's the thing. I don't know how to read Hungarian."

Twenty-Seven

MARIE WAS SO TIRED and hungry by the time she got back to her mother's house from Le Warwick that she ate three Lean Cuisines in one sitting. She just needed to get some fuel into herself before she went on the hunt for what she was pretty sure was in one of the few remaining boxes in the basement. The house was so quiet and still, her ears were ringing with the silence. Marie dropped the tin foil empties into the garbage can under the sink, rinsed her hands and mouth, and looked out the kitchen window. The only activity was a solo mail carrier making her way down the driveway to the Atwoods' old place. Lucy had said she would call her back but hadn't. Marie tried not to resent the fact that her old friend had been doing this for years, and how was it possible that Marie didn't know this history of Mr. Kovak? She felt certain Lucy had never told her—your old neighbor turning out to be a suspected Nazi war criminal is not something you tend to forget. When she had googled "Nazis living in Canada," Marie learned that her country was right up there with Argentina and Brazil in offering a new home for Nazis fleeing justice after the war. She read that many escaped using false names, aided and abetted by her own government, or funneled here by the American government. Marie had researched for a few hours, but despite all her attempts, found nothing about anyone named Kovak. She reminded herself to contact the Simon Wiesenthal Center in the next few days. Or maybe she could try to contact Betty Posner.

Marie left the kitchen and headed toward the basement, her footsteps echoing loudly in the hollowness of the empty hallway. As she descended the stairs, she scanned the last few boxes stacked up against the far wall—the ones she was taking to her house up north. Marie got to her knees and tried to read the writing along the side of one box. This was it—LOUISE'S SHIT was written in her own angry handwriting. For the first time since she'd packed her family's life up, Marie was grateful she hadn't thrown this one out. She lifted the packing tape that sealed the top of the box and opened the flaps. It wasn't even full. Inside were a few of Louise's keepsakes—or at least what Marie's mother had kept for her sake, but Louise had never claimed. A drawing of a little girl holding her mother's hand inside a giant heart. *Je t'aime, maman! xoxo ta fille, Louise* was printed neatly under their feet. A few medals Louise had won in ringette, a game she played in high school that Marie was contemptuous of. It was like hockey, but for girls—instead of stickhandling a puck they pushed a little ring around with a stick. There were two small plaques Louise had won for Best Effort in grades 5 and 6. A few gimp bracelets that she had made, as well as a macramé bookmark that Louise had given their father for his birthday, Marie was amazed to remember. How was it that certain seemingly inconsequential moments are so engraved in her memory, she thought, when she often struggled to remember the details of life-changing ones?

The object of her search lay at the bottom of the box—Louise's high school graduation yearbook. When she opened it, a photo of Louise at her prom fell at Marie's knees. She sat down and examined it. It was the full-on hippie look, circa 1971, that her own kids had imitated for Halloween years later. She had tried to explain to them that being a hippie was a revolutionary way of life, but of course, the words sounded hollow, even to her. It was mostly playacting, as Louise's prom outfit attested to. Her waist-length hair was parted neatly and hung like drapes on either side of her face. Her dress seemed inspired by Twiggy, and the Salem witches. To complete this eclectic look, she had on white go-go boots. Her wrist corsage was the final incongruous detail. Her date had on a striped purple and gray suit with huge lapels and a neon purple tie. He had no chin, but gorgeous long brown hair, a mustache, and muttonchop sideburns. Marie remembers he loved his hair and frequently preened and played with it. She could not, for the life of her, remember his name, but she did remember that he left Louise at the prom dance to drop acid with a bunch of his friends and never returned. Marie thumbed through the pages to the graduating class—until she found the one she was looking for. It was in black and white, of course, but there he was, his head cocked, a confident smile, blond hair falling over one eye. His blurb underneath read:

Ambition: *lawyer*

Probable Destiny: *jail*

Claim to Fame: *his hair*

Pet Peeve: *girls who have nicer hair than him*

Favorite expression: *"I can't get no...satisfaction."*

Activities: *Varsity football, Debating Club, Student Council Vice-president, Red Cross*

He was not in Louise's class, but he was in her year. Tomas Kovak. Marie looked at the photograph more closely. The man at Le Warwick had dimples and a cleft chin. Tomas had neither. The man at Le Warwick also had gorgeous salt and pepper hair, electric blue eyes, and a brilliant smile. We all have a perfect age, Marie thought. The age when we suit our faces perfectly. For some, it's when you're an impish ten-year-old—which doesn't translate well into a fifty-year-old man. Marie's was somewhere around thirty. Her sister Louise actually looked her best when she hit her forties. She had always been a bit matronly. Madeleine's perfect age was about sixteen—before she started drinking. It was all downhill after that. Tomas Kovak in high school was almost too pretty—he hadn't grown into his face as a man yet. If he was this Ennis Jamieson, then he had found his perfect age. And acquired dimples and a cleft chin along the way. Marie closed the book. She must have been mistaken.

On a whim, Marie punched Louise's Calgary number into her phone. She could use Tomas Kovak as an excuse for the call, but it went straight to her sister's voice mail, which announced that Louise, Humphrey, and Bogart could not come to the phone right now, but please leave a message.

It ended with the dogs barking hysterically, and Louise giggling in the background. She wished she actually could *talk* to her sister, but those conversations almost always left Marie feeling worse. The sister Marie had always turned to was Madelaine because of her instinctive understanding, even when she was so sick. About a year before Madeleine died, Marie had discovered her one morning passed out at the base of her toilet bowl, naked from the waist down and covered in dry vomit. Marie thought she was dead. She fell to her knees beside her sister, shaking and slapping her until she opened her eyes. When Madeleine could finally focus on Marie, she asked, "Are you okay, honey?" Marie remembers holding and rocking her while she wept, and Madeleine comforting her.

Marie switched off the basement light and returned to the kitchen with Louise's box. Her phone was lit up with messages—a text from Madame Purdy letting her know that her mother had settled in just fine, and two from Ruby. Roméo Leduc had returned her call, but she'd missed it again. She called his number, but it rang once and went straight to his voice mail. Marie didn't leave a message, figuring she'd text him instead—but what would she say? That a middle-aged man named Ennis Jamieson reminded her of a boy she barely knew many years ago? That he might be that boy, Tomas Kovak? That her oldest friend had informed her that his father was apparently a Nazi? That her mother had identified a murdered woman in her remote Laurentian home as that boy's mother? She would also have to tell him that she had shown her mother the photograph of Anna Newman again, but her mother had no idea what she was talking about. Marie realized this would be a very long and incoherent text and decided against it. This would have to be explained in person.

By the time Marie finished loading all the remaining boxes from the basement into her car, it was already late in the afternoon, and rush hour would be in full swing. The traffic up the Laurentian autoroute to Ste. Lucie would be horrific. Marie decided to spend one last night in her old childhood home and settled into her father's ancient La-Z-Boy with an enormous glass of single malt. She hadn't even swallowed half of it before she was sound asleep, the two newsheads on CNN chattering away to her deaf ears.

Twenty-Eight

ENNIS WENT TO the end of the chapter even though Katie and Liam had already been asleep for several minutes. Although Katie read at three grade levels above her own, she loved being read to and insisted Ennis read her Harry Potter book to her that night. He felt Liam was a bit young for it, but he'd seen all the movies, so maybe it was all right. Ennis had tried to get Bridget to put the kids to bed, but she was already in the bath with a goblet of red wine and a book. She was still angry with him despite the fact that he'd run her bath and opened a very, very good bottle of pinot noir. She refused to speak to him in anything but monosyllables. Ennis extracted himself very slowly from Katie's bed and decided to leave Liam there with her. Although he had a runny nose and felt a bit warm, moving him might wake them both, and then the whole reading cycle would have to start again. He kissed them each on the forehead, switched off the light, and padded quietly to the master bathroom door. He could hear the water running—Bridget refreshing her bath a bit—and figured he had a little window of uninterrupted opportunity. He descended one floor to his office, a large, very masculine oak-paneled room that he had dreamed of having his entire life. He opened his computer and continued the research he'd been hastily doing on his phone while driving back home from Le Warwick. He googled "Marie Russell," and there she was. At first when Josianne said her name, it didn't ring a bell. But then he remembered her sister, Louise Russell, in the same year as him in high school. His old neighbor who had a little sister. Ennis was pretty sure her name was Marie. He hastily scrolled through the few sites where she was mentioned. She had no Facebook account, at least not one that he could find. She did have a website, but it hadn't been updated in ages. From what he could see, Marie Russell was a marine biologist who had mostly worked out of the Monterey Bay Sanctuary—but that was decades ago. She seemed to have done research with humpback whales. She was now a biology professor at Dawson College. He then followed links to Rate My Teacher, to a few papers she'd co-published, and then to a publisher's website. So, she wrote nature books. Just as he started to read her bio, he heard his door open. Bridget stood there in her bathrobe, looking resplendent, and smelling even better.

"What are you doing?"

Ennis shut his computer.

"So, you're talking to me now?"

Bridget didn't change expression. "I came to tell you I'm going to bed. Are you *still* working?"

Ennis nodded. "Just for another little while. I've got a couple of things to take care of, and then I'll be right up."

Bridget remained in the doorway, backlit and framed like a painting. She had an uncanny sense of knowing when she looked irresistible. Then she turned away from Ennis and slammed the door behind her. He hastily reopened his computer and clicked on Marie Russell again. There were several images of her—one making a speech at some kind of Greenpeace hippie event, and one was a publicity headshot for her publisher. But why would Marie Russell, of all people, be leaving him these notes? Ennis just couldn't fathom it. Did he have to go through all that again? Ennis suddenly felt an urge to break something, to smash something—anything. Instead, he grabbed a pillow off his leather sofa and yelled into it with every cell in his body. He would not be the victim of that kind of morbid curiosity again. He would not live through that again. He scrolled back through the publisher's website to profiles of their writers. There she was—in an older and not particularly flattering picture: *Marie Russell is a marine biologist who fell in love with fish as a child with her nose pressed against an aquarium tank—and whose research on the vocalizations of humpback whales earned her recognition early in her career.... She is now a confirmed land-lubber and teaches biology at Dawson College in Montreal. She shares a house in the Laurentians of Quebec with her two dogs, and her backyard with many of the animals she writes about in her books*—Ennis felt his stomach drop. There was no mention of where exactly she lived. He quickly googled 411.ca and entered "Marie Russell—Laurentians." In seconds, her name popped up and an address in Ste. Lucie des Laurentides. Ennis suddenly felt a ringing in his ears. Was he going to pass out? He put his head between his knees and held onto the legs of his chair. He tried to control his breathing, but it took several minutes before he could sit up again. When he did, he stared at the computer screen until he'd memorized the information, then logged off. Ennis felt more than ready to put this to rest, once and for all.

Twenty-Nine

ROMÉO WAS GOING out of his mind. On his desk were the originals of the nineteen letters from Anna Newman to a Mrs. Magda Mayer, spanning almost twenty years. Some were addressed to a private home in Mendocino, California. Several of those letters had been forwarded to another address farther up the coast that, as far as Roméo could tell from the map he had googled, was an even smaller town called Caspar. All the letters had been returned unopened, though one letter looked as if it had been carefully and cleverly resealed. He could be wrong about that—most of the envelopes bore traces of their journeys, slightly battered and covered in ink from the various post office bureaucrats who'd stamped and redirected them several times, ultimately coming all the way back to their sender. Although the most recent was dated just six months earlier, they reminded Roméo of watching an old black-and-white movie, reminders of another time and place. Imagine taking the time to write a letter by hand, sticking a stamp on it, and mailing it now. Roméo poured himself another terrible coffee from the office machine and looked out his window impatiently, although he wasn't expecting anyone. After staring at the letters much of the night, Roméo had fallen asleep at his desk and had woken up with a neck so stiff and sore he couldn't turn his head in either direction. He had drooled all over the pages of loose notes on his desk.

All the letters were written in Hungarian—except for a few words here and there in each of them. Roméo had examined these bits in English, but they weren't enough to construct any coherent narrative. One of his detectives had tried Google Translate, but the text produced was so syntactically convoluted and unidiomatic, it was practically useless. Nicole had finally located a translator from the University of Montreal who was working on the letters already. Roméo was waiting for the ping of an e-mail to signal that the first one was done and in his inbox. He remembered what Marie Russell had said—that her mother had identified Anna Newman as Mrs. Kovak from her old neighborhood in Montreal. Kovak is a Hungarian name, Roméo thought. Why hadn't he pursued that conversation further right then and there? He had tried to reach Marie Russell several times, but they kept missing each other. He was thinking of actually sending a patrol car to pick her up and bring her to his office for a debriefing. He would give it until the next morning. It was becoming clear to him that Anna Newman had most likely assumed a new identity—and very effectively, too. If she had been this Mrs. Kovak, there was no trace of her *anywhere* that Roméo's people could find. Completely changing identity was not an easy thing to do. In fact, for an amateur, almost impossible. Anna Newman/Kovak must have had some serious professional help in effecting this. Roméo returned to his desk and scanned the letters again, which he had arranged in chronological order to create a timeline. The very first letter sent to Magda Mayer was dated September 3, 1995, and was partially written in English:

> *Dearest Magda,*
> *I have started this letter to you so many times and ripped up all my efforts. I keep telling myself, why would she read this? In all these many years, she does not answer my telephone calls, she does not open her door to me. She will not even tell me if she has a child. But I must continue to try because you are my child, and there are things you must understand. Now, my darling Magda, I am thinking that I will not continue these letters in English. I must write in my mother tongue. I am sorry not to write to you in English, but I cannot. That is the language of my long nightmare. I hope you still remember enough from those years of Saturday Hungarian school that you so despised to understand me. But you were the one who learned the language. Your brother had no interest—so quick was he to become Canadian—to cut all connections to the mother country. But you, darling Magda, seemed to understand the importance of one's language. Of one's history. This is why I am writing to you. Because my history is a lie. All of it. From the very beginning, a lie. But was it a lie to save my life? Or a lie to kill everything that matters? My mother. My father. My family. Our story.*

He couldn't make any of the rest of it out—not even close. He tried to recognize one word—one expression that Anna Newman had used in English—but failed. The language looked complicated and like nothing he had ever seen before, written in the hand of someone who had clearly been educated in Europe. Magda Mayer was evidently her daughter and had either changed her name or was using her married name. Of course, they had looked for her number attached to the address, but there was none. They assumed she was then using a cell phone, but none were found in her name. Was this possible daughter of Anna Newman some kind of hermit herself? Was she still alive? They'd finally learned that there was one Magda Mayer who had lived in Santa Barbara, who was divorced from one David Mayer, a retired professor. They had one child, a twenty-six-year-old son, whom Nicole's team was trying to locate right now. Roméo felt relieved that they had finally been able to identify next of kin. Perhaps the huge holes in this case would start to be filled in, and soon. Because there was a killer on the loose. Someone who was capable of throttling an old woman to death. Someone who might very well kill again.

Thirty

BRIDGET PULLED the door shut very quietly behind her and made her way down the carpeted stairs to the kitchen, all buttery yellow in the feeble morning sun. Liam was sick in bed with a high fever that the sticky medicine Bridget had just poured into a tablespoon and down his throat should take care of. For four hours, anyway. Despite Katie's objections to missing school, Bridget had kept her home as she was also running a low-grade fever. Liam was sleeping, and Katie had agreed to watch a few videos in her room on Bridget's laptop while she took a shower and reorganized her day. Of course, Katie insisted on watching *Pitch Perfect,* which Bridget had refused. She found it vulgar and inappropriate for a ten-year-old. Katie was left to sulk and watch *Happy Feet* for the hundredth time.

Ennis at least had fed the ponies before he left for the city. He had to go to the courthouse to get a probate hearing confirming him as the only person who would handle the assets of some new client whose family were all squabbling over her money. He said it was quite ugly, and he had seemed nervous about the impending confrontation, which was not at all like him. He had spilled his coffee all over his suit pants and had to change his entire outfit. Despite how angry she'd been with him, Bridget was never able to hold a grudge long. She retrieved a fresh suit from the foyer closet that had just been returned from the cleaners. She'd kissed him out the door and reminded him to be home for supper. Sometimes she was terrified he'd work himself to death—have a heart attack or get stress-induced cancer. Bridget wanted Ennis to live a long time, retire comfortably, travel the world with her, and then stay home and indulge their many grandchildren.

Bridget cancelled her three appointments for that day and quickly scanned the headlines in the *Gazette* while she allowed herself a second cup of coffee and a few empty minutes before she checked back on the kids. The birds at the feeder were all jostling for position and devouring the seed she'd just put in the day before. A very light snow was falling even in the pale sunlight—but not falling exactly. It was more like an unseen hand was gently swirling the snowflakes in a delicate dance. It was very pretty, pretty enough for Bridget once again to appreciate moving out here to the M.O.N. as Brandon called it. Middle of Nowhere.

She was worried about Brandon. He hadn't come home from school last night, messaging her that he'd be staying at a friend's to study for a big exam. More like smoking pot all night and playing *Final Fantasy*, she thought. Ennis did not tolerate pot-smoking at home—he believed it was a gateway drug and an effective killer of all worldly ambition. Bridget thought alcohol was a much more dangerous drug, but this was a subject about which Ennis could be very stubborn—fanatical even. So Brandon stayed away, and once again, Bridget was caught in the middle. In the Middle of Nowhere, she thought again, grimly. But then, she thought of Ennis early that morning—gently kissing each of their children on the forehead, stroking Katie's cheek, Liam's wild and sweaty thatch of hair. Ennis adored his kids. She knew that he lived for them, and for her.

When they had first met and realized that they would make a life together, Bridget had so hoped that Ennis would love Brandon like his own son. He had tried—and for a few years, before Brandon hit puberty and their own kids came along, to all appearances had succeeded. But then that toxic cocktail of Brandon's adolescence and Ennis's fifties happened, and their relationship became strained to say the least. It was a source of daily sorrow for Bridget—an ache she woke up with every morning and went to sleep with every night. You're only as happy as your unhappiest kid, she once read somewhere.

Ennis had been trying harder with Brandon lately—he had bought him that Mustang. Bridget fantasized about them all going on a long and lovely vacation in—well, anywhere would be perfect, as long as they could get through one day without an argument, without her husband or her son pushing his chair away from the table and storming off in a rage. Lately, though, Brandon had seemed more accepting, less angry. She had even heard him in the garage tinkering on that car. She resolved to make them all a special supper that night—with the little ones sick, they could maybe share a more sophisticated meal and adult conversation.

She slid off her stool and removed a cookbook from the kitchen shelf. Both her men were carnivores, so perhaps a boeuf bourguignon with a full-bodied pinot from Ennis's cellar. She was going over the list of ingredients in this particular recipe and trying to remember what she had in the pantry when the doorbell chimed loudly. She was not expecting anyone, and people did not tend to drop in out here in the country. Bridget tightened the belt of her robe—she hadn't even gotten dressed yet—and went to see who was at the door.

This was *perfect*. Why hadn't she thought of this before? She was so stupid, exposing herself like that at the school. And at the nursing home. This would really hit him where it hurts the most. She had watched him drive off that morning, a bit earlier than usual. She gave it a full hour before putting her car in gear and making her way toward the house, just in case he came back. She parked in front of the four-car garage and took a minute to control her breathing. She walked past the evergreen shrubs now wrapped in burlap that stood sentinel along the paving-stone walkway to the enormous double front door. She could hear the doorbell echoing inside the house, then the blurry shape of the wife peering at her through the frosted sidelight window. It only occurred to her at that moment that the wife might not open the door. People were like that now—suspicious of strangers, scared of psychopaths lurking around every corner. She went to press the doorbell again when the door opened a few inches.

"Yes?"

She put on her most innocuous and sincere voice. "Hello. You don't know me, and…I know this is a bit weird, but I was hoping that Ennis Jamieson might be home?" Susie asked, smiling brightly at Bridget. "I'm an old friend of his from the bad old days out west, and I heard from mutual friends that he was living here now. I'd love to say a quick hello."

Bridget opened the door a bit wider. "He's just gone out for awhile. Where do you know Ennis from? What's your name?"

"Oh! Sorry, of course." Susie extended her hand. "Catherine Kelly." Bridget hesitated. "We both worked in Banff for one summer—many moons ago."

Bridget did another quick scan of the woman. She was the right age and certainly seemed sincere.

"I don't remember him mentioning anyone by that name—"

"Well, it was a long time ago, so I guess that's not surprising."

Bridget sensed the woman's disappointment. "But Ennis almost never talks about the past. He's not one for a stroll down memory lane."

There was an awkward pause.

"Well, then, I guess I'll look in on him another time. Thank you anyway."

Susie took two steps back down the path, as Bridget went to close the door.

"Um. Excuse me?"

The door remained ajar. "Do you think I could use your bathroom? I really need to pee and I'm afraid I might not make it to the nearest restaurant. And there's not too many options around here. The challenges of menopause. Nothing you need to worry about yet!"

Bridget took in the graying brown hair, the matronly coat, and badly applied makeup.

"Sure. The powder room is the second on the right."

Bridget waited by the front door and tried to ignore the sound of a very loud pee. It occurred to her that she could text Ennis right now about this Catherine Kelly—and was about to retrieve her phone in the kitchen when the woman emerged from the powder room.

Bridget escorted her back to the front door.

"Do you think I could leave Ennis a quick note?"

"Um. Okay. Of course."

Susie pulled a business envelope from her breast pocket.

"Oh, you have it all written already!" Bridget took it from her hand and glanced at the name. "But it's addressed to…Tomas Kovak?" She shook her head. "You have the wrong person here."

Susie looked Bridget right in the eye.

"No, Mrs. Jamieson. *You* have the wrong person."

Thirty-One

A DULL ACHE had started in Roméo's stomach—the combination of lousy coffee and the crappy food he'd eaten all morning. He popped a Tums into his mouth and stared at the computer. What was taking so long? The woman had had the letters for hours now. Roméo decided he'd give it another go with Google Translate when his phone started buzzing itself frantically across his desk. It was Marie Russell. Finally. He very carefully pressed the green answer icon.

"*Oui? Bonjour.*"

"May I speak to Roméo La—"

"This is him." Roméo left his desk and began to pace his office.

"This is Marie Russell. I finally caught you—"

"Yes, we've been playing phone tag for a few days now."

"Well, I am sorry, but I just moved my mother into a nursing home and it's been very…busy." Her voice seemed an octave lower than he remembered. The effects of fatigue when you hit a certain age. Roméo heard a ping at his desk and returned to check the e-mails. Nothing from the translator.

"I wanted to ask you a few questions about something you said. At your house—when we were investigating the break-in."

"Have you caught the guys yet?"

"No, Madame Russell. But we are trying."

"Really?"

"Yes, really. Right now, however, we have a homicide on our hands and…. Look. You mentioned that your mother identified this woman in the newspaper, Anna Newman, as your old neighbor, a Mrs. Kovak?"

"Yes—but like I said, my mother has Alzheimer's, and when I asked her about it later, she had no clue what I was talking about."

"Madame Russell, what can you tell me about this Mrs. Kovak?"

Marie explained that she didn't know her well at all—that they were Hungarian immigrants who came to Canada probably in the late fifties, and that their claim to fame was the nuclear bunker they had installed under their house. She told Roméo that her sister Louise knew the older brother a bit, and that Marie herself only knew of him from school, where he'd been several years ahead of her. She told Roméo about the accident—that a girl from her school had drowned in the Kovaks' pool.

"What year was this?"

"Oh shit. I did know this because I just found the obituary in my—1973 maybe? 1974?"

Marie told Roméo everything else she could remember, which wasn't much more than she had already offered. The Kovaks weren't really on her kid radar. Then she repeated the bizarre and unbelievable news Lucy had told Marie about the father. Roméo asked her to repeat Lucy's full name, and then asked her to spell it. He took her cell phone number as well.

"But I did look him up—Mr. Kovak—and found nothing. Maybe he was using another name, but I couldn't dig up anything on any former Nazi named Stefan Kovak, or whatever he called himself back in Hungary, I guess."

"We will look into this now, Madame Russell."

"Could you please call me Marie?"

Roméo hesitated. "Thank you very much for this information…Marie."

"Do you think this is all connected to the murder in some way?" She realized she sounded like a character on *Law and Order*, a TV show she had watched obsessively in its early, superior days. The whole experience was surreal. Or hyper-real. Marie suddenly felt exhausted. Her head was pounding from the Scotch of the night before, and the hangover from the day it had been.

"Oh my God. I almost forgot. At Le Warwick yesterday—that's the…residence my mother moved into? This is going to sound really strange—"

"Nothing would sound strange to me now, Madame Russ—Marie."

Marie tried to say this as evenly as she could. "I was just leaving the residence where I had to…put my mother. A man was at the reception desk. And I thought that *he* was the son, Tomas Kovak. He looked like my memory of him. Except the man I thought was him—his name is Ennis Jamieson. So, it's probably not Kovak. I just thought I'd mention that."

Roméo jotted down the name, as well as the name and address of Le Warwick. Then his e-mail pinged again. He saw the subject heading. It was from the translator.

"Marie, I would very much like to speak to you further. Are you able to come to the precinct later today?"

"I think I've told you all I know—"

"I doubt that. You'd be surprised what memories a few questions can loosen up. Are you in Montreal now? Or are you up north?"

"I'm leaving for Ste. Lucie shortly. As soon as I finish up here at my mother's. The alarm company is coming to install the, the alarm system, obviously. I have to be at my house between four and six o'clock this afternoon to let them in."

Roméo tried to keep his voice impassive. "I have to be back in St. Jerome later this afternoon. I could come by your house this evening. Around eight? Does that time work for you?"

Marie took a deep breath. "Okay. Yes. That can work."

The call ended. Both Marie and Roméo took a moment to remind themselves of the other. The details they each remembered. They both smiled. Just a little. Then Roméo opened the new e-mail.

Thirty-Two

BRIDGET GRIPPED the woman by the elbow and pushed her to the threshold of the front door. "I think you need to leave right now."

The woman grabbed Bridget's hand and held it.

"But I haven't told you the best part—something about your husband. A story from his past you'll really appreciate knowing about. I promise." Bridget now couldn't get her hand away from this woman. She was very strong.

"It took me a long time to find him—but here he was, hiding in plain sight all along."

"Look, I'm going to have to call the police if you don't—"

"He killed my sister."

Bridget finally pulled away and made a run for her phone in the kitchen, but Susie was faster and got to it first. She must have spotted it when she went to the bathroom.

"Give me my phone."

"Not until you listen to the story I have to tell you."

"Mummy?"

Katie stood on the stairs behind Susie, clutching a very loved stuffed dog, her cheeks flushed with fever.

"Katie, go back upstairs, would you?" Bridget said in a high voice without taking her eyes off the woman.

"But I want a glass of juice."

"I said go upstairs right now, honey. I'll bring you one in a few minutes."

"But I want it now."

"Katie, go put your movie on, okay? You can put on *Pitch Perfect*, okay?"

Katie stepped backwards up a few stairs, staring at her mother and Susie. Then she turned around and ran back up the stairs two at a time.

"You have such a nice family. I mean it. You're really lucky. Well, to have two really cute kids."

"I only have my daughter, and Ennis is coming home any minute—he just went to get some milk in town."

"We both know that's not true. You have a little boy. Liam. Is he upstairs, too?"

Bridget remained silent.

"That's why this is so unfair. Because he gets to have a family. He gets to live like a normal person…like he's a normal person. But he's *not*."

"Look. I think you are very upset and clearly not thinking straight. My husband's name is Ennis Jamieson, and I am sure you have mistaken him for someone from your past. Someone you feel very angry with. If it helps at all, I know how that feels—"

Susie grabbed the butcher knife from the wooden block set Bridget had given Ennis for their fifth anniversary and pointed the blade at Bridget's stomach.

"Sit down and shut up. Please."

Bridget sat down at the kitchen table. Ennis's toast

crusts from breakfast still sat there, next to some congealed, unfinished fried eggs and a crumpled napkin.

"Your husband's name is not Ennis Jamieson. His name is Tomas Kovak. It took me a long time to find him. When I first recognized his...face in the newspaper all those months and months ago—it was some stupid charity thing he attended—I couldn't believe it. He was back, and so close to his old hunting grounds. The sheer fucking arrogance of it! He grew up in Beaurepaire—three streets over from mine. He was in my sister's grade. Big Man on Campus. Captain of the football team. Captain of the debating team. Popular. Handsome. Everything came so easy to him. *Everyone* liked him."

Bridget kept her eyes on the woman's face. But she was acutely aware of the knife in her hand.

"Cathy and I were supposed to go straight home from school together that day, but when we got near the Kovaks' house she announced that *Tomas* had invited her over for a swim. She didn't really want her little sister to come with her, but we had made plans and Cathy—Cathy was never the kind of person who'd break a promise. So, I went with her. The father wasn't home, but the mother was. She had this funny accent, so she wasn't so easy to understand. And she fed us this weird stuffed pepper food that looked gross but actually tasted pretty good. Cathy was *so* nervous. She liked Tomas, and she'd never liked a boy before. Not that I ever noticed, anyway. I thought she was maybe a lesbian, you know? She knew she wasn't really in his league—like he was a 10 and she was a 7 at best? She was really smart though—like top marks in math and physics, but book smart, not people smart. I'm more people smart than book smart.

"We ate the weird peppers, then a torte. I remember Mrs.

Kovak calling it that. It had poppy seeds. It was delicious. Tomas had a friend from his class over—and we all ended up in the pool. I remember we played chicken in the pool. Do you know what that game is? Oh. It was a thrill to be on the shoulders of an older guy, my legs wrapped around his body, his hand…gripping my knees. But I remember. Tomas kept watching me. I had a big…chest for my age, and I know I looked good in my two-piece. I used baby oil and iodine that summer, so I had this deep brown tan? Then Cathy went into the house with Mrs. Kovak and the other boy to help prepare some snacks for us, but Tomas stayed and sat in this pool chair beside me. He said to me, 'I thought your sister was pretty. But man, are you ever cute!' I didn't answer. Do you know what it's like to have the most popular boy in school tell you you're cute? It is the best feeling ever. You feel like…*complete.* Like you have achieved something. He put his hand on my thigh. I felt a tingle between my legs. I never felt anything like that before. He said, 'Maybe I should date you. Or do you already have a boyfriend? I bet you do!'"

The woman let out something between a sigh and a groan.

"I let him leave his hand there. It was like an electric current. I was on fire. He leaned in to kiss me—but my sister came out with Mrs. Kovak and that other boy, and he…took his hand away. But the rest of that afternoon I could feel his eyes on me. Enjoying me. Consuming me. I loved it. I *loved* it."

The woman was no longer watching Bridget, who shifted slightly in her chair. Could she get the knife from her? How? What if she failed and she went after the kids? The woman suddenly looked Bridget right in the eye like she knew what she was thinking.

"I knew I should've told Cathy what he did. But it was just a flirt. Guys were like that all the time. But they were all boys in my grade, covered in pimples half of them. Or who hadn't grown into their bodies yet. They walked around with their arms crossed, you know. Shoulders all slumped. Tomas *inhabited* his body.

"At the end of the day, we all posed for a picture sitting in the shallow end of the pool, pretending to be in a boat, all rowing. Magda, Tomas's sister, took our picture with a Polaroid camera—you know, the kind that produced the photograph immediately? There we were. Me, then the boy, then Cathy, then Tomas, leaning into Cathy with his mouth wide open and laughing, like he's about to take a big bite out of her. We all started singing this song." Susie rocked and sang in a melodic, sweet voice: "Row, row, row your boat, gently down the stream…Merrily, merrily, merrily, merrily, life is but a dream."

Bridget felt a kind of horrifying recognition. That was Ennis's song. That was the song he sang when he used to give the kids a bath. But everyone knows that song. Everyone. Who hasn't sung it to their kids in the tub? The woman's eyes were closed. Bridget slowly pushed her chair back from the table to stand up, but the woman gestured her back down with the knife. "I'm not finished the story yet!" Bridget slid back into the chair. What if Katie came back down? What if this crazy bitch wanted to hurt her kids?

"About two weeks later, I went over to Tomas's house. Cathy was totally in love with him by this point, but he kept flirting with me every time she turned her back. I ignored him because of Cathy. But secretly? I loved it and hoped that he would try to kiss me again. I remember his mother was in the basement doing laundry, and Tomas asked Magda—his sister—to show me her room. I wanted to stay with him, but I went off to see her room. She started showing me her stupid Girl Guide uniform or something, explaining to me about all the badges she got—but I could hear Tomas from her window, at the pool, *whining* at Cathy like, like a dog—*Come on, you're killing me. I got blue balls so bad, just help me out here.* I could see him force her head down to his crotch. I watched him try to push his…thing in her mouth. She tried to pull away from him, and he grabbed her. And forced her mouth back on him. She didn't want to. And I watched them. I knew I should go and stop him. Tell her he wanted *me* to do that to him, too. But. I told Magda I had to go home and just ran out the door. I just ran all the way home." Her eyes were glistening. "I know you know it's him. I can see it in your face." Bridget let out a soft, pained breath.

"I left Cathy there alone. And that was the last time I saw her. Until the funeral. It was an open casket and Cathy looked like a freak. She had lipstick on, and, and…rouge—she never wore makeup. Her hands were clasped together like she was praying—and there was a rosary, like laced through her fingers. And Cathy was an atheist. Everyone was crying. My father. My…my…mother collapsed. But I didn't cry. I didn't cry."

"I don't understand. What happened to her?" Bridget asked quietly.

"They *say* she drowned. That she hit her head on…on the edge of the pool. But I know that he killed her. I *know* he did. And he had the…*gall* to come to Cathy's funeral. He was there. I saw him, in the very back row with his…mother and sister and—"

"I think you must be mistaken. Ennis is a *gentleman*. He would never do something like that—"

"Ask him when he gets home! *Ask him*. And if he doesn't tell the truth. Give him this."

She held the envelope out to Bridget. "I *am* sorry. You seem like a good person."

Bridget accepted it with a trembling hand.

"My family fell apart. My parents didn't even last a year. So he doesn't deserve a family. He doesn't deserve you. Or those kids. Or all this!"

The woman gathered her coat and hastened to the front door. "I wonder what all his fancy friends will think of him now. Not to mention all those old women he steals from. Just ask him if he knows Tomas Kovak when he gets home. Okay? It will confirm everything I told you today."

Then Susie remembered she still had the butcher knife, and for a moment looked as though she would give it to Bridget. Instead, she returned it to its slot in the wooden block on the kitchen counter. Then the woman was out the door. Bridget heard the engine of a car turn over, and the sound of the tires backing down the driveway. She began to shake. She could not make herself stop. When her hand steadied enough to pick up her phone, she started to press 911. And then she changed her mind. Instead, she sent a text: *Who was Cathy Kelly?*

Suddenly, Katie was on the stairs, looking very excited.

"Mummy? Liam just threw up all over himself!"

Bridget didn't know what else to do but grab a wash cloth and a towel from the powder room and head up the stairs to clean up her sick little boy.

Thirty-Three

OCTOBER 11, 1997
Dearest Magda,
My biggest mistake, the one I have regretted all my life and will until the day I die and probably beyond that, too, is not to have loved you enough. I know how I worried about your father and brother. How their needs were everything. They took all the oxygen, all the space in my life. What little bit was left over, I tried to give to you. But you were so quiet. And obedient, like a little mouse. Or a little dog. You did not ask for much and so I did not give it to you, either. And on that terrible day, you were obedient once again. I hope now, whoever you are, and whatever you do, you are not so compliant. I hope you are a strong, independent, disobedient woman. Do you have children of your own? They would be grown up now. When I think of this, I feel I might go mad with the desire to know them. But I understand that will not be possible. I know you will never answer my letters, but I must write to you, I must confess to you because that is all I can do. I do not believe in a God. I did once, but

now I see that was all a trick, a great big hoax devised to keep people, and especially women, chained to fantasy and false hope for something better. To be obedient.

I did try to ask for your forgiveness many years ago, when there was still perhaps the possibility of some understanding. I do not ask for it now, because I see how it is impossible to offer. You are probably thinking, who is *this old woman? She means nothing more to me than any other old woman—in the grocery store fumbling to get out her money while all the patrons in line behind her roll their eyes. Or the one sitting alone at the coffee shop, staring out the window and being too polite to the rude waitress? Please,* please, please *just tell me where you have moved.*

I cannot bear the thought of never seeing you again, or knowing you are all right. That you are well, and if not happy, at least have found some sense of safety at times, of satisfaction, of joy that this life can offer. I have found it only alone. In the natural world that surrounds me. Without my birds, my garden and my trees, I should have ended it many years ago. They call this "wildlife," but it is the human world that is truly wild, that is truly savage. Nothing, nothing is more ruthless and vicious than that.

Roméo peered at his computer screen—the original letter had been scanned, and the screen was split between it and the translation. But it abruptly ended. And then continued with a note from the translator.

Detective Inspector Leduc;
The first one is almost done. I am working as efficiently as I can, as I have been made to understand the urgency of learning the content of these letters. After skimming several of them, I realized the information is so dense and so extraordinary that I must go as quickly as I can. I have a three-hour seminar now that I cannot postpone. Are you able to come to Montreal and discuss these with me? I feel that would be the most expedient way, for now at least?

Regards, Dr. Agnes Csatary

Roméo responded with a brief e-mail, saying he could get to Montreal early the next morning. He then asked her to scan the letters for any reference to Tomas Kovak or Ennis Jamieson, and could she prioritize those letters that referred to those two names? In the meanwhile, the second each letter was translated could she please send them to him, one at a time?

Roméo returned to the websites and articles he had flagged in his search for Stefan Kovak, or whatever name he had used in his earlier life. So far, he had found nothing under that name, or any aliases associated with it. He had put in a call to the Simon Wiesenthal Center, who told him that their Canadian Nazi-hunter, a man named Ephraim Zuroff, was unavailable at this time. They also assured Roméo that someone would return his call and respond to his questions shortly.

According to this source, at least two thousand Nazi war criminals entered Canada following the Second World War.

How the *hell* did two thousand Nazis get into this country? The government didn't take action until 1985 when then Prime Minister Brian Mulroney established the Deschenes Commission to investigate. In 1987, forty-two years after the war ended, its recommendations led to the Canada War Crimes and Crimes Against Humanity Act, which empowered Canadian courts to prosecute an estimated twenty war criminals still living in this country. But the results were disappointing, and after eight years without a single conviction, Canada opted instead for the American method of stripping ex-Nazis of their citizenship and seeking deportation. Roméo wondered what had happened to Stefan Kovak, if anything. Had he been deported? There certainly seemed to be little to no record of him. Did the neighbor, Marie's friend—what's her name—get her facts wrong?

Then there were those who had been living for years right under their noses. Roméo remembered the story of a kindly ninety-year-old beekeeper from rural Quebec who was alleged to have been one of the world's most wanted Nazi war criminals. Entering Canada under a false name in 1951, Vladimir Katriuk was suspected of being involved in the massacre of more than two thousand people in Byelorussia, a claim he denied until his death in 2015. Was it there, as he lay in wait outside a barn that had been set ablaze before he opened machine gun fire on civilians trying to escape, that he honed his skill in smoking bees from the hive? It was a horrifying thought.

Roméo discovered that there several more Nazis accused of the most incomprehensible crimes doing very well for themselves in his country. One had been an art dealer living in the very respectable neighborhood of Notre-Dame-de-Grâce in Montreal. One a very well-regarded and popular restaurant owner in Toronto, another a former high-school teacher in rural Ontario. It appeared that many came into this country on something called the "Ratline to Canada," wherein former Nazis were recruited from Europe to provide low-grade intelligence to the RCMP on left-wing immigrants. The government believed it had to get ready for World War Three—that they needed to recruit people who would be useful when the Free World marched back into central Europe and took it back from the Soviet Union. The idea was to turn their World War Two enemies into their Cold War assets.

Roméo was shocked to realize that a former Nazi was more likely to get into Canada after the war than a Jew. He pulled his chair away from his computer for a moment and closed his eyes. He was a bit dizzy from the hours he had spent reading from a screen, but he knew the sudden nausea he felt was not because of the bad coffee and even worse food he had eaten. Not this time.

Roméo checked his watch. It would be another two hours at the earliest before Dr. Csatary would send him the next letter. Roméo rummaged around his desk for the file on Tomas Kovak that Nicole's team had compiled and opened it again. He had committed most of it to memory, as there wasn't much to remember. Born in 1956 in Budapest. Son of Stefan Kovak, engineer, and Maria Kovak (née Hanning), housewife. Emigrated to Canada in 1957. There was nothing unusual after that, until the police report on the death of a Catherine Kelly, seventeen, in 1974 at the Kovak residence. Roméo reread the coroner's report. It was pretty straightforward. Despite the fact that there was little forensic evidence gathered and no DNA, of course, the unambiguous conclusion was accidental death by drowning—after hitting her head and falling into the pool. All witnesses' statements corroborated this—although they were the mother, the sister, and Tomas Kovak himself. The police work was very superficial, shockingly so. Roméo had asked one of the junior detectives on Nicole's team to do some digging into this case. Apart from the backyard tragedy he was involved in, not much was very interesting about Tomas Kovak. He graduated from high school, spent one year at McGill University where he studied engineering, and then it appears he moved out to Alberta. Jobs were so scarce in Quebec in the late 1970s that many opted to work in the Rocky Mountain resort towns of Banff and Lake Louise. Tax records show he worked there sporadically for a few years. And then, he disappeared. All records of his existence more or less stopped around 1992. Roméo closed the paper file, closed his eyes, and tried to visualize the connections here. Where the hell did Tomas Kovak go? Or who or what did he become?

Roméo braced himself and went back to his computer. He usually tried to delegate as much of this research as possible, as he loathed staring into the screen like this. He felt like his soul was being sucked right out of him any time he sat before a computer for more than a few hours. He suddenly felt a desperate need to smoke a cigarette. Roméo opened every drawer, checked the pocket of every jacket and shirt that lay crumpled in his office closet. Nothing. In the old days he'd smoke a butt out of an ashtray when he was desperate, but of course, that wasn't an option anymore, unless he wanted to go pick one up in the parking lot where the smokers hung out in sheepish huddles.

Then almost as violently as it came on him, the craving passed. And without chewing that awful gum. A small victory there, at least. Roméo checked his watch again. Another hour to go. He went back to Google and typed in "Ennis Jamieson." All the information he'd already pored over popped up: his company—Jamieson Investments—which seemed to deal in estate planning. Lots of philanthropic work with the Montreal Children's Hospital before it moved; more recent involvement in Montreal's Irish community. Roméo clicked on *Images* and reviewed photos of his enormous (and in Roméo's mind) hideous nouveau riche mansion in St. Lazare about an hour west of Montreal. It had a turret, for God's sake. He was a very good-looking man, Roméo decided. And very Irish looking. Not what Roméo thought of as Hungarian, whatever that was.

Remembering Marie's confusion about Tomas and Ennis, Roméo decided to do a search of the Derived Record Depository—in Alberta. It turned out that an Ennis Jamieson from Longview, Alberta, had died in 1991. Roméo did a quick check of Google Maps. That was in the area where Tomas Kovak had lived for several years. Was it possible Tomas Kovak had assumed this identity? Maybe when you learn that your father is a Nazi, you want to get as far from that as you can. If this man Ennis Jamieson was Anna Newman's—or Kovak's son—he had to be alerted. He had to be notified that his mother was dead. But why had he not come forward? Is it possible he still didn't know? Roméo grabbed his phone and called Nicole. He frowned when she did not pick up—where the hell was she? He would have to have a word with her about that. Then he ordered a squad car to Ennis Jamieson's office. And a second one to his house. Roméo's phone buzzed in his pocket. Nicole, finally.

It was a woman on the other end of the line, but not Nicole.

"Detective Inspector Leduc? This is Sharon Braverman from the Simon Wiesenthal Center. How can I help you?"

Thirty-Four

ALTHOUGH THE DAY had started pretty badly—coffee all over his lucky court suit and terrible traffic—the morning went better than expected. So much so that Ennis practically skipped out the elevator and down the steps to the parking lot near the courthouse where he'd parked his car. He left his assistant to tidy up the paperwork with the court clerk and decided he would pick up a little something special for Bridget and the kids—maybe a little confection from Madame Clafoutie—a *pâtisserie* near his office that created the best desserts and croissants this side of Paris. Actually, Ennis had been to Paris once and thought their croissants were very over-rated. Their coffee, too.

The probate hearing had gone his way. The family, particularly the son, had challenged Ennis's mandate as executor of their mother's will. The son maintained she had a drinking problem and was estranged from the family. He claimed that Ennis took advantage of that and swooped in on her at her most vulnerable point. It was preposterous. Ennis had known the mother for several years and had done her estate planning while the family was busy pissing away their father's money on dodgy real estate and delinquent grandchildren. He was simply protecting her from their greed. Restoring a kind of justice. The judge had ruled in Ennis's favor. He was used to the outrage and indignation of the family at moments like this, although his poor assistant, Heather, got very red in the face and looked like she was about to cry. He would have to find a special something for her as well. Maybe a trip to the spa and a backstage pass to that godawful girl band she loved so much.

And there it was. Could this day get any better? A parking space right in front of the pâtisserie. This happened about once a year. Ennis grabbed the spot so fast he almost hit one of the many infamous Montreal jaywalkers who'd stepped off the curb in front of him. The guy pounded his fist on the hood of Ennis's car. Then he took in the expression on Ennis's face and hurried across, continued onto the sidewalk, and out of sight. Ennis considered accosting him—he was so pumped up with his court victory adrenaline that he could have given the asshole a good thumping. Instead, he grabbed his phone and headed into the bakery, which was full of customers that kept the place hopping six days a week, fifty-one weeks a year. He feasted his eyes on the sumptuous éclairs *au chocolat*, the *mille feuilles*, the *Gâteau Opéra*, and then selected an assortment of pastries. He was trying to recall which ones Brandon preferred, or visualize if he had ever shown any interest in them. His phone whinnied loudly. Bridget. Ennis was just pulling out his wallet to pay the lovely French-from-France salesgirl while trying to read his text at the same time. The phone fell to the floor. He dropped a couple of twenties by the cash register and glanced at the text. *Who was Cathy Kelly?* Ennis read the message again, unable to believe what he was seeing. He read it again. He pocketed his phone and ran out to his car. The salesgirl called after him, *"Monsieur! Vous avez oublié votre monnaie! Monsieur!"*

Thirty-Five

"THE PERSON YOU REALLY should be talking to is Ephraim Zuroff. I mean, he knows every detail of every file we have. The man is a living legend. But he's traveling now, and unavailable until next week. So, you're stuck with me." The woman, Sharon Braverman, sounded much younger than Roméo expected. She couldn't be more than thirty years old. She spoke very quickly, the way some young people did these days, omitting the final consonants of words entirely. It was as though they talked the way they texted. Roméo was trying to keep up and was taking notes as fast as he could. His English was quite good, but this woman made him feel like he could barely speak the language.

"Could you say his name again, please?"

"Ephraim Zuroff. He is head of Operation Last Chance, which tracks down former Nazis all over the world. Last Chance because that's exactly what it is—our last chance to catch these monsters. Most are dead now, and the few remaining are very old and often very sick. But that doesn't mean they shouldn't answer for their crimes. We are fighting against many who think these old men should be left alone now—that they should be allowed to live out their last few months and years in…dignity. In peace. Peace! They didn't extend their victims the same…courtesy. We believe every single one should be hunted down and brought to justice. We want to find them all before they all…die off. Ephraim, Mr. Zuroff, has tirelessly pursued these war criminals for over thirty years and—"

"And I understand he has a file on Stefan Kovak?"

There was a brief hesitation. He didn't mean to cut her off, but Roméo couldn't wait any longer.

Her voice went brittle. "Yes. I have it right here. I could scan it and send it to you, or—"

"Would you please give me the broad strokes right now, and I would then, of course, appreciate receiving the file as soon as possible."

He heard a rustling of paper. A chair scraping back. Then an intake of breath.

"So, you are interested in Stefan Kovak. His real name is Laszlo Molnar. He served as the commander of the Hungarian police in Kosice—which at the time was Hungarian-occupied Slovakia. He was a police officer and in charge of the ghetto of the so-called privileged Jews. He helped to organize the deportation to Auschwitz of approximately eight thousand Jews from Kosice and vicinity in the spring of 1944. He is accused of executing at least one hundred and ten Jews for resisting their deportation. He escaped to Canada after the war, but was stripped of his Canadian citizenship in 1997, and chose to voluntarily leave the country. His whereabouts were unknown until the fall of…2006 when he was discovered living in Budapest by the Wiesenthal Center—"

"He was stripped of his Canadian citizenship? Can you go back a bit? Walk me through it?"

Sharon Braverman let out a sigh. Not one of exasperation or impatience. Just an exhalation that suggested she had a lot of information to squeeze into a phone call.

"There was another Hungarian Nazi, as it turns out. Named Imre Finta—"

"Oh, yes, I read about him. The restaurateur in Toronto? Very popular guy?"

"Yes. That's the one. He was accused of the torture of and rounding up of Jews for deportation to Auschwitz as well. He was the first prosecuted under Canada's new war crimes law in December, 1987 but was acquitted on May 25, 1990.

"In 1994, the Supreme Court of Canada upheld Finta's acquittal and ruled that the section of the Criminal Code used to prosecute him was unconstitutional. Ottawa then halted its criminal prosecutions and changed tack—it started to revoke citizenship and deport people who lied about their past in order to gain entry to Canada. Finta died in 2003. His trial changed Canadian policy from trying the accused here to denaturalizing them—sending them back to their country of origin. In his case, Hungary as well—"

Roméo was stunned. "How did all these…Nazis get into Canada? It seems incomprehensible—"

Sharon Braverman was very ready with her answer, as if she'd responded to this many times before.

"The Soviet tanks rolled into Budapest in 1956. The crushing of the Hungarian uprising led to over two hundred thousand Hungarians fleeing to Austria. In response to public pressure—it was the Cold War, don't forget—the

Canadian government implemented a special program with free passage. Thousands of Hungarians arrived in the early months of 1957 on over two hundred chartered flights. More than thirty-seven thousand Hungarians were admitted in less than a year. The vast majority of those Hungarian refugees were honest, honorable people. But some—including Laszlo Molnar—came with false papers and false names—sometimes provided by the Canadian government, or through United States intelligence who pushed Europeans with false identities through the immigration stream to Canada. We effectively became a dumping ground for former Nazis who had outlived their usefulness as United States intelligence sources in postwar Europe. Kovak—or Molnar—was one of those. He changed his name before he came over here—but there is no way the Canadian government didn't know what was happening. So, he slips into Canada, no problem. And he lives very well—until 1997. That's when the Simon Wiesenthal Center was tipped off about his past."

Roméo leaned forward in his chair. Closer to the microphone on his computer.

"Who alerted you?" He waited while she flipped through some pages.

"That is not indicated here. It's odd. Mr. Zuroff must have made a note of it somewhere—maybe it was the authorities back in Hungary. I can look into that further if you'd like."

"That would be very helpful—"

"You may want to know that many said the evidence against Laszlo Molnar was flimsy, and the likelihood of a successful prosecution small. They say he was small potatoes—a little fish swimming with big sharks. That they could name two thousand people responsible for worse crimes than he was. Many of them went right back to their lives in Hungary, Germany, and across Europe. Many people, including some Holocaust survivors, believe hunting down people like him is not worth it. That the money would be better spent fighting the propaganda of those who still deny the Holocaust today."

Roméo didn't say anything. There was an awkward silence, and then they both spoke at once.

"Where is Molnar now?" "They may have a point—"

There was another pause, each waiting for the other to speak first.

"We believe Laszlo Molnar returned to Hungary in 1999, was placed under house arrest, and had his passport confiscated. In March of 2005, a Slovak court sought Molnar's extradition to stand trial for his crimes in Kosice. They were somewhat half-hearted about the whole thing. Then he died before it could happen. Complications from heart disease. In 2006. Another one who got away."

Roméo hastily recorded this last bit of information. Kovak had been dead for almost ten years.

"May I ask *you* a question?"

Roméo nodded while he jotted down the last few notes. He forgot she wasn't sitting across from him.

"Oh. Yes, of course, Mrs. Braverman."

"Ms. Braverman."

"I stand corrected."

"Why is a detective chief inspector of homicide in…St. Jerome, Quebec, interested in a long-deceased former Nazi? One *we* haven't even looked at in over twenty years?"

Roméo frowned. She couldn't see that, either.

"When I have the answer to that question, I will be the first to let you know, *Ms.* Braverman," he added.

Roméo ended the call and stared at the wall of suspects without really processing what he was looking at. He knew instinctively that there was a huge hole in the narrative here, that several pieces of information didn't add up. He was trying to process how the hell someone goes from being a Nazi police officer, sending thousands of people—Jews—to their horrible deaths, to a respected husband and father in the suburbs of a nice Canadian city. Roméo had been a cop long enough to know that horror often wasn't found in the margins of society. The most frightening things were masked by normalcy and decency. They say Hitler was a vegetarian and animal lover. Even William Fyfe, the rapist-murderer Roméo had helped put away for the rest of his natural life, was known to be a devoted son to his wheelchair-bound father. Roméo had often tried to understand how those who commit evil can so easily compartmentalize their lives—and then of course, he realized he himself had done it for years. It was a survival mechanism. He guessed that applied to murderers and rapists and war criminals as well. His thoughts were intruded upon by the loud ping of his laptop.

Dear Detective Inspector Leduc,
You requested I fast track any references to Tomas Kovak. This is the first I could find. More to come soon.

Dr. Agnes Csatary

SEPT. 18, 2010

Dearest Magda,

I dreamed of Tomas last night. It is the same dream I have of him since many years now. I am putting you both to bed. You are in your pajamas with the feet attached. You have little daisies on yours, and Tomas has trains on his. I kiss you and you fall asleep right away, as you always did. You were so uncomplicated as a child. I would read you a book—or you would read me one—and then you fell asleep with no fuss. But Tomas. I had to read him one, two, three books—it was never enough—and then sing to him, and then stroke his hair, and then chase the monsters from his closet a few times. Bed time could take hours. In my dream, he will not stay in bed, of course. He keeps escaping out his window onto the roof of our house, like he is going to jump, or play. I do not know. It is very high, and the roof shingles are not attached—they keep sliding off, and I am trying to reach him to pull him back in, but he continues laughing at me, and I am so mad, so angry. But he is just a little boy. I am screaming for help to all the neighbors, and I am screaming for your father, but no one comes. And Tomas then frightens himself and starts to cry and scream, but I cannot get him back in unless I fall myself, and that will not help either of us. We are trying to touch, to take each other's hands, his little hand in my big one. But we cannot. And just as he is trying to grab my hand, he falls. Just disappears. I run downstairs and out the front door to the yard to see if he is still alive. I am terrified to look, but I must. But there is no Tomas. No broken little boy. No nothing. He is gone, like he has flown away. And now

I am screaming and crying, and now all the neighbors come outside to look and judge. They all think I am crazy.

Sometimes. Often. So often. I dream of her. I am sleeping in my bed, and she comes into my room. I know she is there, but I keep my eyes closed. I am too afraid to open them, because this is not a dream. This is real. I know she is watching me. Then she goes to my vanity table (I do not have this anymore, it was my mother's, an enormous dark wooden affair with trick drawers and a beautiful, beveled mirror with rococo carving of angels and cherubs). She begins to brush her hair with my mother's brush, the engraved silver one that I also brushed my mother's hair with a hundred strokes every night. Cathy would be 53 years old. A mother. Maybe a grandmother. Maybe she would call herself Catherine. Or Nana. When I think of this, know the hell I used to believe in as a little girl. The hell where the flames burned you for all eternity, where you lived out of sight of God, where you meant nothing. *But still I wake up every morning like some stupid animal and make my cup of coffee and eat my breakfast and listen to the birds singing and somehow, I convince myself that it was just that. All a dream from so long ago.*

Thirty-Six

MARIE SAT WITH A cup of delicious black tea in one hand, and Shelley's hand stroking the other. She had debated whether to fetch Barney that night or just leave him until the morning, but in the end, she stopped in at Joel and Shelley's to pick him up. Rather than spinning around her ankles in hysterical mini-circles, Barney had looked surprised and then dismayed to see her. He also looked like he'd gained about five pounds in the week Marie had been gone. Marie hadn't planned to visit, but Shelley had taken one look at Marie's face and pulled her into the house. Marie accepted the cup of tea and unpacked her day for them. Although she was advised by the still-smiling Madame Purdy to give her mother a chance to settle in and not visit for a few days, Marie had gone to Le Warwick to say good-bye before she headed home to Ste. Lucie. She'd signed in at the front desk with a different woman—Red Fingers was absent—and proceeded to her mother's room. Her mother had taken a *coup de vieux*—she seemed to have aged ten years overnight. She was less responsive. More resigned. The Social Animator had hovered in her doorway, watching. Marie kissed her mother, reminded her she'd be back in three days, and hurried out, afraid to look anywhere but straight ahead in case the other patients and staff could see her face. Marie *hated* to cry in front of anyone. She had barely left the semi-circular driveway of Le Warwick when she'd had to pull over. She'd rested her forehead on the steering wheel and sobbed. Now Joel and Shelley were looking at her with such concern it made her want to cry all over again. "Why don't you just stay here tonight? It's getting dark, you haven't eaten. And I've made a delicious chicken stew."

Barney was in his bed, oblivious and snoring, like he had always lived with Joel and Shelley. It was tempting. The smell from the kitchen was divine. The house cozy and inviting. Marie thought of her little house. It took at least an hour for it to warm up, the logs cracking and groaning as the heat from the baseboard heaters expanded them.

"If I lived an hour away, honestly, I would. But it's just silly. I'll be home in eight minutes. And I need to get home. The alarm guy is coming at 4:30—and I can't miss him."

Joel looked up from the pot he was stirring on the stove. "I can go let him in for you. And lock up after he's gone. *And* put the new alarm on."

Shelley touched her forearm gently. "You know the old lady on the Fourth Range, Anna Newman? You know she was murdered, right? Joel heard from his buddies on town council that it was a break-in gone awry—which means those assholes are still out there—"

Joel emerged from the kitchen in an apron and oven mitts. "They think she resisted and got clobbered on the head for it."

Shelley shook her head. "I heard she was strangled."

Joel watched Marie carefully. "Then there's Ti-Coune Cousineau—that lowlife on the Third Range Road? I heard he was beaten up very badly, probably by his old friends from the Hells Angels, but still…."

Marie put her teacup back in its saucer. "Did you know Anna Newman?"

Shelley shook her head again. "Not really. She bought chicken from us a few times a year. Wouldn't even stay for a coffee, but she was very polite and friendly—"

"In a very…Teutonic way," Joel added.

Shelley nod-smiled in agreement. "She said what we charged was fair and paid cash. She then announced that we had a very good garden, a very good house. And then she left. A woman of few words, especially adjectives."

"I liked her," Joel added. "I found her kind of fascinating—but I've always been drawn to weirdos. Look who I married."

Shelley swatted him gently. "It's terrible what happened to her. And not so far away. For the first time in all the years since we moved here, I feel nervous if Joel is held up in Montreal and I'm alone at night. I lock the doors now. Can you believe it?"

Marie considered telling them about the strange coincidences surrounding Anna Newman—her mother's identifying her as their old neighbor, Marie thinking she'd seen the son at her mother's nursing home. She just didn't feel like she had the energy for all their questions and speculation. She'd save it for a visit the next day.

"Maybe you should get a dog," Marie suggested, and they all looked to where Barney was sleeping in his doggy bed by the fireplace. He was on his back, his rotund belly exposed, still snoring softly.

Shelley laughed. “Yeah. That would do me a fat lot of good.”

Joel sat down next to Marie. He smelled like garlic and olive oil. “I think what we’re trying to say is we’d really like you to stay with us tonight. Maybe even for a few days. We would feel much better if you’d say yes.”

Marie suddenly handed Shelley her empty cup and stood up. “I’ll be fine. And if I hear anything weird, or see anyone suspicious, I promise I’ll call you. I really need to just get back into my life, you know? And back into my own place. I’ve got this stupid book to write. And a million things to do.” She whistled for Barney, who didn’t budge. He didn’t even wake up. She had to gather him up in his doughnut-shaped bed and transfer him to her car. Shelley followed with his toys and a care package of homemade dog biscuits for Barney, a giant slab of lasagna and half a carrot cake for Marie. As she drove down their winding driveway to the main road, the sun was just starting its descent behind the smaller hills to the west, dyeing the sky a fiery orangey red.

Thirty-Seven

TABERNAC. It was happening again. It was like the stomach flu, except more violent and unexpected. She'd be feeling fine and then suddenly, it was as if her body was turning itself inside out. She practiced her one reliable method of dealing with discomfort and pain—slow breathing in through the nostrils, out through the mouth. She turned off the GPS—it often worsened the nausea when she followed its directions. Nope. She opened her window and inhaled the shock of much colder air. She would not puke again. Would not puke again. Not. She pulled onto the shoulder and barely had time to open her door before she hurled her breakfast and bits of last night's supper onto the highway. She left her door open so at least the people in the cars screaming past her couldn't see. She staggered to her feet, wiped her mouth, and made her way to the flattened swamp grass by the ditch, bent over again, and emptied the last of whatever was in her stomach.

Was this normal? She was past the four-month mark—past her first trimester, and the morning sickness should have stopped. Not to mention the fact that morning sickness was a misnomer—Nicole was sick all day and all night.

What did this baby want from her? She worried it wasn't getting the proper nourishment because she wasn't—then her doctor explained that babies will take from the mother all that they need. "They're like a little succubus!" she pointed out cheerfully. Crushed by exhaustion most of the time, Nicole wasn't even allowed to drink coffee. It made doing her job very challenging.

Nicole thought again about Normand, her baby's father. The man she loved. He liked American TV shows—which he watched in English while he picked at his toenails, to her dismay. He seemed to expect her to do all the cooking. That jolt she had felt when she first met him at the Tim Hortons now seemed like a high school crush. The whole thing was a terrible mistake—but there was no getting off this train now. She'd bought her ticket, it had pulled out of the station, and there was only one direction she was headed in. But Normand did seem thrilled about this baby. He went and bought a state-of-the-art stroller, decorated the walls with adorable animal stencils, and often talked to her belly. Nicole already felt fat and ugly. Her body was not hers anymore. Her boobs, already large, were now grotesquely huge, like watermelons. Normand didn't care. He really did seem sincere when he told her there was more to love and kissed her belly. He was a kind man. He was a gentle man. He would have to do.

Nicole turned into the long road leading up to the house and noted there was only one car in the driveway—and not the Audi 7 registered to Ennis Jamieson. It could well be parked in the four-car garage that was the size of Nicole's entire bungalow in her little town of Piedmont. The house was just gorgeous. She'd never own something like this. It even had a turret. Like the *châteaux* on the Loire valley Nicole had dreamed about since she was little. Another wave of nausea swept over her, which produced an enormous burp. And then, relief. She decided to stay in the car a minute, reviewing her objective here. The shadow of a figure appeared in the sidelight by the front door, then disappeared. She had been observed, then. Interesting that the person did not come out to greet her, to see what a cop was doing in her driveway. Nicole was to inform Ennis Jamieson (a.k.a. Tomas Kovak) that his mother was deceased. That her death was part of an ongoing criminal investigation. And that, as her son, he was now a person of interest.

She was to ask him to come down to the morgue to identify the body. This was not a job Nicole relished. She was also to note his reaction to the news of his mother's death very carefully. Roméo also asked that she watch the wife's response to the news. Nicole closed her car door gently and approached the front door of the house. Before she could ring the doorbell, the door opened, and an absolutely stunning woman stood before her. Nicole was so surprised she opened her mouth and shut it again just as quickly. She stepped into the enormous and inviting foyer and closed the door behind her.

By the time Ennis could see the turnoff onto his road, he had chosen a course of action. Denial. Of whatever and whoever this was. Of whatever she was claiming. He would call the fucking cops on her. He was not going to stand for this kind of harassment anymore. This little game was over. He turned onto the long dirt road that led to his house. And then he saw it. A Sûreté du Québec squad car was parked in his driveway. *What the fuck what the fuck what the fuck.* Ennis hit the brakes hard and skidded onto the shoulder of the road, his heart pounding. Was he going to have a heart attack? He gripped the steering wheel hard, as though it would somehow choose his next course of action. Ennis made a skidding U-turn and fishtailed back in the direction he'd just come from. He checked his rearview mirror. The police car hadn't moved. Ennis turned onto Highway 20. Heading east. He knew where he was going now.

Thirty-Eight

OCTOBER 20, 1999

Dearest Magda,

I woke up this morning thinking of you. Thinking of you and your beautiful long hair that I used to brush—one hundred strokes every night before bed. And then I thought of our battle every morning, when I would tame that mane of yours into one thick braid down your back, and how you hated it! Do you remember begging me to let you cut it, a pixie cut they called it then, just like all the other little girls in your class? I told you your father absolutely would not allow it—but it was not him. It was me. I couldn't bear to think of that thick, curly, gift of hair cut off just so you could look like everyone else. Do you remember that Tomas was jealous of me brushing your hair? He would sit on a chair in front of me, too, and hold the brush up.

"Please Mama," he would say. "Me, too!" I was shocked that a boy would ask such a thing, and of course told him not to be so silly. We didn't believe in such things then.

I wonder if your hair is still long and beautiful and thick. It has probably darkened a bit now. Maybe a few coarse gray hairs? Maybe you have cut it for convenience, or did you give yourself a pixie cut after all these years of deprivation? Then I thought of my mother. I think I used to tell you (many times) that my mother also brushed my long hair a hundred strokes every night. I think she was amazed by my hair—I was very blond, and it grew long and thick all the way to the very ends. She would hum a little song—do you remember I sang it to you? I remember every word of it still to this day. But that woman, the woman who brushed my hair every single night, who held me through the mumps and measles, who sewed me beautiful dresses out of nothing. That woman who went hungry during the war so that I could eat. That woman was not my mother.

I don't know where or how to begin to tell you this story, because even now it is so many bits and pieces. For much of my early life, I believed I was the only daughter of the widow Erzebet Nemeth. We lived on a very little farm about ninety kilometers from Budapest. Her brother, Gabriel, lived there with us, too. My mother told me that a stork delivered me to her after her husband died of influenza, and I was the greatest gift imaginable. I believed this until it was no longer possible. When I asked my mother who my father was, she admitted to me that the nuns from the orphanage near Budapest had brought me to her, to give me a better life—but that it was I who had saved her. She would cross herself and say to me, "Always pray to the Virgin Mary, Maria, for whom you were named. You are the miracle she brought me after all my years of loneliness."

So, I believed my parents were dead, and I thanked the Virgin Mary as I was told to for my good fortune, but my heart belonged to Jesus. He was so beautiful, so selfless—dying for all of us so we could be free of Original Sin. I read every story I could and wept at the stations of the Cross. Why didn't he show the Romans and Jews what he could do? Why did he allow himself to be so humiliated when he could have performed a miracle? When he could have crushed them all? It was because of His love for us. As a result, I felt boundless love for Him. I was the most devout girl in our church. Probably in most of Hungary.

My mother believed I would become a nun, as I was also not interested in boys. Until the day I met your father. His real name as you now know, was Laszlo Molnar. I met him in 1953 when I was almost nineteen years old. He just appeared one day at our farm, looking for work. He was terribly thin, and I could see in his eyes that he had suffered great hardship, but he was very funny in a respectful, intelligent way, and very handsome. He had shockingly blue eyes, just like Tomas, and wavy light chestnut hair—and somehow, a beautiful smile after all the trauma he had endured. He made me feel like I was the only person in the room. In the world.

He had survived a Soviet labor camp in Siberia where he told me he lived on onions and soup water for nearly five years. He did what they called "malenki robot"—little work, but in fact it was slave labor in the most appalling conditions. Many, many thousands of Hungarians died of starvation and typhus. You see, so many Russians—26 million—had died during the war against the Nazis that they had no people to do the work to rebuild the new country—the mining, the farming, the industry—but especially the mining. So, they forced foreign labor into the Soviet Union. They think 600,000 Hungarians were captured altogether, many former prisoners of war and political prisoners. 200,000 died. Your father survived. When Stalin died in 1953, they opened up the camps, and the remaining POWs like your father were finally allowed to return home.

Do you know, I had never any interest in any boy, but the moment I saw Laszlo I wanted to take care of him, feed him, be his wife. I wanted nothing more. He was older—he was thirty-two at that time, but so youthful and different from the boys I knew in our little town—the few that had survived that is. We were married in my church in Arlo in 1954 when I was not yet twenty years old.

Not long afterwards, I broke my mother's heart and left her. We moved to Budapest—it was still being rebuilt after the horrific siege of 1944 when they bombed every bridge crossing the Danube. Laszlo went to work for the new government—the occupying Russian Communists. He was just a clerk, but we were happy. No not happy, but relieved—to live quiet lives and visit my mother and uncle in the country on holidays when we could. He was so talented with his hands, your father. Like my mother, he too, could make something out of nothing. He was, I found out, a brilliant engineer. I loved him, and I wanted to have his baby, because after the war—there was nothing. There were no men. They were all killed or damaged. I wanted to have a baby to make new life.

We somehow managed to live fairly well—Laszlo was always able to procure a little extra, he always had an angle he was working. He had a sharp mind and was quite fearless, about some things. I gave birth to your brother, Tomas on November 5, 1956—the day after the Soviet forces attacked Budapest and put an end to our hopes of a free and democratic Hungary. No one—not the Americans—no one came to help us. No one had the courage to risk war with Russia for little Hungary. We had been so hopeful, and then it seemed overnight, everything went dark. I had Tomas—I was so in love and exhausted that I couldn't really understand or process the impact of what had happened. But your father could. And he hated the Russians. They say their soldiers raped fifty thousand Hungarian women when they occupied Hungary. After the war.

Laszlo insisted we must get out of Hungary—that we had no future there and that we start anew, with new identities. He heard of a chance—a wonderful chance to get out. To Vienna. And then of all places—Canada! Canada to me was snow, and Niagara Falls. And bears, I think. In those days you did not question your husband's decisions. And so, I broke my mother's heart a second time. When I asked Laszlo why Canada, he told me because Canada wanted him to work for them, against the Communists. And that he had done that all along in Budapest—for the Americans!

As people seeking asylum from Soviet-occupied Hungary, we were seen as so virtuous. It was the Cold War, you see, and because we were anti-communist no questions *were asked. We joined thirty-seven thousand other Hungarians who came to Canada. In less than one year! So I changed my name again. This time: I was Anna Kovak, married to Stefan Kovak. I asked no questions, too.*

But I can tell you that my name is not *Anna Kovak. It is* not *Maria Molnar.* Not *Maria Nemeth. I wonder if you are ready to hear the story of my name, and of course, yours as well. Please, my Magda, write me. Call me.*

Your always loving mother.

Thirty-Nine

MARIE SAT AT her desk looking out her enormous front windows into the darkness starting to close in around her little house. She sipped a single malt from her favorite writing mug, trying not to inhale the carrot cake Shelley had packed for her. Scotch and carrot cake—a surprisingly delicious combination. The sun had long since set, and her lake had changed color from a deep blue to slate black. She could just make out the silhouettes of the balsam trees that were the last to disappear in the overcast and darkening sky. They were calling for temperatures well below zero that night. Marie had built a crackling fire in the woodstove and could almost see the damp slowly leaving her house.

She was having a hard time focusing on her work, though. In fact, she hadn't even opened her laptop yet to start reimmersing herself in the world of nature for kids. She couldn't even force herself to look at her handwritten notes. Instead, she stared out at where the lake had been just hours earlier and tried not to succumb to the intense irritation she felt—the alarm guy hadn't shown. He'd called at 5:59 to inform her that he was stuck on another job and was now done for the day. The alarm installation would have to wait until the next morning, but he assured Marie she would be his first client of the day. Marie stabbed at another huge chunk of cake and finally opened her laptop, to her most recent chapter about migratory birds. She'd been rereading the study about whooping cranes' skill in navigating the best migratory route, which is entirely based on one factor: the wisdom of their elders. Maybe this could open a chapter entitled *Listen to Your Grandparents—They Know More Than You Think!* Marie thought of her mother, who could no longer find her way to the elevator of Le Warwick, let alone navigate across a continent. She wondered how her mother was doing now. It had only been about ten hours since she'd left her. Was the perpetually smiling Mrs. Purdy haunting her? Was she being forced to listen to that old geezer pianist play "Feelings" all night long? "What do I do now, Marie?" she had asked when Marie had first left her at Le Warwick, her mother's veiny, arthritic hands grasping her arm. I don't know, Maman. I don't know.

She watched a fly lazily examining a crumb from her cake. She had a fly chapter in her book—*Males sometimes dance around a female fly carrying a little silk-wrapped package. If the female accepts it, the male does the deed while she's distracted unwrapping it. By the time she's finished, so is he. Most of the time, the package is empty.* So what else is new, Marie thought. Which reminded her of that cop. Roméo Leduc. Didn't he say he'd be dropping by for a quick interview? It was now past eight o'clock, and he still hadn't shown up. Marie realized that that was why she hadn't stayed at Joel and Shelley's—she'd hoped to see Roméo. Now, she felt a low-grade rage starting to simmer. She had a feeling

Detective Chief Inspector Leduc had delivered a few empty packages himself. Why don't people just fucking do what they say they're going to?

Marie closed her computer again and scraped her chair back from her desk. Maybe she should call someone. Lucy? No. She was always too busy, too distracted by her demanding life. Her kids? She hadn't spoken to Ben in a few days, but Marie found that anyone under forty was taken aback when she actually called on a telephone. They always asked if something was wrong, like a live phone call now meant bad news. Marie yearned for the days when she could have a meandering chat on the phone, navigating the emotional landscape of a friend's voice. She slipped another log into the stove and knelt by Barney, who was sleeping as close to it as he could without getting singed. She stroked his long, mismatched ears and wondered when or if anyone would ever touch her again. Of course, Roméo Leduc had a partner. His wife. *Sa blonde*. Men like him were not allowed to be single for very long. But maybe he had never found the right person for him. Maybe Marie and Roméo were fated since birth to be together. Oh my God, she thought, What's wrong with me?

Marie had never been sentimental about romance before—why was she allowing this stupidity to colonize any brain cells? She had witnessed too many of her women friends pine for a man, wait slavishly for him to *text* them, let alone call. Never getting the clear message that the guy was just not interested. Marie thought the kids these days called it *ghosting*. And if he did answer? Nine times out of ten it was a booty call—which was fine, Marie decided. As long as that's what both parties were interested in.

Barney suddenly opened his eyes and looked almost alert—not enough to actually rouse himself, but he had definitely been stirred from his deep sleep. He looked alarmed.

"What's wrong, Barney?" Marie asked in doggy speak. "Did you have a bad dream?"

Barney scrabbled to his feet, his nails clawing along the wooden floor. Then he hurtled through the two rooms to the back door and started barking. Marie would have felt alarmed herself if this wasn't something he did about ten times a day. But tonight, she was on high alert. All the doors and windows were securely locked. Still, she flicked on the outdoor lights, peering through the darkness out at the lake. There was nothing there that she could see, and Barney had already forgotten what he was barking at and had returned to his spot by the fire. He was scratching at and making tight little circles on the rug before he finally settled into himself, his nose tucked into his tail. He looked like a furry doughnut. Marie glanced at her front door and reminded herself that the ax she used to split her firewood was still in the closet there, leaning against the wall. Should she call Joel and Shelley? What would she say? That Barney had started barking? The police had assured her that it had been teenagers who'd broken into her house—and they got the only thing they could resell. There was nothing left here for them. Still, Marie wished once again that Loki were alive and here with her. She was never nervous when he was in the house with her. Never. Marie remembered that her cell phone was charging in her bedroom upstairs and started heading toward the stairs to retrieve it when she heard a noise.

Or did she? Sometimes the house groaned with the wind or cracked when it was heated up enough by the fire.

Marie couldn't place the sound exactly. She got very quiet—not even breathing—and strained to hear if it would repeat. As she started to climb the stairs heading to her room, she thought she heard the back door open. It made a very annoying grinking sound that reminded her it needed WD-40 again. Marie hesitated, then ran to get the ax. Clutching it like a shield, she made her way toward the back of the house. She tried to calm her voice as she announced herself. "Hello? Is somebody there? I've called the police and they're on their way!" But the door was closed tight. Marie threw it open and peered into the darkness until the motion-triggered light blinked on. Nothing. No one.

Marie checked that the door was locked again. Had she forgotten to lock it in the first place? Not a chance. She pushed a chair up against the door and stuck a ski pole through the door handle. She steadied her racing heart with deep breaths and then walked into the spare bedroom and threw open the closet door, jumping back in case someone tried to grab her. A scruffy pillow and a few old blankets sat on the shelves. She made her way back to the front door and listened again. Nothing. Marie opened the front hall closet and returned the ax to its place in the corner. Barney was sound asleep by the fire again. Marie went back to the stairs to retrieve her phone from her bedroom and had one hand on the first banister when she realized something wasn't right—Marie felt the chill air before she could process what had happened. He stood just inside the door, and without taking his eyes off her, closed it gently behind him.

"Hello, Marie. I heard you were looking for me."

Forty

ROMÉO HAD BEEN on his way to Marie Russell's house when he got the call. Even then he was very reluctant to miss the interview with her again. But after talking to the woman at the Simon Wiesenthal Center, he couldn't overlook any possible connections between what he was now looking at and the murder of Anna Newman. Before him stood the remains of Rabbi Isidore Stern's summer cottage in Val David. He was the very elderly and widely respected spiritual leader of several hundred Hasidic Jews who spent a few weeks of the summer in the Laurentian Hills, getting away from their relentlessly urban lives. The fire was now out, but still smoldering. Three walls of the house were charred and starting to buckle, and the front was completely gone. The interior was gutted. The forensic team that Roméo had called in to work the crime scene were on their way from Montreal. He needed them to comb the property for any evidence linking the two crimes. Was there some conspiracy of neo-Nazis that were now roaming the vacation communities of Ste. Agathe? A gang of idiotic teenagers out to relieve their boredom? Or were these a bunch of outliers?

Despite the freezing temperature, the air felt seared and sweltering, the area too hot to be taped off and secured. Several Sûreté du Québec cruisers had blocked off the access road, and of course the rabbi had been informed of the attack. Roméo moved away from the main house itself and down the driveway to a series of smaller wooden cabins that lined both sides of a gravel road leading behind the rabbi's house. None had been torched. But on every front door of each identical little log cabin, a giant swastika was painted in blood red. Like an evil inversion of Passover, Roméo thought. Not saved from destruction but marked *for* it. An SQ officer was busy taking photographs of each cabin. No one spoke. It was as if each police officer in his or her own way was respecting the significance of this attack, and the horror of past crimes it evoked. Roméo felt an intense shame. At least none of the members of the Hasidic Jewish community were here, thank God. They were all ensconced in Roméo's old neighborhood in Outremont, or long since returned to New Jersey where many of them lived. If the criminals who did this meant to terrorize, or intimidate, or to impress their psychopathic friends, they'd chosen not to do so when the residents were actually here. Roméo felt grateful for that small mercy. At least he was not dealing with another homicide. Or possibly several more.

A young, very overweight, and out-of-breath man—his badge identified him as a Ste. Lucie Volunteer Firefighter—approached Roméo. "You're from the Sûreté du Québec? Violent crimes?" Roméo nodded. The man held up an empty gasoline jerrycan. "There were a few more hidden up in the woods behind those cabins. Maybe they were planning on torching the whole compound?" Roméo didn't respond.

The young man seemed very excited. "You think they got spooked? Lost their nerve?" The man tried to punctuate this observation by hiking up his firefighter pants over his enormous belly, but failed. Instead he opted to pull his uniform shirt over the mound of fat. "Anyway, I thought you would like to know right away that we found the probable accelerant." Roméo thanked the young man and watched him walk with splayed feet back to his fellow volunteers. Roméo remembered his uncle once telling him that the nuns at his elementary school taught them that all Jews have horns. This was in a midsized town in rural Quebec, maybe around 1965 or so. Roméo refused to believe him. His uncle lifted his right hand and declared every bit of it was the God's honest truth. Roméo remembered Easter mass when he was an altar boy. The priest would remind the parishioners every year that it was the Jews who had killed Jesus. When Roméo had later pointed out to a classmate that Jesus himself was a Jew, he laughed and corrected him. "Jesus was a Catholic, you idiot."

Roméo's memory was interrupted by an armada of vans pulling up, filled with the news teams from several TV stations in Montreal. CNN would be sending someone local any minute now, too. As he approached, he could see the mayor of Val David was being prepped for an interview—and behind her more camera crews arriving. For the most part, Roméo despised the media. They would glom all over this story until they'd sucked it dry. But did it change anything? Roméo understood that the press was important—vital to the functioning of a healthy democracy, but the rapaciousness of journalists on the hunt for a story was often repugnant to him. He could see several clamoring before the mayor, microphones thrust in her face. They'd be coming for him next. Roméo checked his watch and remembered he'd better call Marie Russell. Their interview would have to wait. Again.

Forty-One

OCTOBER 9, 2000

Dearest Magda,

This is the story of my name. Please be patient, as it will take a few words to explain. When we first came to Canada, to Montreal, of course it was difficult. Your father spoke English quite well, but I had only Hungarian. In those days you could get by without French, so we only ever learned enough to buy groceries or exchange greetings. He got a job two weeks after we arrived. Two weeks! At an engineering firm downtown. We lived in a little flat in Cote des Neiges for a year, but we saved every penny, enough to buy the house on Woodgrove fifteen months after we set foot in Canada. It was a dream. More than I could ever know, of course. Tomas had the run of our beautiful garden, I had a few friends, good neighbors who at first would not speak to us, but eventually accepted and welcomed us. Then you were born, my darling Magda—my longed-for daughter. When I first saw you, I cried because I missed my own mother so much and wanted her to know that I, too, had a baby girl. Your father was at that time, to all appearances, a good man. He was a good provider. He did not drink too much like so many did on our street, and he was never violent with me. He made sure I had enough money every week, and was to my knowledge, always faithful to me. We worked so hard at this project called the Canadian Dream, we never talked about the war, and I never asked. We were so happy. So often we don't even know how happy we are, but I did—until that terrible afternoon. The afternoon of the accident. I have no defense for my actions except to say that I would do anything not to lose that which I believed we had. Your father had given me a life I didn't even know was possible. I would protect him and Tomas no matter what.

After that day, I lived by putting one foot in front of the other, day after day. I knew the family of the girl had been ruined and, of course, so had mine. But your father and Tomas pretended as though it was not so. Tomas went off to university, your father promoted up the ranks of his company, his picture in the newspaper marking each achievement. Only you and I knew the truth—that we could never be really ourselves again.

What you do not know, is that I had learned the truth about your father this man I truly did love—years before I turned him in but after you and Tomas had left home.

It started with a television program—one of those ones that uncovers secrets about the past. It was all about former Nazis who had escaped to different parts of the world, but especially to Canada. A camera crew followed this "Nazi Hunter" they called him. Who had found a former Nazi and ambushed him outside his home. He was already an old man who looked quite pathetic and hardly capable of the horrors he was accused of—and I remember thinking they should just leave him be. At the end of the program, a man announced they were still looking for many suspected Nazis—and a slideshow of faces came up on the screen. I was ironing, I think, and just glancing at the TV—and there was your father's face. Not who he was now, of course. But it was him, no mistaking. Of course, I didn't believe it. I had refused to see certain things—how easily we got out, how we had to change our names and histories/identity—I was so stupid not to ask even why we changed our name! How quickly he found work in Canada. The government—the Canadian government—helped these men—all these men who had done these terrible things, to have a new life, and your father because he had worked for the Americans after the war—they protected him and got him into Canada. Your father spoke fluent Russian—because of his time in the labor camps. A Nazi turned American spy.

I know it is all so implausible, all such an absurd movie. But this is what happened.

I did not know what he was. But can you understand why I did not pursue this? Why I still did not ask questions? Because I did not want *to know. That is why.*

So, we lived like this. You and your brother gone. Oh, still calling on birthdays and Christmas, but gone from us. Each one of us, except your father, knew why. Ironically, he was the only innocent person on that terrible afternoon. And the girl.

I suppose he had his secret, and I had mine. And we would have continued like this—one foot in front of the other, probably until my death, because denial is one of the most powerful forces in the world. Then one day, I was invited by Mrs. Posner—do you remember? The people who owned the butcher shop? I volunteered with her at the Beaconsfield library—I was invited to her grandson's bar mitzvah. This is the coming of age ceremony in the Jewish religion. It was at their synagogue. I had never seen such a thing. I had never really known a Jewish person. In Hungary we knew the terrible things that had happened to them, but many, even after the war, believed they were just rumors. But no one really talked about it. No one. So, I am at this beautiful synagogue, and the boy—the grandson—starts to sing at a big altar, like in our church in Arlo. But he sang in Hebrew. A language I had never heard before, a dead language that Israel brought back to life. When I heard this singing, this prayer. It was like I flew out of my body, and floated over myself, like I could look down on my body, but my soul was flying. And as I listened to this music, this old prayer, I remembered something from when I was a child, something before words, before conscious memory. I knew that I myself had sung this music. Magda, I cannot really describe how this felt. Except to say that I felt…returned to myself. Like I had never been a real person until this moment.

I needed to know my provenance. I investigated

who I was. I learned from a center that locates missing children from the war, that I had an aunt who had been looking for me for many years. When I finally did find her—and this was all by letter of course and a few long-distance phone calls—this is the story I was told.

My real name is Hannah Neuman. I was born in 1934 in Budapest, the only child of Rivka Caplan and Yitzak Neuman. My mother died giving birth to me due to complications of RH factor. My father tried to raise me alone, but he was affected by the anti-Jewish laws passed in 1938 and could not continue in his law practice. Jews were banned from most professions. He was already vulnerable to depression after the death of my mother, and he saw the writing on the wall for Jews. He understood that what was happening in Poland and Germany to the Jews was coming—even though Hungary had made a deal with the devil and were allied with the Germans. Of course, it was coming to Hungary. When I was five years old in 1939, my father knew he had to give me up. He begged the nuns at a convent near Budapest to take me in. So, my father saved my life by giving me away. For what purpose? I don't know.

When I was eight years old, the nuns decided it was too dangerous to hide me at the convent, so they found me a home with my new "mother," who was childless. I learned that my father Yitzak survived the early deportations of 1941, and my aunt explained he had promised to come back for me. I was ten years old in 1944, when from May to July—in fifty-six days—450,000 Jews were deported to Auschwitz. It was called the Hungarian Operation, a tidy name for the filth and horror they dedicated themselves to. Almost half of all the Jews gassed at Auschwitz were Hungarian. Almost the entire Jewish population of Hungary. It was punishment you see, because the Hungarian leaders saw the writing on the wall and were desperate to make a good peace with the Allies.

My father, Yitzak, did not come back. He died there, along with my entire family, except for my maternal aunt. Her name is Sara Caplan. She is still alive and still living in Israel. This is the one who looked for me. I often wonder...in those days, if I would have had the courage to hide someone, like those old nuns did for me. They knew I was a Jew, and they risked their lives for me. They say when there's a pack of wolves, you howl with the wolves. I wonder if I would've been brave enough to leave the pack. Or at least not to howl with the rest of them. I never had much of that kind of courage. They call it moral courage, but it is actually the strength to face the terror of torture and death. It is great physical courage then, too. And I do not have it.

It was September 3, 1997. The day I finally wanted to know the truth about your father. I looked up the Simon Wiesenthal Center—this is named for a famous Nazi hunter—and there he was. Your father. In their book. A photograph. It was him. There was no mistake. He was accused of—well, you know what he was accused of. Your father was an officer in something called the Death's Head Division, responsible for overseeing the deportation of 170,000 of Hungary's Jews. They said he was not even a big rat. He was a little mouse. Not so important. But little mice can do a lot of damage. At Auschwitz? They gassed 12,000 Hungarian Jews in one day.

I finally confronted your father. He was accused of things that were not possible. Not Laszlo. I had to hear his story from his own lips. He was very calm, very measured in his response. That yes, he did participate in the overseeing of people to labor camps, but certainly not death camps. That yes, it was terribly hard, but no one was tortured or murdered, and he had no idea where these people were going. That he only did what so many also did—they were police officers under occupation and had to do as they were told, or they too would be shot.

It was like he had punched me in the face. In the heart. He admitted it. I remember I began to cry and scream at him. I don't think he had ever seen me like that and he was shocked. Truly shocked. And then, it was as though the Laszlo I had known and loved with my body and my soul, it was as though he was gone. Vanished. He said to me, "Do you think these victims… your Jewish victims were all so wonderful? You think they were heroes? Saints? That they were morally superior? No. What I saw was the opposite. They were just like us. Out for themselves, out to do anything to protect their families. Like us. They'd kill for a crumb of bread, a morsel of food. And so, if you want to feel superior, or feel like you've been wronged terribly by me, then feel that way.

"But I know what I saw, and I know what I know."

It was when he blamed his victims. When he said they were somehow—as bad as he was—no one was right or wrong—no one was blameless—as though he *were the victim, almost. He was wrongly accused. When he said that, I knew he was who they said he was. And I knew I had to turn him in. Imagine then when I found out the government knew all about him—that they had brought him to Canada on that so-called Rat-Line— When I learned that our government,* my *government had known all about your father, I knew I would have nothing to do with government. Ever again. I left him and my life and everything I knew and disappeared. When Tomas learned what I did, he did not speak to me for many months. It was as though he blamed me for who your father was.*

For many years after, I feared for my life because there was a network of old Nazis—not just in the movies—but very real. They are all very old now, but they have their supporters and sympathizers. I was always afraid they would find me and come after me. People don't talk about this, but where do you think all those Nazis went? They went right back to their former lives. Teachers, doctors, lawyers, businessmen, alive and still running the world. Of the 5,000 officers at Auschwitz, only fifty were ever arrested.

There is a big difference between learning the truth and accepting it. It took me a very very long time to accept that I had loved a man, had made babies with a man, had protected a man like Laszlo. On many, many days, I wanted to die. To kill myself. On many days I thought of all those women and girls in Auschwitz whose hair was shaved—and sent to fill mattresses, or upholster furniture… and I thought of my mother in Arlo, where I was safe, brushing my long, blond hair every night. And I wanted to die. Instead, on the day I called the authorities about your father, I cut it all off. I have kept my hair short since then, like a penitent. Until I decided I could finally atone for what I had done.

I remain always your loving mother,
Hannah Newman

Forty-Two

THE MAN MARIE had seen at Le Warwick was standing just inside the threshold of her front door. Despite how unbelievably handsome he was, Marie felt her blood tingle. "What the hell are you doing in my house. Get *out*." The man smiled. He had amazingly white teeth that almost glowed in the dim light. He took one step closer. He gestured to the air and started to chuckle.

"Do you think—do you think I'm *breaking into* your house? I've been knocking on this door for at least five minutes. I finally let myself in because I saw your car and all the lights on. I came all the way up from Montreal—I'm not just going to turn around."

He started to remove his overcoat but changed his mind after he took in the expression on Marie's face. He shrugged it back onto his shoulders. He moved a bit closer.

"May I come in?"

"The police are on their way. So, unless you want to be arrested for—"

The man smiled, more broadly this time, and shook his head. "The police? No, Marie, we both know the police are not on their way here."

Marie was trying very hard not to show how scared she was. She felt like she might throw up. "How do you know my name?"

"Marie." He sounded like a parent admonishing a child. "Of course, I know who you are. We're old neighbors." The man stepped into her foyer. "Wow. This is a very nice place you've created here. You wouldn't think much of it from the exterior—but this—" He gestured to the room. "This is *very* charming." Barney had finally woken up and found Marie. When he saw the stranger in the house, he stopped a few steps away from him, planted his four feet, and barked with everything his twenty-one pounds could produce.

Marie heard the man's knees crack as he squatted and held his closed hand out to the dog.

"Hey, buddy. Come here. Come here!"

Barney thought about it for a second—there was always the possibility of food in a human hand—but he didn't budge. His bark turned to a low whiny growl.

"You know who I am, Marie. You've been asking about me." Marie glanced quickly around the room. She needed a weapon. The fireplace poker. A log. Then she remembered the ax in the hall closet.

"What the hell are you talking about?"

"You know who I am. You recognized me at the Warwick—"

"I thought I did, but the girl at the front desk said you were...someone else."

He smiled. "Well, yes. That's true. I certainly am someone else. Now." He pointed to the dog and frowned. "Is there any way to shut that dog up?"

Marie shook her head. "Not unless you get the hell out of my house."

"Shut him up. Or I will." Marie backed away without taking her eyes off the man and called Barney to her. Of course, he ignored her, so she just grabbed him. He trembled and growled in her arms.

"Lock him in that closet." She didn't move. "*Do* it."

Marie moved carefully to the closet door, opened it, and gently dropped her dog inside. His whining was muffled by a dozen winter jackets and unsortable junk. As she closed the door, she eyed her ax, leaning in the corner.

Marie's obedience emboldened him. He walked right into her living room and took in the whole effect. "Yes, very charming. And inviting." He picked up the photograph of Marie and the Swedish boyfriend from the 1980s. "You have had quite a charmed life, too, haven't you? Is this your husband?"

Marie didn't answer. He kept talking anyway, one eye surveying the space, and his peripheral vision on her.

"You know, I am surprised at you…your…resistance. Women usually like me. I've always had a kind of power—control—over them. Well, that's where the money is."

Marie tried not to react, but somehow a truncated snort emerged from her nose.

The man turned to look directly at her.

"But you did leave me a heartwarming note. Several, in fact—"

"No, I didn't—"

"A series of little letters, right? Anonymous, too. That was naughty of you.

"Let me see if I can remember them all: *Remember me?*

A blast from the past! Tell the truth. Nice kid. How did that happen? And of course, the kicker: the obituary. That was a nice touch."

Marie was completely baffled. "I have no clue what you're talking about. I wrote no letters to you. I don't even know who you are. I thought I recognized you at Le Warwick, but I was wrong. What letters?"

The man removed his overcoat and laid it on the back of her overstuffed armchair, which he sank into, his gloved hands gripping its arms. Then he slowly picked up the bottle of Glenfiddich and refilled Marie's Scotch glass for himself. He took a sip and smiled at the glass, surprised. "For a cheap Scotch. That is not bad."

Marie made no response. It began to occur to her that this situation was pretty ridiculous. "Look…there's been some misunderstanding here. I *thought* you were Tomas Kovak, the son of our old neighbors. But you are, apparently, someone named Ennis Jamieson. I don't care, frankly. I just want you to leave my house. Now."

He crossed one long leg over the other. "You want me to tell the truth, right? So here I am."

Marie could still hear Barney whimpering in the closet. "I'm just going to let him out, okay—?" But before she could take two steps, the man had smashed the Scotch glass on the ironwork of the woodstove, leapt out of the chair, and grabbed her arm. It hurt like hell.

"Sit the fuck down. You wanted the truth? Here's the truth: If you ever come near my kids again, I will kill you."

Marie started to protest, but with his free hand he walloped her across the mouth. Marie saw pinprick stars and fell to her knees. He picked her up off the floor and shoved her into the matching chair to his. She struggled to clear her head. She was trying very hard not to cry for the second time that day.

"At first I thought you were just a disgruntled client. Or the child of a client. You can't imagine the flak I take for basically *saving* them. Making their lives manageable. I mean, what I do for those people is entirely legal. It may skirt the border of ethical, yes. But it is legal. I do more for those old ladies than their children and all their so-called friends. They would be entirely lost without me. I *deserve* every cent I earn."

Marie was tenderly touching her jawbone. She didn't think it was broken.

"I thought you were—it sounds so funny, now—*blackmailing* me. I thought maybe you had something on me—that you were after *money*."

Marie said nothing. Her jaw was throbbing. She was trying to figure out what he wanted. What he was accusing her of. What she should do.

"But then, you leave me this." The man pulled a yellowing piece of paper from his pocket and unfolded it carefully. "The obituary for Cathy Kelly. I see you kept it all these years. That *is* impressive. And I realized…it's not the money. You want to rehash *that* old story—"

Marie tried to speak, but her swollen jaw made her sound like a drunk. "Please. I don't know what you're talking about—"

He smirked and imitated her slurred speech. "'*I don't know what you're talking about.*' All you…*girls*." He leaned forward in the chair. "You were friends with her, weren't you?"

Marie shook her head. "Yes, you were. You were all the same. Always hanging around me, pretending that you didn't want something. But especially her. Everybody thought she was so…sweet. And such a victim! But I just gave her what she wanted. Or at least I tried to." He took a long swallow of Scotch straight from the bottle and jabbed a finger in Marie's direction.

"Oh. And her little sister? Her little sister *was* creepy, am I right? She came onto me really hard. Well, I didn't respond to her the way she wanted me to? And she kinda went berserk. That whole family was crazy, you know. So, I would just like to set the record straight. What happened that day was an accident. Okay? She hit her head on the concrete edge of the pool, and fell like a stone. It was a freak accident. I didn't push her. I didn't make her fall. We were just fooling around and she slipped.

"And…and…okay, she didn't fall in. But there was no pulse. You understand? There was nothing. My sister—she was the calmest one. She said we should call the police. She said it was an accident. I wanted to call the police, too, but my mother said no. I was seventeen years old. A kid! What would you do?

"And my mother. My long-suffering mother. What people don't know? She said we had to hide what happened. She said they'd never believe us. She said it was too late anyway. Put her in the pool. When the autopsy report came back, and proved that she had died by…drowning, I knew my mother had killed her. I did not kill Catherine Ann Kelly, if that's the truth you want me to tell, you crazy bitch. I am the *victim* here!"

As though on cue and in sympathy, Barney started

howling from the hall closet. Marie tried to straighten up in her chair, but her head was just starting to clear from the blow. He took another long pull on the Scotch bottle, grimacing as he swallowed.

Marie was trying hard to keep her voice even, despite the pain.

"Can I let my dog out of the closet. Please."

He continued to stare into the dying fire in the woodstove, ignoring her request.

"We all paid for what happened that day. Things were never the same. And then my mother. My crazy old bat. My mother who…disappeared after she *destroyed* my father, and our family. My mother all these years later, she wants to confess to the police what happened. To clear her conscience. She's found *God* now—now that she's old and about to die. Her *Jewish* God. No atheists on death beds, right?" He turned to look at Marie. For a moment, she saw him as clear as though 1974 were yesterday. His face as a teenager. "Did you know her? My mother? She lived not very far from here."

There was a pause, as they both took in what he'd just said. Marie suddenly felt very warm—like she might pass out. He turned to look at her. He looked directly into her eyes. She tried to betray absolutely no information. No understanding. She could tell he didn't buy it. In one huge impossible effort, Marie dashed to the closet, flung open the door, and groped for the ax. She felt the solid wooden handle meet her hand, as Barney scrambled through her legs and out. She knew it would be close, and she was right. Tomas Kovak was right behind her.

Forty-Three

SEPT. 11, 2015
Dearest Magda,
I wanted you to know that several years ago, I found your brother. We had not spoken in many, many years. After your father was deported back to Hungary in 1999 Tomas never spoke to me or had any contact with me again. I thought he was still living out west, but it turns out he too returned to Quebec. Just on the other side of the Ontario border. It was as though each of us had to come back to the source of our shame. He now calls himself Ennis Jamieson. I understand he is a very successful and respected businessman, which of course makes sense, as Tomas always got what he wanted. He has a family. I have two small grandchildren. I will not write their names here as I know I will never meet them.

But I do know one thing. And that is that I must and will say the truth about that day those many years ago with Tomas, and you. I decided last year that I will not spend one more Yom Kippur without atoning for my sin. This is the holiest day for Jews—where we ask forgiveness from those we have sinned against. Not from God. But from the people we have hurt…damaged… killed. My offense against that girl and her family—we must tell the truth. Another Yom Kippur has passed, and I did nothing. I thought it was because of the two children. His two children. What will the truth do for them? But as you know, I never had much courage. And I made the excuse of my grandchildren not to do what I know must be done. I recently contacted Tomas—and informed him that I intend to go to the police and tell the truth about that terrible day. He begged me not to—and I very nearly agreed again to deny the truth. But then Tomas started to explain again that the "accident" was all the girl's fault. That she was the aggressive one, that she caused her own death. When I think of your father—that man—blaming his victims for what happened to them, I realized—my God, Magda I can scarcely write this—we did the same thing to Cathy. We blamed her for her "accident."

But now I know what I saw. When she said no to your brother—he doesn't like when people say no to him—he grabbed her by the throat to tease her I think. He called her a "cocktease"—but she struggled and fell. Please understand that I would never never hurt that girl. I thought she was dead. I thought Tomas had killed her. We put her in the pool not to kill her—but to save Tomas. Tomas begged me not to call the police right away. I cannot explain it, except that I could not face Tomas in trouble. In jail. Your father. It was animal. It was biological. I protected my child. And I sacrificed another for that. I have lived (if you call it living) with this all my life. Please understand that I never wanted to involve you, I never wanted to hurt you.

I will be 81 years old this November and I will not go to my grave with this on my heart. I will contact Tomas and demand that he meet with me. I hope he can see why this must be. Please know if you ever read these letters, that I have loved you. That in the end, I tried not to be a coward. I knew when I discovered the truth about your father that I had to tell someone. I didn't with your brother. But that is why *I had to with your father. I know you loved your father. I know that broke your heart in ways that could not ever be healed. I hope that you go through your life, the good part left of it, with no fear. With no lies. Take this life for yourself, because it is the only one you have.*

Now I am like the old King Lear, and you are my darling Cordelia. The only one who would tell the truth to her foolish father. And like the old king, I ask for your forgiveness. Although I dream that you will answer as she did "No cause, no cause," I know that you will not. I don't even expect you will read this letter.

With much love always,
Your mother.

Although Roméo stood a few yards away from the scorched ruins of the rabbi's house, awaiting any further evidence, he had read through the letter twice. He was still staring at it, considering its contents, when he was startled by the phone ringing in his hand.

"Hi, boss." She sounded breathless, like she'd just sprinted ten blocks.

"Did you talk to Jamieson?"

"No. He wasn't home—but *tiboir* you should see his house. *C'est un château!*"

Roméo recalled the photos from the Internet. Then he remembered that Nicole loved to ogle ostentatious displays of wealth. She had once insisted they drive by Céline Dion's palatial estate in Laval just to gawk.

"*En tout cas*, he wasn't home. But the wife. You should see her, too. Tall, redhead, a body like Wonder Woman. *Much* younger than him. When I asked her about Tomas Kovak, she said she had no idea who that was. But boss. You should've seen her face. She was freaked. Like I'd just told her aliens had landed in her backyard. I asked her a few questions, but I think she has no clue about much. Jamieson was in court, apparently. I've put out an ATL for his car. I'm heading to his office now." Suddenly, Nicole gasped as she felt something she never had before. It was like a moth fluttering inside her. She clutched her belly.

"Detective LaFramboise? Nicole? Are you still there?"

"I think...I think the baby just moved."

Nicole felt a thrill she had never known. She had a baby inside her. She was growing a human being.

"I remember that moment well when it happened with Elyse and Sophie."

There was a pause. Nicole went first. "I'll let you know when we find Jamieson."

A hazmat-suited officer approached Roméo and held up a single, mud-encrusted sneaker for him to examine. Roméo pocketed his phone and took a look. It was a size 10 pimped-up Nike. Expensive.

"I think he was on the run and got it stuck in the slush from the heavy snow last week. Guess he decided to leave it behind." The man slipped the shoe into a transparent plastic bag. Roméo nodded at the shoe. "Now all we have to do is locate a man missing a size 10 left sneaker. Our little Cinderella. Piece of cake." The young officer looked at Roméo quizzically, trying to read his expression. Was he kidding? They were all so nervous around the famous Detective Inspector Leduc that no one wanted to risk offending him by misinterpreting his sense of humor.

Roméo looked away as the last news vans were pulling out of the crime scene. He checked his watch. It was latish to drop in for an interview now. But he was in the area, and he could be at Marie Russell's house in about twenty minutes. The young cop was still standing in front of him, awaiting orders. Roméo had forgotten he was even there. "This is the work of delinquents with nothing to do and a lot of rage in their small hearts and even smaller brains. Tell Officer Juteau to take a look at the usual suspects here. I have a feeling these little assholes are known to us." The cop almost bowed to Roméo and walked briskly to a police car. Roméo pulled his phone out and pressed Marie Russell's number. It rang four times, then went to voice mail again. He decided to text her that he was on his way. Roméo knew this interview did not have to happen right at this moment. She might be in bed already or even have company over. But he wanted to see her again.

Forty-Four

"AN *AX?* Are you kidding me?" Marie gripped the wooden handle of the ax tighter and raised it, like a baseball player preparing for a pitch. Ennis Jamieson leered at her.

"Go on. Take a good swing at me. Swing that ax, baby!" Marie held her position, not taking her eyes off his. She was desperately trying to remember her self-defense moves from a college course many years earlier. Jamieson took a step closer, his arms outstretched. He was still wearing his leather gloves. Marie had always wondered if she could bring that ax down on a human being and really connect, but she had no doubt now. She just wanted to use it with maximum effect. She figured she had one shot and had to make it count. He took another step to her left and started to circle her, grinning his perfect and very white teeth at her. Marie responded in kind, like a mime before a mirror, circling each other around her massive oak coffee-table—the one she'd inherited from her grandmother. Barney barked and barked, dodging Ennis's kicks. Marie was breathing hard, her fear audible. She forced herself to speak.

"What happened to your mother?"

"She fell and hit her head."

"Like Cathy Kelly?"

He smiled again, but this time she could see behind the mask. Unmistakable rage.

"I told you. She wanted me to go to the police and confess 'our' crime." He gestured with two fingers from each hand, putting *our* in quote marks. "I was seventeen years old, for crissakes. I am not sacrificing everything I worked for, everything I have for an old lady's guilty conscience."

"Of course not. That's not reasonable."

"I mean, is she out of her mind? I have a family. A house. A *life*."

They continued to circle the coffee-table. Marie gave it one more try. "Maybe you should just tell the police what happened. It was an accident, obviously. I'm sure if you explain everything—" Ennis made a grab for the ax. Marie pulled it away and swung it at his shoulder with everything she had. And missed. The momentum of the swing threw her off balance, and she pitched forward, practically into Ennis's waiting arms.

Roméo pulled into Marie Russell's driveway, past her recycling and garbage bins, past the little sign with the address hidden behind an overgrown fir tree. There was no moon out and no stars, just a gray-black sky swollen with impending rain or snow. He stopped his car and thought it over. Maybe this was way too obvious. If there were lights on in the house he'd definitely stop in. If there were *many* lights on. Roméo took his foot off the brake and continued slowly up the gravel road, his tires crunching audibly. As he made the last turn up to Marie's door, he was surprised to see two cars. The one parked behind Marie's was an Audi 7—the same make and color as Ennis Jamieson's. Roméo opened his glove compartment and pulled out his gun. Then he started to run.

She had never felt pain quite like this—paralyzing pain that left her unable to take a breath. He had her by the hair and was dragging her to the door, which he was trying to open with one hand. With the other he held her so tightly she couldn't move. Marie could just see the ax lying harmlessly on the floor where she had been forced to drop it. No way to get it now. Ennis shoved her up against the door, they were face to face, her hair still woven through his fingers, the pain unbearable. She could feel whole chunks of it being torn out at the roots. He gathered a bigger handful, and with his free hand placed a thumb and forefinger around her throat, squeezing with shocking force. Marie knew she was going to die. He leaned in close to her, so close she could smell her Scotch on his breath. She stared into his blue eyes, holding his gaze. Just long enough to free one hand and grab his balls with every bit of power she had left in her oxygen-deprived body. Marie squeezed harder and pulled. Ennis fell to his knees, releasing her throat. Marie gasped for air and pulled the ax toward her, but she could barely lift it. Ennis howled on her foyer floor, clutching his testicles. Marie staggered over to him, holding the ax aloft, while Barney started humping away at Ennis's ankle. Marie knew she couldn't pass out, that she had to hit him with the ax. And not miss this time. And then, her front door burst open, and Roméo Leduc appeared, just like in a movie, his gun pointed at Ennis Jamieson. Also known as Tomas Kovak.

Forty-Five

HE WAS RUNNING with every bit of his body he had left, pumping his arms to propel him faster through the thicket of trees, their branches whipping his face, twigs snapping underfoot. He knew he couldn't look back—he just had to keep going, dodging treacherous roots and rocks, grateful that his eyes had adjusted enough to see every few feet in front of him. They were right behind him—any moment he expected his legs to crumple as someone tackled him or an arm grabbed his shoulder and stopped him dead. If he could just find an upturned tree from the last blowdown, he could hide himself and manage to breathe. But he was too old. Too slow. His legs staggered to a stop and he doubled over in agony, gulping air into his empty lungs. He slowly straightened up, hands on hips to ease the pain. It was over. But when he turned to face them, there was no one there. No one. Just the sound of the wind playing in the brittle, bobbing branches. Where the hell did they go? He felt a gentle squeeze on his shoulder. "Inspector Leduc? Boss?" A steaming cup of coffee slowly came into focus. Followed by Officer Juteau, looking strangely solicitous and maternal. "Have you been here all night?" Roméo sat up and wiped the bit of drool pooled in the corner of his mouth.

He was at his desk. It was daytime. He looked out his office window and saw the rain had finally stopped and a smudgy sun was just working its way above the horizon. Two squad cars sat idling in the parking lot, the exhaust clearly visible in the chill of the early morning air. Roméo sipped at the awful, watery coffee and nodded his thanks. It took him a few seconds to clear the sleep cobwebs and recall the events of the night before.

After Ennis Jamieson was taken away in a squad car to the holding tank in St. Jerome, the team was called in to photograph and gather fingerprints and evidence. An ambulance was called for Marie Russell, but she insisted they cancel it. Roméo himself took her to the little hospital in Ste. Agathe, where he managed to skip the queue and get her seen to right away. She had lots of bruising on her cheek—but it was not broken—and a very black and purple eye.

The doctor checked her for concussion and her bruised throat for serious damage to her trachea. Several angry red marks where Jamieson had throttled her remained like stains, nasty reminders of how very close it had been. The doctor insisted on keeping her overnight and, despite her protests, put her on an IV drip. Marie told Roméo everything that had happened, everything she knew. He kept insisting it could wait, as she was in shock and needed to rest, but it all poured out of her—the story of Cathy Kelly's drowning, Ennis mistaking her for someone else, her belief that Ennis Jamieson had killed his own mother. Roméo offered to call Marie's children, but she did not want to disturb them so late at night. She promised she'd reach them in the morning.

She did ask that someone contact her neighbors, so that they could go and let her dog out for a pee. Then she was done talking, so exhausted she could no longer form words. Roméo felt an overwhelming urge to hold her hand, still trembling with exhaustion and adrenaline withdrawal. He wanted to kiss her bruised eye, her swollen and damaged throat. Instead, he assured her someone would retrieve her cell phone from her house, just as his own buzzed for the umpteenth time that night. It was one of his team informing him that they'd caught one of the suspects in the arson attack—the idiot had gone back for his lost running shoe and someone recognized his truck. It had a Confederate flag on the front licence plate. They picked him up a bit later, when the same truck was spotted parked outside the imaginatively named Danseuses Nues! strip bar that is a feature of almost every small town in Quebec. Roméo was expected to make a statement, and although he tried to, he couldn't find a junior member of the team to do it. Roméo had finally taken Marie's hand and given it a gentle squeeze. Despite the IV and the circumstances, it was a thrilling sensation. And entirely unrequited, Roméo decided. What was wrong with him? He felt like he couldn't bear to leave Marie Russell alone in the hospital. But he did.

Ennis Jamieson was charged with the assault on Marie Russell. He was awaiting a bail hearing, but they decided to keep him in detention until his court appearance, while Roméo's team hustled to gather evidence concerning other possible charges. Marie was convinced that the alleged murder of his mother would be harder to prove, but they were reworking the evidence and reviewing all the potential witness interviews. Someone might have seen Jamieson in the area the night of the murder. Just before he collapsed at his desk, Roméo had watched a detective do a brief prelim interview with Jamieson. But he had clammed up, refusing to say a single word until his lawyer arrived. He did not seem like someone who would offer any kind of confession to anything, ever.

Roméo scratched at his two-day-old beard, sipped at his sludge coffee, and for the first time in about thirty years did not automatically pat his breast pocket for his cigarettes. Was this a breakthrough? Is this what kicking the habit felt like? For a moment, a vision of his stepfather came into focus, a pack of Export A's perpetually tucked up his T-shirt, a dangling cigarette stuck to his lip. Had Roméo stunk like him all those years? He pushed his chair back with an overwhelming urge to go to his cubicle sink to brush his teeth, when there was a knock at his door, followed by Nicole LaFramboise's entrance. She was very pale and had dark bluish circles under her eyes. He'd heard through the grapevine that she still had terrible morning sickness. Couldn't they come up with something for that? Roméo remembered the thalidomide babies of the 1960s—that had been a terrible tragedy, but surely there was another medication that might work? Nicole dropped heavily into the chair facing him, without asking permission. She didn't speak for several seconds, then pulled a letter from her breast pocket and slid it across the desk to Roméo.

"This arrived the day after Anna Newman was killed. It's dated just ten days ago. We just found it in her post office box. Along with a few fliers and a bank statement."

It was addressed to Mrs. Anna Newman, in the block print letters of a primary school teacher. The sender was a

Ms. Magdalena Mayer, the return address in Mendocino, California.

OCTOBER 21, 2015
Mother,
I know you may be shocked to hear from me after all these many years. I am a little shocked myself. You can't imagine how many times I answered your unopened letters. I would even seal them and put a stamp on them, but I could not send them. They all said the same thing—do not contact me again—but just as I couldn't completely sever all connection to you, I just could not allow myself to reconnect to you—it was too dangerous. Do you understand? I had to preserve myself.

But I finally did open your most recent letter. I don't know why. Maybe I felt I had punished you enough—for nearly thirty years. I'm ashamed to admit that in the end I sealed it up again as carefully as I could, so you wouldn't know I'd opened it. It had been quite some time since your last letter, so I thought you'd finally given up on me. Maybe I was amazed you were still alive—could it be that heart of yours was still beating so stubbornly? When you wrote that you were going to tell the truth—that you were meeting with Tomas to persuade him to tell the truth—I wanted to feel relief. I wanted to feel blessed relief. But I felt such an intense rage instead.

Do you remember the times I told you and Daddy that I had seen Tomas—I had seen him—be too aggressive with girls, too grabby, too nasty?

You said nothing. Like somehow it would pass, or it was okay for him to behave like that. And Dad? He was proud—and told me to my face that he was a chip off the old block—girls were drawn to Tomas like they were to him in the old days. And they were chasing Tomas, not the other way around. When Cathy drowned...when Cathy was killed, I should have seen it coming. I should have warned her. And so, I too, am guilty. It took me many years to be able to write that—to actually put it down on paper.

When I left those many years ago, I ran as far away from you all as I could afford. I was stopped by the Pacific Ocean. There I spent a long time with people who either could not imagine a future in which they mattered or had long since given up hoping. I got lost in a fog of addiction for years. Until I met a very kind man who told me that I did matter. I never wanted children—never—but he did, and to thank him for his kindness and for saving my life I allowed myself to get pregnant. He was a devoted and generous father and I was as happy as was possible for me. But of course, sooner or later, the demons that I thought I'd left behind when I snapped that suitcase shut so long ago escaped and found me. There were so many—I never could trust or get very close to anyone. I tried. I did marry my son's father. But because of his essential goodness, I had to destroy the relationship with the only person who mattered, and in the end, we divorced. We shared custody until our son turned eighteen and he moved out of state to college. Your grandson is a very handsome, very bright and joyful young man. He was born on September 11, 1991, and his name is Samuel Jacob Mayer. Yes, it is ironic that the grandson of a Nazi has a Jewish father. I never told him about our family's past. He thinks I'm an only child, and that his grandfather died right after the war. He has asked about you so many times over the years, and I have always explained that we are estranged and not in contact. It is a funny word—estranged. We are like strangers, although we have shared the most intimate and intense experience possible.

I want to tell you that I will be coming to see you as soon as I can get away from my obligations here—sometime in the next 10 days or so. I will call and let you know exactly when. I do not expect your meeting with Tomas will be very successful, or that he will even turn up for it. He always gets what he wants, and I feel certain he doesn't want this. In fact, I would be very careful how you approach him with this. I see no reason for him to want to acknowledge his guilt now. Please take care with this matter. I also want to let you know that Sammy wants to meet you and know you, but he cannot make this trip—he just started a new job and cannot get the time off right now. But he will. One day he will meet his grandmother.

Your daughter,
Magdalena.

Roméo looked up. Before he could even make the request, Nicole informed him that Madame Mayer had finally been located and informed of her mother's recent death. She was flying in the following week, and arrangements had already been made to interview her. Roméo handed Nicole the letter, which she returned to the Ziploc evidence bag.

They both sat silently for several seconds, letting the content of the letter sink in. Roméo suddenly thought of the chai necklace in its own evidence bag and made a mental note to be sure it was returned to Madame Newman's daughter. There was no doubt now that it had belonged to the dead woman.

Roméo was about to ask Nicole how she was feeling, but the pallor of her skin told that story. She remained in her chair. It was obvious she had something more to say, something personal. She slowly pulled a second folded paper out of her pocket. "I'm sorry, Roméo. I know Ti-Coune—Cousineau is an old...acquaintance of yours, but," she leaned forward and placed a single piece of paper on his desk, "this just came in."

Roméo scrutinized the paper. He nodded and folded it in half. Nicole hesitated, then made her way to his door and out into the now bustling office. Roméo looked out his window into the parking lot again. He watched as a young woman trailing a toddler exited a squad car, led by a policewoman. She had a bleeding nose that had been staunched with Kleenex and led the child roughly by the arm. Then she fell to her knees, hugged him, and started to cry. Roméo closed his eyes and steeled himself for the task he knew he had to face.

Forty-Six

FIRST THERE WAS the astonishing, stupendous, satisfying beyond *all measure* news, that he'd been arrested. The deliciousness of his arrest on the TV when the detective—a very tall and distinguished one—placed his hand on Ennis's perfectly coiffed salt and pepper hair and lowered it into the back seat of the squad car. His refusing to look out the window, but straight ahead as though he were just being driven to some fancy party. The cameras following the car as they took him away—the press was all over it—highly respected local businessman and philanthropist involved in bizarre incident. Then the shock that it was not for the murder of her sister, but for an assault on Marie Russell. *Marie Russell.* That girl who went to her school who lived on his street. Susie vaguely remembered her—a skinny girl with curly hair who was good at dodgeball. What did she have to do with this? They were calling it *bizarre*? Well, that it was for sure. *She* was the one who found him. *She* was the one who made it all happen.

She made certain she was at the "appearance," as they call it, which was disappointing, not at all like on TV—no gallery of spectators, just two young reporters, a few stragglers, his family, and her. The room itself was very small—it looked like the stupid office where she worked. The judge seemed overworked and in a hurry to move on. But the best part was Tomas coming out in a crumpled suit and a thinning shank of hair hanging into his eyes. What? No hair gel in jail? The second-best part was his wife, who glanced at him briefly, unsmilingly. Then she refused to look at him or anyone. The next best was his son, the older one, his eyes burning holes of rage into the back of his stepfather's head. She supposed the little ones had been sent to school. Their lives would be shattered, too. She spent quite a while trying to catch his eye—but when he finally had looked right *at* her, there was no flicker of recognition, no awareness whatsoever. But The Wife had seen her and looked startled. Frightened, even. Susie barely had time to take everything in before it was all over. She saw him pleading not guilty. She saw him turning back to look at The Wife, who would only nod at him. She saw him reaching for her hand as best he could, but she did not reach back. She saw him escorted from the courtroom and into some back room. In the time it took her to grab her jacket and purse, they had left the courtroom and disappeared. Susie went looking in the Ladies' Room, but The Wife was not there. No matter.

Already today she had replayed the entire scene in her mind twenty, maybe thirty times. It was like a fine wine that just got better and better with each swallow. She had already decided to book off the necessary time from work so she could attend every single minute of his trial. Of course, she had considered telling that detective everything she knew, but decided instead to wait. The trial wouldn't be for months, but she would be patient. Then, at the right moment, she would reveal to the court the other crime Ennis Jamieson had committed, and she would announce it in a spectacular way. She would get the attention of all those bitches at work, that she would.

Just thinking about it made Susie smile, but she forced herself to return to the present. She had a date tonight, and she hadn't even done her face yet. Reluctantly she stepped into the bathroom. For the first time in many years, Susie had not woken up to the image of her sister lying in her coffin. The rosy cheeks, the pink lipstick, the hair already lifeless, brushed over her forehead like an old movie star. Instead, she'd woken up that morning rested. Clear. Now, she examined her own face in the bathroom mirror. She thought she looked pretty good. Glowing, in fact. So much so, she decided to wear no makeup. Leave the mask off. But her hair... she hated it. It was too long and too thick. The women at the office said she wore it like a little girl. Susie rifled through her vanity drawer for her scissors. She lifted a huge shank of hair by her ear lobe and cut it off. Then she snipped away at the rest of her hair, until it was all gone, lying in helpless piles around her feet on the bathroom floor. Much better. And tonight, on her date? She was even using her real name.

Forty-Seven

THE WEATHER JUST could not make up its mind. The day before had been unseasonably cold, with well below freezing temperatures. Now the sun was so brilliant it almost hurt, and it was fifteen degrees warmer than yesterday. Roméo drove past the little patches of November snow clinging stubbornly to the yellowing lawn that flanked the main road to the hospital. They'd all be melted by the afternoon. He flashed his badge to the parking lot attendant and drove right up to the front door. Ti-Coune was already waiting, smoking a cigarette and chatting up the nurse, who held onto the handles of his wheelchair like she was ready to push him and it off a cliff.

Roméo thanked the nurse, took a pair of crutches from her, and dropped them in the back seat. Then he eased the patient into the front of his car. Ti-Coune edged his bum onto the seat. Then he very gingerly lifted his right leg inside. He turned and grinned at Roméo—one front tooth was missing. But he gamely raised a thumb and said "*Zigidoo! Let's go.*"

Roméo pulled away from the entrance and headed

out onto the short road to the highway. Despite his shattered jaw, Ti-Coune still kept up a lively, if slurry one-sided conversation.

"I was thinking. I'm gonna change my life. Completely, you know?" he declared, his eyes on the road ahead. "For now, I'm gonna get the disability until I'm back on my feet. *Ça va prendre du temps.* Then maybe I'll go to school again. Get trained to do something." Roméo nodded his approval, if not his conviction it would happen. "*Criss,* I'm glad to be out of that hospital. But, I have to say...there was this one nurse. Sexy like hell. And I think she liked me. But..." he gestured to his knee and touched his still stitched-up face, "right now, I'm not at my best."

Roméo smiled grimly. He had to find the right moment to tell him. Ti-Coune took a breath and watched the sun dazzling the bits of snow by the road. "But maybe...I was thinking...when I get some money saved up, I'll go out west. I can still do drywall, I think. I done that many years ago. They're still looking for drywall people." He winked at Roméo and said in a thick accent, "My English, it's pretty good, too." Ti-Coune took a pack of smokes from his breast pocket and offered one to Roméo, who shook his head. Ti-Coune lit up anyway and blew a perfect stream of white smoke through his nostrils. "Then I'm gonna find Hélène. She's still out there, you know." He took another long drag, then lowered his window and flicked the lit cigarette out. "Did you find her, Roméo? Did you tell her about what happened to me?"

"I didn't get a chance yet," Roméo answered.

"I thought maybe me and Hélène—we can get a place together out there? That's what I'm thinking."

Ti-Coune glanced at Roméo and then fiddled with the brace on his knee until he was comfortable.

"Hey, I wanted to tell you, *detective inspector.* About the old lady?"

Roméo glanced at him briefly.

"What about her?"

Ti-Coune took another cigarette from his pack, stuck it in his mouth, but left it unlit.

"That guy—Batman? The big rich guy, there? He wanted her to sell him her land because—okay—he was trying to sell his house, and the guy who wanted to buy it didn't want to see her little *cabane* or anything that stopped the view… her house and a few trees of hers blocked his view of the lake—can you believe it? So, they asked me to…scare her a little bit—but I did not do that to her! *Je te jure!*"

Roméo said nothing at first.

"I take it your buddies who beat you up thought that you'd attacked her and taken her money?"

Ti-Coune shook his head. "I'm not talking about that." Ti-Coune stared out the window in silence.

Roméo saw the sign for 100% Beef on the highway up ahead. He decided to pull over. Ti-Coune looked as pleased as a little kid. *"Ben, merci, mon ami! J'ai pas mangé un bon hamburger depuis chais pas combien de temps. C'est bien gentil."*

Roméo pulled into the packed parking lot and turned off the engine. Ti-Coune leaned into the door and started his preparations to extract himself. Roméo stopped him with a gentle hand on his arm.

"Jean-Michel. I have to. Tell you something—"

"You're calling me *Jean-Michel*? Shit, this can't be good."

Roméo looked right at him, but Ti-Coune could not meet his eyes. He stared straight ahead through the windshield.

"I did look for Hélène. Did a quick search, but nothing came up."

Ti-Coune let his breath out. "Is that all? Okay, I'll find her myself. Now, I could use a cheeseburger and poutine—"

"But then yesterday, this came through the office." He pulled out the paper Nicole had shown him and left it on the seat between them. Ti-Coune glanced at it. Then he held it and read it. Every word.

"She's been reported missing. Near Prince George. That's where they have what they call the Highway of Tears, because so many women have gone missing or been… killed there. Most are First Nations women. It is a disgrace—a disgrace of this entire country."

Ti-Coune said nothing. He closed his eyes and did not reopen them for several minutes.

"Prince George? That's in Alberta?"

"No, Ti—. Jean-Michel. It's in British Columbia. I guess she moved there."

Ti-Coune turned away from Roméo, leaning his head against the window. "But she's…not dead? She's just missing?"

"Yes. The report was made just a week ago. So, that could mean…anything. And not necessarily a bad thing."

Ti-Coune did not respond. Roméo added, "I'll do my best to find her. But it's not my province. Not my jurisdiction. I have no control there."

Ti-Coune just said very quietly, "Take me home."

Roméo started up the car engine. "I'll do my best, Jean-Michel."

They drove the rest of the way in complete silence, until Roméo pulled into Ti-Coune's overgrown driveway.

"I got you some milk and bread. A few apples. Some frozen dinners." Ti-Coune still had not moved, his head tilted against the glass of the car window. Roméo had to open his door for him and gently sit him up. Then he got him onto his crutches and to the front door. As he put the key in the lock, they could hear hysterical barking from inside.

"I also got your dog back from the SPCA. I thought you would appreciate that."

Ti-Coune finally looked Roméo right in the eye. "Pitoune? She's home? *Merci*, Roméo. *Merci*." The little dog skittered out the door and wove herself in and out of Ti-Coune's legs and crutches. It was only then that he began to weep.

Forty-Eight

SHE BRIEFLY ALLOWED him to touch her fingers. Then she withdrew her hands and returned them to her lap. He reached across the table to pull them back, but he did not insist. He doesn't look so bad, she thought. He was wearing a gray T-shirt and baggy gray sweat pants, but still…the man could wear a plastic bag and pull it off.

"How are the kids? Katie? Is she okay?"

Bridget sat back in the plastic chair and looked him straight in the eye.

"How do you *think* she is, Ennis?"

"How much does she know? How much do they know?"

Bridget stared past Ennis to the corridor behind him. A giant, shimmery *Joyeux Noel!* sign was stuck on the wall above a stick-on cartoon of Santa Claus. For a second, she felt like she was going to start crying and never stop.

"I can't talk about the kids right now, Ennis. We have other things that need discussing."

Ennis made another grab for her hand that she'd nervously put back on the table. He thumbed the enormous diamond on her engagement ring.

"Listen, Bridge. As soon as you get bail posted, I promise you. I swear to you I will sort this all out. It's very tough to do any business from—in here. And this is all…well, a joke, frankly. The whole thing."

Bridget watched him rub her diamond. Then she looked him straight in the eye.

"They've subpoenaed Heather. *Heather!* Why would they subpoena your assistant, Ennis? I mean, it was one thing when you went after that fucking crazy woman for threatening us…I understood. I did. It was a misunderstanding somehow. But this. Ennis. They took your computer, all your files—all our bank accounts are frozen! I can't even pay the heating bill right now—"

Ennis raised his hand to quiet her and lowered his voice to a stage whisper.

"Listen. There's about ten grand under a floorboard in the bedroom. Take that. I've marked it with—"

"And just how far do you think that will take us? We have *bills* to pay…school fees. Fucking *ponies* to feed—"

"Lower your voice. *Lower* your voice. Use your own money. You have that private account." His eyes bore into hers. "Right?"

"I have no idea what you're talking about. My lawyer—"

"*Your* lawyer?" Ennis pushed himself away from the table and smirked at her. "And just who is *your* lawyer?"

"She is looking into some things for me."

"Oh. Good. Look, talk to her about those frozen accounts—you hold some of those with me and—"

Bridget cut him off, her voice calm and measured. "Did you steal from old ladies? Is everything we have stolen from their savings? From their retirement money? From their children. Their grandchildren?"

Ennis scraped his chair back and got to his feet. He lurched in Bridget's direction until the guard stopped him dead and returned him to his chair.

"I did not steal from those people. I help them settle their estates. I *relieve* them of the worry and anxiety of managing their affairs—old women who've never so much as written a check! And—and those other ones—the ones who let me invest for them? They invested with me because they thought they'd get a little more—they were the greedy ones, not me. Didn't they wonder when every year—every single fucking year they got a return of 12 percent? Did that not ring any *fucking bells* for them?"

"Ennis, keep your voice down."

"I've worked hard, Bridget. Worked my ass off. How many weekends? How many? I deserve everything I worked for."

He just would not stop talking...would not shut up.

"Why, Ennis?"

"I did it all for you. For you and the kids. So you could have what *you* deserved."

Bridget knew it was over. All of it. The house gone. The land. The ponies. The cars. The life free of financial worry. She was old Bridget...again. She'd been there before, and she could be there again. What she could not bear was the public shame. The humiliation. The lunch dates—over. The PTA—over. Running the school fashion show—over. She would lose it all. The kids, their father. And Brandon was just starting to come around.

Ennis returned to his chair and looked at Bridget indignantly.

"I can't stay here another fucking night. You need to post bail. Use the house as collateral—"

"The house? Are you insane?"

"I am not guilty, Bridget. *Not* guilty. Try to remember that."

"They're asking about your mother—remember you told them that you were home with me that—night? But you weren't. You went out, remember? And I was asleep when you got home—"

"I was home all that night. We watched the *Princess Bride* with the kids. Remember? We made hot chocolate. Katie had a stuffy nose and there was Kleenex all over the place. We sat on our old sofa because the new one hadn't been delivered yet and you said you felt sentimental about that sofa and would miss it—"

Bridget wasn't listening. She opened her handbag and removed an envelope.

It was addressed to Tomas Kovak. Wordlessly, she slid it across the table to him. Then she stood up and tucked her chair neatly under the table.

"Good-bye, Ennis."

"Bridget. Are the kids coming? Bridget? *Bridget!*"

But she was gone. All Ennis could hear were her heels tapping and echoing along the long, hard corridor before the automatic door closed and muted the sound of her entirely.

Forty-Nine

SPRING LASTS ABOUT one week in Ste. Lucie. One day there's two feet of snow on the ground, and you can still see your breath suspended in the chill air, the next day the newborn leaves are already unfurling themselves and everything is a pure, greeny green. Suddenly this geophony of melting snow is transformed into biophony—the urgent singing of frogs, the whine of mosquitos, the ecstatic trill of the winter wren, the first soul-stirring cry of the loons, the swaying, sighing sibilance of trees in full summer leaf, all the way up the food chain to anthropophony, when the lawn mowers and weed whackers and chainsaws come to life. But not yet. Although it was mid-April, winter was still clinging to southern Quebec. Marie looked at the bird feeder outside her kitchen window. She had spotted two goldfinches the day before and was watching for them to return. Claire used to call them wild canaries, the bright yellow beacons of spring. There they were, four at the feeder, inhaling thistle seeds like their lives depended on it, which strictly speaking, they did not.

Marie slipped the veggie casserole into the oven and

then almost tripped over the dog, who liked to wait and watch her for any scrap of food that might come his way. Marie had picked him up at the SPCA—a five-year-old mix of God knows what—a Gargantua of chestnut fur and pointy ears and bushy tail. Barney was furious with Marie for getting a second dog who wasn't Loki—and he punished her at every opportunity. Today he had ignored her and planted himself on Claire's lap, practically daring the new dog to try the same. They were a study in opposites: Barney spoiled, indignant, and world-weary, the new dog grateful, earnest, and delighted with everything.

Marie grabbed the kitchen counter to prevent her fall. "Dog. Please go sit somewhere else. I promise you I'll save some for you later." Marie had yet to name the new dog, and now the name *Dog* was really growing on her. He was just about the doggiest dog she'd ever met. Marie topped up her glass of wine and then pushed open the door to her porch to check on her mother. Claire was bundled up past her chin in an old faded afghan she herself had made many years earlier, staring out into the forest. Every now and then she would shift a bit, and Barney would grumble and readjust his position on her lap. Marie was not sure what exactly her mother was staring at, or what she still could really see. It didn't matter, as long as she was warm, and fed, and safe. About four weeks earlier Marie's phone had rung at three o'clock in the morning, and someone shrieked, "Because seven ate nine!"

Marie was so deep-sleep foggy that she almost hung up and then realized the voice was her mother's. She was calling to tell Marie the punchline to a joke she had forgotten from a visit a week before. She was very pleased with herself and totally unaware of the time. Then she started to sob and once again asked, "What do I do now, Marie? What do I do now?" Marie felt crushing guilt for not visiting in several weeks and had promised to see her the next day. But Marie was not prepared for the woman who was once her mother. The brilliant minds at Le Warwick had apparently been treating "excessive weeping with underlying Alzheimer's dementia" with a drug that rendered Claire weak, exhausted, and practically catatonic. Under the alert gaze of the still smiling Madame Purdy, Marie took her mother in her arms, and this time, Marie had wept excessively.

She tucked the afghan away from her mother's mouth and ran her hand along her mother's soft, dry cheek. So she had moved her. Not in with her, of course, but into a brand-new old folks home in Ste. Lucie. It was part of a government initiative to revive the town—if they couldn't bring the young people back, they could at least bring back the old ones and give the young some jobs. It had very few potted tropical plants, and no Victorian wing-back chairs, but it was bright and clean, the attendants were kind, and the woman in charge sometimes seemed overwhelmed and not inclined to smile constantly. Marie could drop in on her mother daily, and on special occasions, like today, she could easily arrange to bring her mother home.

Marie frowned as a screeching blue jay assaulted the bird feeder, scattering the chickadees and nuthatches. They were known to imitate the call of a hawk to frighten smaller birds off their nests, and then to eat the eggs.

"Did you see the jay, Maman? Nasty old birds. But they sure are smart. And beautiful."

Marie's mother turned her head and looked at her. Then

she opened her mouth, but just as quickly shut it again. She spoke less and less frequently now.

For some reason, the memory of her mother's voice the summer her father died came to her. Marie had been traveling in Greece and hadn't called home in six weeks. She finally decided to call on her birthday. She waited seven hours in a Greek post office for her call to come through from Montreal. When it finally did, it was not the joyful happy birthday she was expecting. Her mother, sounding terribly vulnerable and angry at the same time, just said, "We've been searching all over for you. We couldn't find you. Your father is dead. Come home." That was too painful a memory to linger on. Instead, Marie marveled that all those many years ago, she could *not be found*.

Now, between Google Earth watching, or CCTV cameras installed everywhere, where could anyone go, really? We've lost the ability to get lost. Marie thought of the early explorers who started off with maps filled with white spots of *terra incognita*—which they slowly filled in over time. Were there any left anywhere? Yes. In her mother's mind. The great unknown, her mapped journey now returning to white spots, her *terra incognita*. Marie had just finished the last chapter of her book, which discussed how white spots are appearing on the migratory maps of birds as climate change and habitat destruction have altered the landscape beyond recognition. Birds who have navigated this planet for millions of years are getting lost. They cannot find their way home.

Marie's reverie was interrupted by a shout and then a peal of low-pitched laughter. The screen door squeaked open and then Ben was leaning behind her and pecking a kiss on her cheek. He smelled like a fresh shower. His girlfriend waited and watched in the doorway, then came over and delicately kissed Marie on both cheeks.

"Jesus, Mum. Could you please get rid of that creepy doll? Or at least put her someplace else? Scared the shit out of me—"

"He screamed," his girlfriend observed.

Marie had offered to send the Chatty Cathy doll to Louise in Calgary—it was her doll after all—but Louise had refused it. It often did give people a bit of a fright.

"God, I didn't even hear your car, you guys. I must have been completely *dans la lune*."

Ben returned to the foyer, picked Chatty Cathy up, and shoved her in the closet. "There!" he said. "Out of sight, out of mind."

The girlfriend turned to Marie and smiled. "We brought appetizers and I made a cake. Vegan, though. I hope that's okay." In spite of herself, Marie was really starting to like the girlfriend, and just in the nick of time, too. She was five months pregnant.

Ben returned to the porch and kissed his grandmother on the top of her head. "Hi, Grand-mère." Then he turned to his mother. "How is she?"

Marie had never seen Ben so fully himself. It was as though now, finally, he was starting his actual, own life. She would never have thought him capable of fatherhood at his age, but now she had to admit, it was like he was the man he was meant to grow into. A little prematurely, maybe, but she had to thank the older girlfriend for this, who now was bustling around Marie's kitchen, her belly slightly swollen and preventing her from moving freely.

"Is Ruby coming for supper?"

Marie shook her head. "She's writing her LSATs on Monday. She's buried in her apartment and not coming up for air until June."

A little part of Marie was grateful Ruby was absent—she and Ben often erupted into painstaking analysis of American politics, and Marie just didn't have the stomach for it tonight. It looked like Donald Trump was going to win the Republican party nomination for president. Everyone thought he was a joke, but Marie had her doubts. Marie remembered him from when she was in grad school in New York City. He was a buffoon who talked about being president then, and about how stupid the American people were—that they'd believe anything. If Trump became president, then anything was possible…in the worst way. This was true anarchy.

Ben opened his beer on the countertop, took a deep swallow, and then lifted it in Marie's direction. "I heard the book is finished—and Ruby told me you managed to get the rights to the work of Anna Newman. Congrats, Mum!"

Marie had attended the memorial service Anna's friends from the Artists' Co-op had held, where a lovely young rabbi said *kaddish*, the Jewish song for the dead. Many of Anna Newman's charcoal drawings were beautifully displayed, and Marie could scarcely believe how exquisite and skilled they were. When she asked Anna's daughter if she could use her mother's illustrations for her new nature book, she had said yes immediately.

Marie heard a sound from the porch, like a child softly singing to herself. She left Ben and Maya in the kitchen and stood in the porch doorway listening.

Il y a longtemps que je t'aime, jamais je ne t'oublierais. Her mother sang the chorus over and over again. Marie knew better than to try to have Claire sing the verse—dealing with Alzheimer's patients was like the improv games Ruby used to excel at in high school—just say yes to whatever the other actor throws at you. In this case, whatever the loved one throws at you. The key is not to force them into our reality, but to join theirs. It wasn't always easy, but it was the only way. Marie glanced out at the yard, and noticed the snowdrops popping up through the thawing grass. Marie had learned recently that galantamine, a compound found in snowdrops, is used to treat Alzheimer's. The snowdrop was also, she remembered from some college course many years ago, the antidote Ulysses used to protect himself from Circe's poison. Marie inhaled deeply. The nostalgic smell of melting snow and balsam. Spring was definitely coming—she could almost feel the stirring of millions of creatures underground. And the birds that stay will soon be joined by hundreds of songbirds, some found, some lost, sharing their little forest.

Claire had stopped singing. She tilted her head coquettishly and grinned. "Hello!"

Marie already knew who got that sort of response from her mother. She didn't need to turn around.

"Did you park the car in the garage like I told you?" Claire asked.

"Oui, Madame. Of course."

"And did you pick up the milk and bread?" Roméo smiled and winked at Marie.

"Just the milk. The bread wasn't fresh."

"Good," Marie's mother declared, satisfied.

Sometimes Claire thought Roméo was Edward. Sometimes she thought Ben was Edward. Sometimes she talked about sex at inconvenient times. But that didn't matter, really. Roméo very gently touched the back of Marie's neck, and leaned in for a kiss. Marie looked up at him, her brown eyes smiling.

ACKNOWLEDGMENTS

There are so many people to thank for their help in making this happen.

To my children, Alice and Isaac, for their unwavering certainty that I could do this.

To my big brother, Brian, who is such a superlative sibling that he hasn't made it into my stories. Not yet.

To my early readers for their encouragement, invaluable opinions and insight: Alice Abracen, Louise Arsenault, Sally Frances Mann, Lia Hadley, Linda Iny Lempert, Emma Lambert, Mirlla Lambert, Michelle Ledonne, Sasha Mandy, Rebecca Million, Richard and Susan Mozer, Michelle Payette-Daoust, Cathy Richards, Maila Shanks.

To Andrew Katz who connected me to William Levitan and Debra Nails, two strangers who offered their expert eye and passionate insight, and whom I hope to meet one day.

Corrina Côté for a great story. Megan Williams for the great tip.

To my editors, Wendy Thomas and Kathryn Cole, and all the people at Second Story Press.

I am so very grateful.

ABOUT THE AUTHOR

During the course of her almost twenty-eight years at Montreal's Dawson College, ANN LAMBERT has taught English literature to literally thousands of students. For the last twelve years, she has co-written, directed, and produced plays with the Dawson Theatre Collective. The Collective is proud of the fact that they welcome students from all backgrounds and abilities, often have casts as large as thirty-five, and play to enthusiastic and non-traditional theater audiences every year.

Ann has been writing and directing stage and radio plays for thirty-five years. Several of them—*Two Short Women*, *The Mary Project* (with Laura Mitchell), *Very Heaven*, *Parallel Lines*, *Self Offense*, *The Wall*, *Force of Circumstance*, *The Pilgrimage*, and *Welcome Chez Ray* have been produced in Canada, the United States, Ireland, Greece, Australia, and Sweden. Ann is the co-artistic director of Right Now! which produced her plays *Two Short Women*, *The Assumption of Empire*, *Jocasta's Noose* and *The Guest*, by Alice Abracen. From 2001–2005, Ann adapted and directed plays for The Roslyn Players, a children's theater company that specialized in performing Shakespeare's plays. From 2002–2004, Ann headed the Playwriting Program at the National Theatre School of Canada. In the spring of 2019, she launched a new theater company called Theatre Ouest End in Montreal.

Ann is also the vice-president of The Theresa Foundation (www.theresafoundation.com), dedicated to supporting AIDS-orphaned children and their grandmothers in several villages in Malawi, Africa.